Julie Highmore is the author of *Sleeping Around*, *Play It Again?*, *Pure Fiction*, *Country Loving*. She lives in Oxford.

Praise for Julie Highmore's previous novels:

'Funny, original and dazzlingly assured' *Jill Mansell*

'A witty, wry, observant tale of mixed relations' *Bookseller*

'A real feel-good read, full of funny scenes and one-liners, [a] seductive story of love, music and family life' *Publishing News*

'Highly addictive' *Bookseller*

'A funny and compulsive read' *Choice Magazine*

'Welcome new life is breathed into a familiar scenario' *Woman & Home*

'A fun little romp' *Star Magazine*

'I like her totally unsentimental angle on country living and eccentric and quirky characters . . . It will do well' Rosamunde Pilcher

'Compulsive reading' *Daily Express*

'Classic, warm-hearted comedy' *Bookseller*

'A tangled, complicated tale of love and life' *Closer*

Kiss Me Quick

Julie Highmore

headline
review

First published in 2006 by HEADLINE REVIEW
An imprint of HEADLINE PUBLISHING GROUP

First published in paperback in 2006 by HEADLINE REVIEW
An imprint of HEADLINE PUBLISHING GROUP

A HEADLINE REVIEW paperback

1

Cataloguing in Publication Data is available from the British Library

0 7553 2119 7 (ISBN-10)
978 0 7553 2119 3 (ISBN-13)

Typeset in Garamond by Palimpsest Book Production Limited,
Grangemouth, Stirlingshire

Printed and bound in Great Britain by Clays Ltd, St Ives plc

Headline's policy is to use papers that are natural, renewable and
recyclable products and made from wood grown in sustainable forests.
The logging and manufacturing processes are expected to conform to
the environmental regulations of the country of origin.

HEADLINE PUBLISHING GROUP
A division of Hodder Headline
338 Euston Road
London NW1 3BH

www.reviewbooks.co.uk
www.hodderheadline.com

For Chris and Kate

APRIL

SATURDAY

Tim While I was waking up with coffee and a cigarette this morning, I stared at my eyesore of a garden and considered my current situation. I haven't had a client in months, or a proper girlfriend since my divorce. My glasses are broken, I have no decent clothes, and I can't for the life of me give up smoking. After a long drag, I exhaled, coughed a morning cough and gulped down more coffee. What a mess.

On top of everything else was the cash-flow issue. Would I have to resort to selling the house? The place is 'rank', according to daughter Alice, so I'd have to do it up, and that would involve money, not to mention energy. I stubbed out the cigarette and thought of going back to bed. It's a common sign of depression, I know, but I wouldn't have classified myself as depressed, just tired. Maybe an hour or two's kip on a chilly spring morning was all I needed to get me going. I'd wake up refreshed, then tackle the kitchen and sweep the path. I'd buy the *Shelcombe Bugle* and look for a proper job, get a haircut and definitely, definitely sort out the study.

Yes, a little snooze sounded tempting. Although, on reflection, it would involve standing up, turning the heating down and mounting two flights of stairs. I wondered if being too knackered to go back to bed meant I really was in a bad way. When the phone rang it was all I could do to haul myself from my chair and cross the room.

'Yhaallow,' I said through a yawn. I put my mug down and gave one temple a rub. Too much booze again last night. But, what the hell, it always helps put my troubles into perspective, or at least out of sight for a while.

'Oh,' said a woman, 'I wonder if I've got the right number from the Yellow Pages. I'm after a Mr Cash.'

I stopped rubbing and blinked. A potential client! I cleared my throat, scanned the debris for a pen and said, 'Yes, that's me. Timothy Cash, life coach. How can I help you?'

We met for a cup of tea in the Imperial Hotel, a once-dignified but now down-at-heel establishment that rumour has it is about to become seafront apartments. Debbie Clinker was as she described herself: dark shoulder-length hair, over forty, beige top, glasses. Behind the thick makeup, long fringe and tinted tortoiseshell specs there could be a pretty face, but first she'd have to lose some weight.

I watched her empty three sachets of sugar before she sighed and said, 'Well, where shall I begin?'

'Do you work?' I asked, to get her going.

'Down in one of the arcades. I gives people change for the machines. You know, in a little booth?'

'Ah, yes.' Alice used to love those machines, but then one day decided she'd no longer hand over her money, or even mine, to 'some like huge rip-off, global-warming corporation'. She was ten at the time. 'And do you enjoy it?' I asked Debbie.

She stirred her tea and snorted. 'Yeah, it's my dream job. Listen, do you mind if I go out for a fag?'

I raised a disapproving eyebrow. 'No, go ahead.'

After rummaging in a cream tasselled handbag, Debbie pulled out my preferred brand. 'Do you?' she asked.

'No,' I told her, hands gripped in my lap. 'Thanks.'

'Wise man.' She got up and hooked the bag over her shoulder.

I indicated to the waitress that we'd be back and followed. 'So how long have you worked there?' I asked once we were out on the pavement.

'Um . . .' Debbie lit up and swirled smoke around teeth and tongue, then blew out. She didn't inhale, I noticed, '. . . must be fifteen years.'

'*Christ*,' I said. 'I mean . . .'

'Oh, you get used to it. The noise, the abuse what gets thrown at you when the machines don't pay out. I wear earplugs and take loads of magazines. Anyway, it ain't for much longer. They're making me redundant, now they're putting in cash machines and change machines and what have you.'

'I'm sorry to hear that,' I said. I got my little notebook out and jotted things down, wondering, heavy-heartedly, how Debbie Clinker was going to afford me. 'And are you married?'

She nodded then shook her head, then shrugged. 'Oh, I don't know. Yeah, yeah, I am. To Gary. He ain't never been husband of the year, though. Sort of comes and goes.'

'What does he do?' I asked, hoping Gary might be the source of my fees.

'Dodgems in the summer, signs on in the winter.' She flicked ash on the road, then took another long drag. 'I'm dead lucky my arcade stays open all year round,' she said, exhaling over me. 'Well, *was* lucky.'

I couldn't detect sarcasm, so wrote 'Glass-half-full type?' while at the same time thinking I ought to just go home now. A person with a bank account might be trying to get hold of me. 'Children?'

'Paul, twenty-two. Serena, twenty-one. Nicky, twenty.'

'OK,' I said, pointlessly listing them.

'And little Gary, eighteen.'

'Uh-huh.'

'A right handful, I tell you. Always have been, always will be.'

'Oh dear.'

The cigarette I'd been trying to passively smoke was finally ground out by Debbie's big brown buckled shoe.

She picked up the butt and threw it in a litter bin. 'I really *really* want to give up,' she said. 'Can you help me?'

'Absolutely,' I told her. 'All it takes is a little willpower.'

We returned to our table, where I finished my tepid tea, then sat back and summed up. Four useless children and a dead-beat husband. Debbie Clinker – scruffy, unemployed, barely educated, out of shape and a smoker – was more in need of life coaching than any previous client – all three of them. But, as much as I'd like to, I don't take on charity cases. I slipped my notebook in my pocket and began planning my escape.

'I liked your name,' she said, pouring herself a second cup of tea. 'Cash. That's why I chose you in the Yellow Pages. It just seemed like fate, you see, since my main problem is what to do about my financial situation.'

I raised my watch to face height. 'Goodness,' I said, 'that can't be the time.' I gestured to the waitress and took out my wallet. I'd recommend Citizens' Advice to Debbie, as a starting point. Then Relate. But not now. Over the phone. 'I'm afraid I'm going to have to shoot,' I told her. 'Another appointment. I'm so sorry.' I felt her gaze but avoided her eyes. 'Tell you what, I'll give you a call—'

'Thing is,' she said quietly, 'I've had a bit of a win on the Premium Bonds.'

'Oh?'

'Quite a substantial one.'

'Really?' Five hundred, I was guessing. A thousand.

Perhaps she wanted to blow the lot on life guidance. I suddenly pictured my car back on the road and a new pair of glasses, or a holiday with Alice. No, maybe not a holiday with Alice. 'Tell me more,' I said, as the waitress approached, ripping the top sheet off her pad.

'Look, I've kept it to myself, so promise you won't repeat none of this.'

'Of course not,' I protested. We'd hardly move in the same circles. 'When you say substantial . . .'

Debbie Clinker leaned across the table and cupped a smoky hand around her smoky mouth. 'Got the jackpot,' she whispered smokily. 'A million. Tax free.'

When the bill landed on the table, I handed it straight back and put my wallet away. 'Come to think of it,' I said, 'we might like some lunch?' Debbie nodded but then I ran my eyes down the menu and regretted my rashness. If I'd known I was meeting a millionaire, I'd have arranged to meet at the Lobster Pot; not exactly five star, but Le Manoir aux Quat'Saisons of Shelcombe. 'I'll have the gammon, chips and peas,' I told the waitress. 'Hold the pineapple ring.' I handed Debbie the menu.

'I'm trying to lose weight,' she said, patting one of her spare tyres, 'so just the beans on toast, please. Make that twice. Oh, and maybe a poached egg. No, two.'

The waitress curled a lip, then when Debbie and I were alone again I said, 'A million is a lot, but not a huge amount these days. Easy to squander.'

'You mean I could buy my house off the council, get

me and the kids a flash car each, have a holiday or two in Spain and then be back where I am?'

'Exactly.'

'Obviously I've thought of all that, otherwise I wouldn't be here offering to pay you bucketloads of money.'

My spirits soared but I smiled cautiously. Some buckets aren't that big.

'What I want you to do,' she continued, 'is make me a completely different person, so's I can have the kind of life what I've always dreamed of. I want to be sophisticated and talk posh. Have nice things and a dead impressive job. I want to spend the summer in a place that don't start with Shel and end with combe . . . Know what I'm saying?'

'I know exactly what you're saying, Debbie.' She wanted miracles.

'I bet you're thinking, blimey, that's a tall order!' She slurped her tea then tilted her head at me. 'Excuse me for asking, but you are qualified, aren't you?'

'Of course,' I said firmly. Somewhere in a pile of bills and junk mail, up in the study, lies my Diploma in Life Coaching Skills from Distant University Inc. – now so distant, its website is untraceable. I had to self-certify that I'd spent two hundred hours on assignments and case studies. Two might have been closer. No one has yet asked to see my qualification. 'I took a diploma course,' I told Debbie. I didn't tell her my credit card is still recovering. 'I could give you a reference if you want?' There's the one my cousin did, eulogising about Timothy

Cash and how I'd changed his life: 'I highly recommend his dynamic yet sensitive approach.' When the client signed up, I gave my cousin a cut.

'Oh, don't worry about a reference,' Debbie said. 'You've got an honest face, Mr Cash.'

'Really?' Now I felt bad. I wasn't Cash at all, I was Downer; a name less suited to life coaching would be hard to find. I decided on Cash when listening to Johnny one day. 'Please, call me Tim,' I said. 'Tell me, is Clinker your married name?'

'Yep.'

'What were you before?'

'Oh,' she said, as though trying to recollect. 'Duval.'

'Debbie Duval. Nice.'

'Yeah?'

'Mm. Quite sexy.'

'You think?' she said with an unexpected smile. Considering everything, she had very good teeth.

The food arrived, complete with tinned pineapple ring. I thought I wouldn't make a fuss and began talking fees. After more than doubling my normal hourly rate, I told her what I'd charge and she didn't wince, so I said, 'Plus expenses.'

'Sounds reasonable.'

'Er, the expenses could be quite high?'

'That's OK,' she whispered. 'I'm rich, remember?'

Thinking I might have died and gone to life-coach heaven, I wondered where I should start with this new client. Diet or elocution? Job or relationship? In some ways, she'd be easier than most. No need for all that time-consuming preliminary assessment business: gap analysis, confirming strengths, getting the client to establish and prioritise goals and create her own Purpose, Vision and Mission Statement. Debbie's life appeared to be one big gap and, as far as I could see, all goals had equal priority.

'What I'd ask,' I said, sawing at overcooked gammon, 'is that you hand yourself totally over to me.'

'Sounds good.'

I caught her eyes twinkling behind the tinted glasses. Was she flirting?

'You see,' I continued, 'too much resistance on your part would only slow down your progress. Of course, if you violently disagree with any of my suggestions . . .' She was smiling at me, oddly. I wasn't sure I liked it. 'I mean requests. I mean . . . Look, why don't we start with your name?'

'Sorry?'

'Why not go back to Duval? More dignified than Clinker.'

'Not to mention sexier?'

'Er, yes, ha ha.'

'Debbie Duval. Huh. Haven't been that since I was eighteen, walking up the aisle, huge with Paul.'

'Of course, *Deborah* Duval would be even better.'

'Yeah, right, and make myself a laughing stock at bingo nights?'

'Debbie,' I said, giving up on the gammon and clasping

11

hands under my chin. 'I don't think there'll be any more bingo nights.'

'No?' She too put her knife and fork down and echoed my pose. Her hands were rather lovely, I noticed. 'Oh, well,' she said with a shrug, 'it's not like I needs the money. You know, I ain't spent a penny of my win yet, not even on a celebration drink.'

Poor thing, I thought. No family or friends she felt able to share her news with. Worried, no doubt, that they'd all try to benefit in some way from her new-found wealth. Unlike myself, of course.

'I think you were right not to tell anyone,' I said, the idea of a drink suddenly appealing. 'How's your meal?'

'Horrible.'

'Mine too.' I pushed my plate aside. 'Fancy that celebration now?' I called the waitress back and stood up. 'We could go to the Lobster Pot?'

Debbie suddenly looked anxious. 'It's a nice idea. Only . . . well, I'm sure they've got a bit of a dress code there.'

'Oh, don't be silly.' I pulled a tenner from my wallet in the hope we'd be going Dutch. 'You look perfectly OK.'

'Um,' she said, purse open, a twenty-pound note in her hand. She smiled, sort of apologetically. 'I was thinking more of you.'

With the best part of a bottle of champagne in me, I took the promenade route to Erica's house. Shelcombe is currently in limbo. After a flurry of activity over the

Easter period, a lot of things have shut down again, waiting for the season to start properly in May. Other businesses are soldiering on bravely, hoping for an early heat wave. Just about every seafront building is having work done on it. As I hurried along past the crazy golf (closed) and the whelk stall (open), a cold Atlantic wind whipped my right cheek and the sound of drilling and hammering assaulted my ears, but I didn't care. Debbie Clinker was going to pay me lots of money and save my bacon. I could keep my house! Now, all I had to do was impress my new client and, more importantly, hang on to her. That was where my ex-wife was going to come in. I prayed she was home, and that she was in her usual good mood.

Having passed the stationary toddler rides and the Richard- (formerly Punch) and-Judy stand, I crossed the road, then turned left and strode past the drab pastel houses along Drake Street, with their frosted-glass doors and scalloped net curtains. 'No Vacancies', 'No Vacancies', 'No Vacancies', they announced, which is hard to believe in Shelcombe in April.

I stopped at the last house on the right, painted a defiant bright blue, with sunshine-yellow woodwork and a red front door. Neat white blinds half covered each window. There was a poster for music at the Anchor: 'The Gay City Rollers'. Some hilarious tribute band, I guessed, wondering if Erica's taste in music has reached new depths.

I banged the big brass knocker, which was so shiny I could see my reflection in it. As I took in the little piggy eyes and the huge bulbous nose, hoping it was a distortion, the door swung open and there stood Erica, in rubber gloves.

'Come in,' she said, leading me towards her kitchen. 'Did you know you're wearing odd shoes?'

I looked down and swore. I really should have opened those bedroom curtains.

'So long as you don't dress like that to meet clients,' she said laughing. 'Come on through. I'm just sorting out the fridge. Is it money?'

'No, not this time.'

'Woman problems?'

'I wish.'

I sat at the table while Erica reminded me of how effortlessly she keeps on top of things. Not only does she run a successful dating agency based in London, but she also finds time to sustain a long-distance relationship with someone in New York, be a mother and keep her fridge-freezer pristine. The thing was wide open before me, glowing cheerfully while Erica placed little jars of this, packets of that, back on their shelves; all parallel or at right angles to one another.

'There,' she said finally, closing the fridge door and running a tea towel over it, before bundling up the cloth and popping it in the washing machine. Then she turned – five-six, slim but curvy, overdressed for housework, and with that curtain of blonde silky hair that half hides her left eye and stops somewhere near her shoulder. 'What can I do for you?' she asked.

I wasn't sure how to broach the thing I had in mind. Ten minutes ago I'd been high and clear-thinking on champagne, positive Erica would be amenable. But now the bracing walk was beginning to take its toll, as was the lack of breakfast or a proper lunch. 'Food would be nice,' I said, and the fridge came open again.

Erica pulled a face. 'Debbie Duval . . . a bit older than me, you think?'

'Said she was forty-one.'

'And she definitely grew up in Shelcombe?'

'That's the impression I got.'

'Well, there was only one school and it wasn't big. So, even if she'd been a year or two above me, I'd have known her; who she hung out with, went out with. That sort of thing'

'Hm,' I said. I've never been keen on the incestuousness of Shelcombe. Erica seems to have a connection with everyone, but then she did grow up in the place. How different our childhoods were. Hers was council estate camaraderie, scary rides, candy floss – a day at the beach, in fact. Mine was prep school, alcoholic mother, boarding by eleven. When I was loathing Latin and trying to avoid rugby, aged sixteen, she was pissed on cider and skinny-dipping at midnight, aged fourteen. I often wish I'd had Erica's good start.

She said, 'Gary Clinker doesn't ring a bell either.'

'He signs on, so you may have come across him when you worked at the Jobcentre?'

'Nope. Weird, eh? Anyway, what's your client planning on doing with her million?' I'd finished eating and, in the blink of an eye, Erica had spirited everything away, wiped the table and put the vase of flowers back. She sat down and tucked the curtain of hair behind her ear. 'Or should I say what are *you* planning?'

'I'm not sure yet. Trouble is, Erica, I'm expecting quite a few consultations with her and, well, you know what my place is like these days. Hardly—'

'Impressive? No. So you want to meet her here? Pretend it's your place, even?'

'Well . . .'

'That's fine,' she said. She was even smiling. 'One condition, though.'

For a silly second, I thought she might demand sex. 'What?' I asked, bracing myself for some painful chore. Having Alice for an entire month again. I love my daughter dearly, but that had definitely tested our relationship.

'Get Debbie to sign up with me.'

'With Opposites?'

'Yep. Sounds like her marriage is dead. What better way to change her life than to find a new partner? Someone completely different from herself.'

I nodded and tried to think who the opposite of Debbie Clinker might be. One of the Royals, perhaps. A few years back, Erica decided there must be people who'd benefit from being with someone quite unlike themselves. She then went on to prove this with Opposites, an agency that mostly matches highly strung, big-bonus city types with placid, rural or suburban homebodies – folks who'll have a hearty stew on the go but won't complain if you miss dinner. Often, the ones with the stew are guys, the ones calling to say they'll be late, women.

'It's an idea,' I said. 'Only I have one tiny condition too.'

'I'm not sleeping with you.'

That was hardly what I'd been about to ask, but I managed a dejected, 'No?'

'We stopped doing that, remember? When I got together with Kurt?'

'Ah, yeah. OK, but what I'd really appreciate is if Opposites could sort of keep a low profile. I'd like my client to think she'd found him herself, as a result of my life coaching.'

'God, you're devious,' she said, 'but all right. Only there'll be a higher fee if we're not going to get the credit.'

I shrugged. It would still be a drop in the ocean. I reached over and put my hand on hers. 'Thanks,' I said, and she didn't move. I smiled too – attractively, I hoped. 'Listen, are you sure you wouldn't like to—'

'Oh, Tim,' she sighed. She wriggled her hand away from mine and stood up. 'Come on. Follow me.' I obeyed, unable to believe how my day was going. When we got to the bedroom, Erica reached up for my shoulders and swung me round to face her full-length mirror. 'Take a good look,' she said, before heading back downstairs.

MONDAY

Deborah After breakfast, I sat on the bed typing notes into my laptop: 'Why choose Cash? Makes him sound greedy.' I was told his real name is Downer – confirmed when his library ticket fell out of his wallet in the Lobster Pot. Greedy or just in need of money? I remembered his face when I said I wanted help with my finances. He'd been about to do a runner, that was for sure. Then somehow, from somewhere, came the Premium Bond idea. What on earth made me say a million, though?

Trustworthy? Hard to have unerring faith in a man who claims not to smoke but has mustard-coloured fingers and a cigarette burn in his shirt pocket.

Bit of a drinker? He raced through that champagne – plus what sober person uses his pocket as an ashtray?

Likeable? Yes, strangely.

* * *

I sank back into the pillows and looked out at the bay. It was a good find, the studio flat; owned by someone called George, a friend of my features editor, Stefan. The offer of accommodation had decided the location of my investigation, and the life coach too. George said he knew a woman called Erica, whose ex-husband was a life coach. 'Calls himself Cash,' Stefan was told. After Stefan and I looked up Timothy Cash – one of six life coaches in the area but the only one not giving an address – all I had to do was move in and call him.

After five days, the tiny flat is beginning to feel like home. It's clean, modern and, more importantly when you're on Shelcombe's seafront, efficiently heated. Despite the biting wind and the lack of anything the hell to do in the town, I consider myself lucky to have got 'L is for Life Coach' in our 'A to Z of Helpers and Healers' series. I could, like my London flatmate, Mel, have got 'F is for Fruitarian', and be investigating the woman in Derby, who puts you on a raw-food diet and can literally smell when you've strayed from it.

No, it isn't such a bad gig, Shelcombe. And 'L is for Life Coach' might make an interesting article, after all. For a start, Timothy Cash is something of a surprise. Appearancewise, a total mess. Forty-something? Long, unbrushed hair. Stubble that doesn't look deliberate. Beneath it all, he's got a nice face, though. Dark brown eyes, good bone structure, a warm, full mouth. I'd imagine he was quite a looker at one time. But now, in his raggedy old clothes and that pallor . . . and what was with those shoes? He must have realised. Could it, I wondered, simply be a ploy? I pulled the laptop towards me.

Is it just part of the programme? Has Timothy Cash worked out that you take one look at him and instantly feel better about yourself?

My legs were beginning to tingle, so I got off the bed and went out on the balcony. It was too nice a morning to be inside. Cold, but nice. There were figures on the beach already and several dogs playing fetch, charging into the waves with abandon. It looked inviting – not the water, but the beach – so I went back in and grabbed my jacket from a chair. While I was slipping it on, the foul smell of cigarettes hit me. It was coming from the hideous wig, lying curled up on the seat of the chair, like a big black cat with a forty-a-day habit. I picked it up between finger-tips and took it outside. 'God, I hate you,' I said, drop-ping it on the balcony. Smoking, when I actually don't, is painful, as is wearing sponge in my cheeks and second-hand glasses. But the torture of the hot and itchy wig is the worst thing. How can Dolly Parton bear it?

After locking the sliding window, I went to get my trainers. Half the wardrobe houses things I found in Shelcombe's charity shops last week: lots of baggy tops and trousers, two bland and shapeless calf-length skirts and a couple of stretched-in-the-wash cardies – all in different shades of beige. From one hanger dangles the strap-on padding I've concocted to go under my new outfits. Not that I'll need it if I carry on taking three sugars in my tea. What's been most depressing about this assignment so far, is discovering how easily I can pass for forty-one, seven years older than I am. I put the trainers on, ran a brush through my longish, some might say red but I say auburn, hair, and went out to see what a Monday morning in Shelcombe has to offer.

This turned out to be more or less the same as any other day. The centre is a clone of every small English town, the seafront attractions are few, and the beach, when you see it at close range, is grubby and littered. In the end, I headed for the Lobster Pot for a spot of lunch. Everything goes on expenses.

'You'll probably need a couple of weeks,' Stefan said. 'The flat's a freebie, but spend the money on your life coach, not on Nemesis rides.'

From my window table, I could just see the funfair. Shelcombe's answer to Nemesis is the Wild Mouse: an oxymoron of a ride with two-seater mice carriages, currently being painted a terrifying lemon. At its highest point, the ride is shorter than the bingo hall and cafeteria.

I had four hours to fill till I had to get into my Debbie gear. I wished I'd brought my laptop. Then I could have put some final touches to my homeopathy piece, due to go in the July edition of *Zip!* Provided we last that long. Month after month the readership's been falling. In fact, if I had any sense at all, I'd have spent those four hours job hunting.

*   *   *

Tim's shoes were canvas and worn out, but at least they matched today. He probably hadn't combed his hair since Saturday.

'Come in, Debbie,' he greeted me. 'Let's start in the kitchen with a cup of something, shall we? Then move into the sitting room. Can I take your jacket?'

'Ta,' I said glumly, not wanting to smile and crack the makeup.

He took my horrible jacket and wandered down the hall. 'Lovely day, isn't it? They're forecasting a scorcher of a summer for the UK. Mind you, how many scorching summers do you remember in Shelcombe, eh, Debbie?' He stopped, turned and stared at me, obviously wanting an answer.

'Well, there was 1976,' I said, knowing I couldn't go wrong with that.

'Ah, before my time,' he chuckled. He seemed much more upbeat today. Perhaps he'd realised how much he's making an hour. 'I'll just hang this up for you.'

He opened a door under the stairs and peered in. I joined him. It seemed to be a broom cupboard, with ironing board and other household items all neatly arranged. I was impressed.

'Um . . .' he said, moving on to the next door. Now we were looking at a toilet. 'Er, loo,' he said. 'Should you, you know . . .'

'Thanks.' Was he going to show me every cupboard in the house?

He took the first step down into the kitchen, then

cried, 'Ah!' and backtracked, almost bumping into me. My jacket was hung in a little alcove. 'Coat rack,' he said, almost to himself.

Although he'd told me on Saturday that he'd been in his present house for fifteen years, I had to show him how the back door unlocked when I lit up my first cigarette. Had he never been in his back garden? Odd, I thought, but then it got odder. In the cloakroom were bottles of handcream, moisturiser and perfume. On a shelf in the sitting room sat a photo of a fair-haired man, posing on a beach in only shorts. 'With all my love, Kurt' was handwritten across the bottom. If Tim was gay, he had good taste in men, but I suspected he wasn't, and that I was in the home of a very tidy woman with a muscular boyfriend.

The game was finally given away, though, when the front door bashed open and a tall young girl with Tim's features popped her head in the room and said, 'Oops, sorry. Mum said you'd be gone by the time I got back from school.' She nodded in my direction with a 'Hi', then added, 'It reeks of your fags in here, Dad. Mum'll go mad.'

Tim was forced to own up. He was using his ex-wife's house, it being a little more – he searched for a word – 'roomy' than his own. And OK, he was a smoker, but intending to give up very soon. 'We could do it together?' he suggested, then whispered, 'Sorry about Alice. Going through a bossy phase. You know what they can be like.'

'Tell me about it,' I said, and he did. All about the years he'd spent teaching adolescents, or trying to. He'd moved into estate agency but hadn't been much good at that either. 'And then I found my niche.'

'Oh, yeah?' I said. 'What was that?'

'Well . . . life coaching.'

'Ah. Right.'

But perhaps I shouldn't pass judgement too quickly, I thought, as I lumbered home along the promenade like an overweight, middle-aged woman. This gait wasn't because I was still keeping up the pretence, but because I couldn't help it. Looking that way made me walk that way.

Back at the flat, the wig came off first. 'I hate you!' I said, flinging it on the balcony and rubbing my scalp. Then came the glasses, the tights, the skirt, the padding, the blouse and the stuffed-with-itchy-napkins bra. I went to the bathroom, hooked the small sponges out of my mouth and looked in the mirror, thanking God for the power shower. I turned it on, stepped in and blasted my makeup off.

Jonathan The sound of a sliding window and 'I hate you' woke me up. Then came the loud swish and clunk of the window shutting. I put my hands over my ears in case she did it again. I can't stand loud noises.

I thought my neighbour must be talking to her wig, because I've heard her do that before. I think she's a bit mad, but I wouldn't mind getting to know the girl next door. She's quite pretty, when she isn't in those terrible clothes. No, very pretty. And not really a girl. I think she must be about ten years older than me. Which is OK. I like older people. I like younger people too. It's the ones my own age I'm not so keen on. I don't know why my neighbour sometimes dresses that way, but I've got more important things to think about. With my parents paying for private tutors and the bedsit and everything, I'm supposed to pass my exams this time.

Anyway, my neighbour and I have had just the one 'Hi, I'm Deborah', 'Hi, I'm Jonathan' conversation on our balconies. Well, not quite a conversation. I couldn't think of anything else to say, so I just went back in and played computer chess. That was last week. She certainly looked good then: tall, lovely shiny hair, tight T-shirt and short skirt, nice legs, big brown eyes. It's amazing how she changes into Mrs Drab. I wondered if she was an actress. My favourite actress is Angela Lansbury.

When it went quiet and I was sure Deborah wasn't around, I got up off the sofa, stepped over the pile of books and went outside. There was the wig again, lying on her half of the divided balcony. I still wasn't sure if she was an actress or a madwoman. I'm sure my friend Clive would be able to tell. Well, he's a sort of friend. He comes round to play computer games sometimes and is always trying to sell me drugs. My parents don't give me enough money to buy drugs, and anyway, the two times I tried smoking stuff it made me 'fucking paranoid', as Clive put it.

I went back in, feeling hungry, but couldn't find any food so fell on the sofa and zapped the TV on. It was *Murder, She Wrote*. I'd forgotten. Which is strange, because I don't usually forget. But it was one I'd seen seven times before, so I knew who'd done it. Truthfully, I prefer crime dramas when you know who did it right from the start, like *Columbo*. Because then you don't have to try and work out people's motives or try and understand their reactions when they're being interviewed, etc. When I was younger, my sister would say things like, 'It's so obvious he's the murderer, Jon, from that look he just gave the victim's wife.' What look? I used to think. I expect my sister was winding me up. People are always doing that.

Tim 'So who's the woman in the hilarious wig?' Alice asked. We were at her mother's kitchen table. It was covered in the maths homework I said I'd help her with but then couldn't.

'Who do you mean?'

'Your client or whatever.'

'She wears a wig?'

'Duh.'

'Really?'

'Dad, it's so obvious.' She laughed cruelly. 'God, men are so dumb.'

I wondered if she was basing this on a large sample, or just me and that plonker of a boyfriend she's had for a while. Rupert is so different from Alice, it's almost as though her mother had a hand in it.

'Men have', I said confidently, 'been known to invent computers and mobile phones.'

'Things that give off toxic particles and cook your brains?'

'Yes, but.'

'I rest my case.'

I tried to remember the last time I won an argument with my daughter, or told her something she didn't know. These days the roles have reversed. 'Dirigisme?' I had to ask the other week. She'd sighed and said, 'State control of economic and social spheres?' shaking her head as though despairing of me. I do so hope this is just a phase and that one day soon she'll get into shopping, and only shopping, like normal daughters.

'She's called Debbie,' I said, guessing that wasn't breeching client confidentiality. 'Debbie Duval.' I'll stop there, I decided.

'And you're life coaching her?'

'Yep.'

'What does she do? I know this is uncharacteristically classist of me but she looks as though she might clean the bogs down on the front. I mean, has she got enough money to pay your extortionate fees?'

'I charge no more than is recommended by the Federation,' I bristled. 'Normally. And besides, she has plenty of money, I assure you. Plenty.'

'How come?'

'Well, she—' *Stop*, I told myself.

'Robbed a bank?'

'No, she . . .' *Don't.* 'So how are you and Rupert getting on these days?'

'Maybe she's on the game,' sniggered Alice. 'In fact, no way. Not in those clothes.'

'Are you both still doing the conservation work on the coastal path at weekends?' I'd been meaning to go and help but hadn't found the time. It's odd how doing bugger-all can stretch to fill an entire day.

'I know, she was some rich recluse's housekeeper and he left her tens of thousands in his will.'

'And how about the t'ai chi?' I asked. 'You and Rupert still doing that on the beach before school?' I suspect Rupert isn't as keen on these activities as Alice, but doesn't have much say in things.

'Maybe *hundreds* of thousands,' Alice said. Her big brown eyes were boring into me. I hate that. It always wears me down in the end. 'Hey,' she went on, as I knew she would, 'you've found a client in Shelcombe with hundreds of thousands of pounds. You have, haven't you? I can tell by your face. Ha! Wait till I tell Rupert.'

'Actually, she's got a million,' I said, suddenly heart-warmed to have Alice feel proud of me. 'A windfall. She's about to lose her job and lives in a council house. Her husband's a no-gooder and her kids are a nightmare. She wants me to give her a complete makeover and point her in all the right directions for a life change.'

Alice continued to stare at me and I returned her gaze. How like myself at that age, eighteen, she looked, with her dark and unruly shoulder-length waves. Exactly the style I sported through adolescence. And, in fact, not unlike my current mop. Must get it cut. Alice is always bemoaning the fact she didn't inherit her mother's fine pale hair. 'And you reckon you're capable of that?' she asked.

I laughed. 'At ninety pounds an hour, I think I have to be.'

'*Ninety?*'

'Er, yeah.' I felt a cold breeze coming from somewhere. Across the table, maybe.

The eyes narrowed. 'Dad, that's *totally* obscene. I hope you're going to donate some to a good cause?'

'Erm . . .' I said, unable for the moment to think of a better cause than Timothy Cash.

'Have you any idea,' Alice enunciated, 'what even one pound would mean to a family of ten in Bujumbura?'

I hadn't heard of Bujumbura. It sounded vaguely Australian, but from the look on Alice's face it wasn't in Queensland. Perhaps when Debbie Duval pays me, I'll go there. Anything to get away from my scary daughter.

I decided on a long and circuitous route home because I didn't really want to arrive. If only those two bustling women from that TV programme would come and work their lemon juice and vinegar magic on my house. Alternatively, I could look in the Yellow Pages for someone, now I'm going to be flush. I fingered the ninety pounds in my pocket, still inside the envelope. Debbie had insisted on cash payments only, saying, 'I ain't paid no tax, so I don't see why you should.'

As I meandered round the streets, I decided a plan of action was needed. Aside from working on her double negatives, perhaps I'd try being more assertive and directional with her: 'Get rid of the wig!' – that sort of thing. 'Hire a personal shopper!' Actually, I could do that myself. Borrow Erica's car and take Debbie into Bournemouth to a department store. My head did the sums. About five hours' work in all. Four hundred and fifty pounds! Well, just over four hundred, what with the ten per cent for the family in Bujumbura. Alice had made me sign a pledge.

TUESDAY

Erica I'd work from home, I decided when I got up. But would also find time for a jog, a nice healthy lunch and telephone sex with Kurt, probably in that order as it was currently around two a.m. in New York. I'd thought up a great little fantasy for us, involving Kurt and myself, a box at the Royal Opera House, a tub of Häagen-Dazs and a good-looking usher. Being a classical music buff, Kurt would love it. I've been genning up on opera to make it more authentic.

It's always lovely not having to catch the train to London. I took my coffee to the computer and picked up a dozen or so emails. Although a lot of our clients are happy to do it themselves via Opposites' website, many choose the option of having us sift through possible matches and perhaps arrange the first rendezvous. People seem to feel comforted by the old-fashioned approach and don't mind paying a bit extra for it. Well, didn't. New clients aren't exactly queuing out the door these days. But they should be. We (one part-timer and myself) offer counselling – the dating game can be so bruising – and insist on meeting everyone who signs up so we can weed out all the oddballs and pervs. Not that we catch all of them.

I rattled off some replies, then checked the day's stars. I'm Aries, Kurt's Libra – perfect opposites. It's funny how I always go for Librans. Today, apparently, I was going to discover deception, and he, the bastard, was going to reach a new level of intimacy with a lover. I panicked, but only briefly, as Alice had appeared at the door with mug in hand and a look that told me I'd done something wrong.

'Good morning, love,' I said.

'No, actually, it's not a good one, Mum. The Fairtrade tea's all gone, and I can't stomach the exploitative bleached-bag stuff you drink.'

'Oh . . . try the green caddy. I put your teabags in there.'

'Yeah?'

'Mm, yesterday.'

Alice looked doubtful, then sniggered at the computer. 'Sorry to interrupt your, er, work.'

'Libra' was still on the screen above a set of scales. 'Just doing a bit of research. I've got a client who's into astrology and she's desperate to meet an unattached Libran.'

'Oh, yeah? Dad's a Libran, isn't he? You couldn't get much more unattached than him, plus he's going to be in the money soon, now he's getting ninety pounds an hour.'

'How much!'

'I know.' Alice shook her head. 'You should see this new client of his.'

I was, in fact, planning to bump into her later; see if I recognised her. 'What do you mean?'

'Well, she blatantly wears a wig. Only Dad didn't spot it, of course.'

'That might be because he sat on his glasses. Do you remember? They were all taped up for a while and now I haven't seen him in them for ages. Unless he's got contacts?'

'Yeah, *right*.'

I laughed, although Tim always being skint and never getting his act together has gone way beyond a joke. Mostly, though, I try not to dwell on it, and when Alice wandered off, my thoughts returned to Kurt. Now it was almost three a.m. in New York. I pictured him in his loft, reaching a new level of intimacy with some tartlet from his law firm. I wanted to ring and interrupt them but instead tried a different online astrologer. 'As an Aries, you value honesty in others above all else. However, today you'll discover . . .' I quickly hit Libra. 'A day for whispering sweet nothings, or even somethings, to that special . . .' 'Fuck,' I whispered. 'I'll kill him.'

I went back to the Opposites website and was having a trawl through, checking that it was up to date and working properly, when Alice slouched in with, 'Nice try, Mum,' and tipped the contents of the tea caddy on my desk.

Alice It comes as something of a shock when you realise your mother's completely shallow and not very informed. I've kind of got used to the fact now. Dad's different – he reads real books and is lovely and well-meaning, and doesn't place much importance on appearance and possessions and things. In fact, no importance. But, all the same, I do often wonder where I get my intellect and depth from. If I didn't have Dad's face and hair, I'd probably think I was Gabriel García Márquez's secret daughter, conceived on a holiday in Colombia. I wouldn't put it past Mum to have his baby, but never to have read his books. Mum reads magazines – and I don't mean *New Scientist* – or she might take a cookery book to bed if she feels like being stretched. She likes any TV programme that involves voting people off and thinks modern music peaked with seventies disco. As much as she mocks poor Rupert, at least he knows John Donne was a metaphysical poet, not a Radio 2 DJ. God, she was *so* embarrassing at the Anchor quiz, especially in that literature round. 'Yeats?' she called out to the quizmaster, laughing. 'I think you mean *Yeets*?'

I sometimes wish my gran was my mum. Gran's a widow and still lives in the council house my mother grew up in. It's fifteen minutes from us, if you walk, or three in the car, but you'd think Gran lived in Yorkshire or somewhere from the number of times Mum visits. I go and see her a lot because she always seems so proud of the things I do – 'You got to the second round of the tennis tournament? Well *done*, Alice.'

I was actually horribly embarrassed at being knocked out so early on, and Mum didn't help. 'You must get it from your father. I was always *so* good at games.' But not much else, judging by her three O levels.

God, I was pissed off with her this morning. I give her money each week from my allowance so she'll buy Fairtrade and free-range stuff when she does the big shop, but so often she forgets. I'll get them myself from now on. Anyway, after drinking only water for breakfast, I cycled to Rupert's, then we cycled together to school. Rupert lives in a huge Victorian house with his lawyer father, who's always in London, and his brittle mother, who's always at home, unfortunately. I think Mrs Gerrard is depressed, and so would I be if my husband didn't hide the fact that he had a Monday-to-Friday-and-some-times-Saturday mistress in Swiss Cottage.

I think having a man is like having a dog. If you let them know from the start that you require loyalty, respect and a certain amount of obedience, you won't end up like Mrs Gerrard. It's what I've done with Rupert, and he practically worships me.

When we reached school, which is now on its new site in the suburbs and an extra two miles for me to go, all I had to say was, 'Rupert, I'm famished,' and he was off to the Baker's Dozen round the corner for me. He came back with an egg and bacon roll and a cup of tea.

Of course I feel guilty eating these things. The eggs aren't free range, the bacon's from pigs who never see daylight either, and the tea . . . Well, a person has to eat. Anyway, I've made Rupert *swear* not to tell Mum.

Deborah I arrived at Tim's, or rather Erica's, at midday, as arranged. He was going to take me out to get me some new outfits. I'd tried hard to wriggle out of it, of course. If anything was going to blow my cover it would be Tim popping his head in the cubicle while I tried things on.

He opened the door, head to toe in ancient denim. 'Come in, come in,' he said joyfully. 'Let me just get the car keys. This is going to be such fun!'

'Hm,' I said. Could Tim be the one man who likes shopping with a woman?

While he was in the sitting room and I hovered in the hallway, picking up one of his leaflets from the hall table and trying to avoid my hideous self in the big mirror, a person with long, very blonde hair, a red off-the-shoulder jumper and leather trousers appeared from the kitchen.

'Hello,' the woman sang out as she strode towards me. 'I'm Erica Jones-Downer.' A powerful perfume arrived just after her.

I shook the outstretched hand. 'Hiya, I'm Debbie.'

'Here to see Tim?'

'Yeah.'

Erica gave me a lipsticky smile and said, 'Do you want

to go through?' A few faint lines fanned out from her bright blue eyes, and big hoop earrings shone beside her cheeks. She was pretty, well-groomed and looked squeaky clean. How could she have been married to Tim?

'Actually, we're going out,' I said. 'He's just getting his car keys.'

'His? Ha ha.'

Tim reappeared saying, 'Right. Let's shop till you drop.'

'Did I hear "shop"?' Erica asked.

Tim slipped arms, then head, into a tired-looking green ribbed jumper with shoulder and elbow patches. 'Yes,' he said when his stubbled face reappeared. 'I'm taking Debbie into Bournemouth for some new clothes.'

'What?' Erica shot down the hallway and returned with a suede jacket. 'Not without me you're not. You'll be hopeless, Tim. Ready?'

'Ah . . . um, is this all right with you?' he asked me.

No it bloody wasn't. 'Ouch,' I said, one hand flying to my stomach. 'Oooh . . . ow. Oh God, not again. I'm sorry, could I use your cloakroom?'

Erica looked appalled. 'I'll show you where—'

''S alright, I know,' I said, hurtling towards it.

I sat on the toilet and counted to a hundred, and when I came out they were both standing by the open front door, murmuring.

'Are you all right?' Tim asked, looking genuinely concerned.

'Not really. Something I ate, I expect.'

'Can I get you anything? A glass of water?'

'No, ta. Think I'll just go and get some rest, if that's OK.' I squeezed past both of them. 'Sorry. Look, I'll give you a bell, yeah?' I clutched at my stomach again.

'OK,' said Tim. 'But can't I drive you home? You look really sick.'

'Don't worry, it ain't that far.'

'Well, take care. See you tomorrow?'

'Yeah.'

Tim waved me off, while Erica stood with her arms folded, half smiling in a way that I didn't like at all.

When I reached the beach, having regularly checked that I wasn't being followed by anyone in leather trousers, I sat on the sand in front of a row of huts. It was another warm sunny day but there was little seaside activity. One man, one spaniel and two schoolboys were all I could see, so I removed the sponges and pulled my wig off without fear of frightening anyone. Next came the glasses, then the awful cardigan I'd been sweltering in, the clompy shoes and the elastic-waisted trousers. That left me in shorts and long baggy T-shirt, chosen in case I'd got caught half dressed by Tim. I undid the padding around my middle, tugged it out and wrapped it and the wig in the cardigan. I then lay back on the sand and let the sun work its way through half an inch of makeup, while I tried to think what to do next.

There was no denying I'd screwed up. Erica was on to me, and maybe Tim too. I realised what a crap idea this whole disguise business had been. 'Ridiculous,' I whispered, as my eyes grew heavier. 'What was I thinking?'

The honest thing would be to return to London and admit defeat, but then I pictured Stefan's face. Stefan knows nothing about Debbie Clinker, thank God. 'Ridiculous,' I said again, then, 'Bugger.' I couldn't go back to the office empty-handed. I'd have to write something, but realised as I lay there that I've actually learned very little about life coaching in the past couple of days. What I have found out is that Timothy Cash is a nice guy. That he had a miserable time at boarding school, tried several careers before his present one, is pretty hard up, longs to have his little girl back, aged six or seven, and that he's still a bit in love with his ex-wife. Some of this he's told me, some I've deduced.

So what exactly does a life coach do? I deliberately hadn't researched the subject in order to meet Tim with no preconceptions. I could check out more local life coaches, but there wasn't one actually in the town, and with no car . . . ugh, could I be bothered? I'd go on the Internet, I decided, and find out more. After I'd had a bit of a rest in the sun. All this pretending to be someone else was exhausting.

Tim Erica said, 'I tell you, Tim, that was no Shelcombe accent.'

'It wasn't?'

'You've lived here twenty years, can't you tell?'

'Obviously not. Actually, I think I've always been more visual than aural.'

'That's true,' she sighed. 'I don't remember you being very oral at all.'

'I don't remember you asking me to be.' When Erica gave me an exasperated look I kicked myself. A silence followed while I worked out how to get back on subject. 'Perhaps her parents were from somewhere else?'

'Hmm. It's not just the accent. I only saw her for a couple of minutes but I thought she didn't really gel as a human being. The wig, the lovely hands. No lines on her neck, I noticed. Unusual for a forty-one-year-old. Look at mine.'

She lifted her chin and I peered. I hadn't noticed my ex-wife's lines before, so perhaps I'm not that visual either. 'Oh, yeah.'

'God, Tim, you're really squinting. Would you like me to buy you some glasses?'

'Don't worry, I'll be able to get some soon.'

Erica said, 'That's assuming this Debbie hasn't got a screw loose,' as she tried stroking her lines away. 'Could be she hasn't even had a Premium Bond win.'

My heart stopped. I'd just booked Shelcombe Scrubbers to come and blitz my house. 'No, no, I'm sure she has. Anyway, I'll try and find out more tomorrow. We've arranged daily appointments for this week.'

'Right. You know my stars this morning said I'd come across deception in a person. Amazing, yeah?'

'Mm.' Erica and her stars have been part of my life for so long, I no longer deride them.

'So you're seeing her tomorrow, eh? That's good. She's got me intrigued now.'

'But you'll be in London tomorrow?' I almost pleaded. If it wasn't for Erica I'd now be four hundred quid better off.

'I don't have to go, if you need me to—'

'I'll be fine.'

Deborah I woke up frozen and with a hairy dog licking my toes. 'Get off!' I cried, disgusted.

The owner called, 'Here, Ben!' with a clap of his hands and the dog did as he was told. I jumped up, grabbed my bag and broke into a jog, mainly to warm myself up but also to get to the sea quickly to wash my foot. Where had the sun gone? I couldn't believe it was the same day.

Paddling in the waves of Shelcombe beach was as I'd expected – shocking and painful – but it well and truly woke me up. I jogged back to the promenade, bought a pair of flip-flops and a sweatshirt saying 'Shelcombe-on-Sea For Me!', then went into the Paradise Café. It had red and brown sauce in plastic bottles, tarnished placemats and a menu that didn't mention a single vegetable. Perfect.

I took a window table and drank a mug of milky tea, thinking about letting Tim down, and how shitty that was of me. He ought to be paid for today, and maybe more. But how? It had to be cash – I could hardly write him a cheque – and a lot of it. Stefan would be suspicious if I hadn't used much of what I've been allocated.

A generous amount, as it turns out. Perhaps he's being a bit what-the-hell, suspecting, as we all do, that *Zip!* is soon to fold. Of course, I could always just go on a clothes-buying spree . . .

No. I got out my notebook and wrote Tim a short letter. Later, I'd get money from a machine. Then much later, the middle of the night perhaps, I'd put the cash and the note through Erica's door.

I stared out at the incoming sea and shivered. How did people swim in it without fearing a heart attack? I pictured Tim frolicking in the icy waves with his little girl each summer, building sandcastles and getting buried up to his neck. I felt almost sad that I wouldn't be seeing him again. I really rather like my wreck of a life coach.

Erica 'Hi, Kurt.'

'Hey,' he said affectionately, and I instantly felt better. Of course he wouldn't screw around.

'I've thought up a great fantasy,' I told him. 'You, me, a hunk of an usher at the Royal—'

'Sounds great, hun. But listen, let me just take you off speakerphone. Got a bit of a meeting going on here.'

'Oh, not again. Sorry.'

'That's OK, Dan and Frankie are getting used to it.'

I heard distant mirth. 'Am I off yet?'

'Yep. Shall I call you back when it's, er, more convenient?'

'Sure. I'll be home all day.'

'OK.'

'Oh, and I probably won't be wearing knickers.'

'I'll keep that beautiful thought in mind,' he said, and hung up.

Another Bridget Jones moment. I sometimes wish I was anything but a ram, charging into situations without thinking. You wouldn't find a dreamy fish or a wary crab doing that. On the other hand, I wouldn't have set up my business if I'd been another star sign. How they all laughed. 'Good plan, Erica. An agency that finds you exactly what you *don't* want.' But I've shown them. OK, I've bent my original rules a bit – had to, really – and the 'opposites' thing can now apply to hair colour, skin colour, height, reading tastes. Or just the fact that one's a man and the other a woman, if need be. Desperate measures, you might say.

I switched on the computer and got up my website, hoping to find a match for Debbie Clinker. Ray the accountant? Fifty-three and . . . oh, no . . . looking for someone in her early thirties. He'll be lucky, I thought. Or perhaps he will be. Strangely, the younger women tend to be less fussy than those in their forties and fifties. 'No smokers or nose pickers,' one older divorcee insisted. 'No country-and-western fans, motorbike enthusiasts, snorers, binge drinkers or wearers of white trainers. No caravaners, red-top readers, Internet porn users, TV-remote hoggers, car-booters or pub quizzers.' I got her together with Bill, who pretty much matched that description, and now they're so happy, I use them in my promotional material.

I scrolled down the page through the assorted faces.

Vic the dentist, who was turning out to be a serial one-night-stand guy. I'm not into pimping, so won't be renewing his membership. Mind you, the way things are going, I won't be renewing anyone's.

Lance the hairdresser? *The* perfect man for Debbie, who must feel desperate about her hair to wear a wig that bad. I made a note on the pad beside the keyboard, then moved on to Stefan.

Ah, Stefan. An excessively good-looking journalist, working on a magazine but moonlighting as a novelist. I've had trouble keeping this one out of my head, ever since he walked in the office a month ago and told me he was looking for a blonde extrovert. 'How about me, me, me!' I wanted to shout.

He's been in several times since, always with the same opening line: 'Found me a blonde extrovert yet?' He stays and chats for a while, asking me lots of questions about myself, what kind of men I like. It's all looking rather hopeful but, as yet, he hasn't asked me out. I realised he might be waiting for me to make the first move, so when he asked what Shelcombe was like, I said, 'Why don't you come and find out one weekend? We're not Cannes but we've got good fish and chips.'

He told me he might just do that, and I found myself, against my own rules, giving him my address and home number.

'Fire away then,' said Kurt. 'No wait, I just have to get something out.'

I breathed impatiently. 'Is it out?'

He gave a little groan. 'Yeah . . .'

'OK, we're at the opera.'

'Great. Which one?'

'Toss . . . ca.'

'You're wicked,' he drooled. 'What are you wearing?'

'Tight strappy red dress, fur wrap, lacy hold-up stockings, high-heeled shoes . . . no underwear.'

'Mmmm . . .'

'You're in a dinner jacket, looking blond and gorgeous. It's the Royal Opera House. We have seats in a box, but we're having trouble finding it.'

'Oh, yeah?'

'Mmm. So . . . we stop and ask this usher. He's tall and dark and mouth-wateringly handsome. After stripping me with his eyes, he—'

'Is it this Stefan guy again?'

'Well . . . yes. Do you mind?'

'Kinda. But carry on.'

Deborah I could see Jonathan, the young guy who lives next door, peeking from behind his curtain as I walked up to our building. I almost waved but thought that might embarrass him. What I decided to do, as I mounted the stairs, was to invite him round for a cup of tea or coffee. Now my secret mission was over, I might as well be sociable. Also, in the week I've been here I've only heard him go out once, and then he was back half an hour later. I sort of felt sorry for him.

After changing my cheesy sweatshirt and washing the makeup off, I knocked on his door and waited, but there was no response. I knocked a bit louder, then again, but still he didn't come to the door. I'd definitely seen him at the window, and I could hear his TV. All I could think was that in the time I'd taken to climb the stairs, he'd got into the shower or put headphones on, or something.

Oh, well. I returned to my flat and phoned Mel to see how she was getting on with her fruitarian, but she wasn't answering. Probably out flat-viewing. Our lease is expiring soon. I tried my parents, realising I hadn't told them where I was, but they were out. I tried my sister then my brother, with no luck. What were they all doing on a Tuesday in April?

I switched the laptop on, made myself tea and got on with some work. Through the wall I could hear movement, but I wasn't going to try again, no matter how much I fancied company. And, anyway, maybe he had a girl in there.

WEDNESDAY

Tim I was trying to make a bit of an effort, just so Shelcombe Scrubbers won't be too horrified when they turn up tomorrow. I moved the empty cans and the pile of bills from the kitchen table, then swept it with a dustpan and brush. In went empty fag packets, ash and butts, apple cores, crumbs galore and the remains of a chow mein. I felt truly disgusted with myself and tried to work out when exactly I'd become a slob. Surely not the minute Erica left? God, how the place used to glow. Floors got waxed, surfaces were clear and gleaming. You could see through the windows. There were always vases of flowers . . . then one day there weren't.

It was the lack of an explanation that hit me the hardest. 'I don't know, Tim,' she'd said, waving arms in an I-give-up way. 'I just can't be with you any more. I'm sorry.'

I wasn't able to buy her out of the house, but she took lots of the furniture and then somehow bought Drake

Street. How had she done that? It wasn't as though her widowed mother could help. Then there was the cost of setting up a business, although she once said something about a commercial loan. That's the thing about Erica: she makes stuff happen.

I tipped the rubbish into the black sack on the floor and was about to put the dustpan down when I remembered the fridge. I went over, opened it, wondered what the smell was and began sweeping the bottom shelf, the one all the bits of gunk had fallen on. As I emptied the dustpan again I heard the surprising noise of a key in my front door. Surprising, because only Alice has a key, and – I checked my watch – she was at school.

Apparently not, though. She came into the kitchen, followed by Rupert. Both were in T-shirts and jogging pants, and Alice was carrying a rucksack. 'Dad?' she said, stopping abruptly. 'You're not doing housework!'

I chose to ignore this and said, 'Hi, Rupert', but the kid was plugged into something and couldn't hear. 'Is it an inset day or something?' I asked Alice.

'Er, no. Listen, why don't you sit down. We've got something to tell you.'

I ran an eye over Rupert and felt dizzy. 'You're not pregnant?'

'Duh. I am on the pill, you know. Here.' She pulled a chair out.

I swept newspapers off and sat down. 'What?' I asked. 'Is it your mother?'

'No, no. Rupert, *sit*.' He did, and Alice pulled his

headphones out. All three of us were now at the newly cleared table.

'Whassup?' said Rupert, jabbing a hand my way. 'How's it going witch you, man?'

'Fine, thank you, Rupert. Now tell me what's happened, Alice.'

'OK. We were on the beach doing our t'ai chi this morning, right? When a dog came running up with . . .' she delved into the rucksack and pulled out a black wig, '. . . *this*.'

'Isn't that . . . ?'

'That's what I thought. So Rupert and I went and had a bit of a search. Honestly, Dad, the council's got to do something about that beach. It's like half of Shelcombe thinks that's where you leave your recycling. Newspapers, cans, sweet wrappers. There's dog poo everywhere, disgusting used condoms—'

'And did you find anything?' I asked. It's always best to cut her off early.

'This,' she said, tugging a chunky cardigan out. Debbie's cardigan. 'And this,' she continued, holding up a big brown shoe. Debbie's shoe. 'And these.' Debbie's trousers.

'But,' I said, then heard myself gulp, 'it might not necessarily—'

'There's more. Isn't there, Rupert?'

'What?'

'Tell Dad what we found on the doormat first thing this morning.'

'Oh, yeah. A leh-ah.'

'A letter?' I said, wondering if Erica should be letting Rupert stay over on school nights. 'Who to?'

'You, man. From laak the woman what's done herself in. We fought we dint ought a read it, but when we went back wiv da clothes we couln't help it, even though it had laak yous name on it.'

'And?'

'There's a wad of cash in there, I tell you, man.'

'Really?'

Alice pulled a face and handed over an envelope. 'Sorry,' she said. 'A bit rude, I know. It's just that it was ripped half open already, bulging with the money. I kind of guessed it was from Debbie.'

Alice didn't often apologise, so I said, 'That's all right,' as a lot of fifty-pound notes fluttered on to the table. I took out the letter and unfolded it. 'Dear Tim,' it said, handwritten. There was no date or address.

I'm sorry to do this. I've made a right mess of things, so it's best for everyone if I just bring the whole thing to an end. Wish I could explain.
    Debbie
    P.S. Hope this covers a couple of weeks' lost dosh for you.

I read it again, trying to work out what she meant. It was ambiguous, that was for sure. 'Do you really think . . . ?' I asked Alice. She tended to know everything these days. But she just shrugged.

'You must be proper gutted,' said Rupert. 'Losing laak a millionaire client.'

Alice said, 'Shut up, Rupert,' while she counted the money. 'Five hundred. Is that what she'd have paid you for a fortnight?'

'I dunno. Maybe.' Why were we discussing money when Debbie was . . . ? 'Oh God,' I said, hanging my head. 'She's topped herself.'

'You don't know that, Dad,' Alice said. She put a hand on my shoulder and squeezed. It felt odd, having her touch me. 'Maybe she just left town.'

'Naked?' I asked.

'That woundna been a pretty sight, man,' said Rupert. He did a pointing thing with all ten fingers. 'Not judging from them laak huge clothes.'

I stared at my daughter's conundrum of a boyfriend. He was undeniably good-looking – fair hair, clear blue eyes, no spots – and apparently a high-flyer at school. Straight As and brilliant at English, even though he couldn't speak it. Odd, because his parents were plummier than you'd think possible for Shelcombe. 'Why the fake rapper talk?' I once asked Alice, and she'd said, slightly puzzlingly, it was because his father wanted him to be a barrister.

'We should get to school,' she was saying. 'Shall we leave these with you? Maybe you'll want to take them to the police; report her as a missing person.'

'Yes, I suppose I should.' I piled up Debbie's things, then bundled the money in my shirt pocket.

Alice stood herself and her boyfriend up. She hooked the rucksack over her shoulder and gave me her warmest smile for years. 'Well, we'll be off. Are you going to be all right?'

'Yeah,' I said, reaching for my cigarettes. How lovely she was being to me. All it had taken was a death. 'Thanks.'

Rupert slapped my hand and was plugging himself in again, when Alice swung round and said, 'Hey, Dad. I think you've forgotten something.'

'What?'

She came back to the table, arm outstretched. 'Ten per cent?'

Alice If Dad's house wasn't so minging, as Rupert describes it, I'd move in with him. But it takes you half an hour to find anything in that kitchen, and then it's usually covered in fungus, in the dishwasher he filled a week ago and forgot to switch on.

There would be plusses, though. Dad does *listen* to me. Properly, not the way Mum half listens while she's spitting on her mascara. And he'll offer to help with homework. Dad did a sociology degree, so environmental studies, economics and maths are a bit beyond him – 'Got any long division? I always liked that' – but sometimes it's just nice to have someone to think out loud to.

He looked really worried about his client this morning, not surprisingly. As Rupert said, just when he finds a rich one, she disappears. It would be nice, for once, if something worked out for Dad. As much as Mum seems to despair of him, I think she likes the fact that she's the successful one. Well, if she gives it any thought at all.

Mum's not exactly reflective. Lots of things pop into her head, but I don't think they hang around for long. It's all live-in-the-moment with her. She's got a zillion so-called friends, mostly from way back, but hardly sees them and doesn't even like most of them. After she's chatted all sympathetically on the phone – 'What a pig, Paula. But then you're far too good for him' – she'll say to me, 'God, that woman's a doormat. Always has been.'

The annoying thing is, everyone loves her. People are always telling me my mother's amazing, and I know for a fact Rupert's got a crush on her. Still, she can some-times come in handy. *Will* come in handy, I hope, now I'm going to start a clean-up-the-beach campaign. Mum might not give a toss about the beach, but she does like the limelight.

Jonathan I was standing on the balcony, aiming bottle tops at a saucepan in the middle of the flat, when I spotted my neighbour in the street, about to enter the building. 'Hi, Deborah,' I called down. 'Lovely day.'

'Don't speak too soon,' she said with a nice girly giggle.

'Would you like a cup of tea?' I asked. I don't normally do this, so I was a bit shocked. Just as I was shocked and didn't know what to do, or what I would say, when Deborah knocked on my door yesterday evening. I knew it was her because I heard her door open and close, then open and close again afterwards. It's got a bit of a squeak. I've never had a girl in my flat. I've only had Clive, and my parents when they moved me in.

'OK,' Deborah said. 'See you in a minute.'

I dropped the bottle tops and ran to the kitchenette. Did I even have tea? Milk? I opened the little fridge. Shit, no milk. I went through the things on the worktop, then searched the cupboard. No tea, either. Now she was knocking on my door. Shit.

'Hello,' I said, swinging it open. 'I've run out of tea. Oh, and milk.'

Deborah said, 'Ah. Well, black coffee would be fine.'

I said, 'I don't like coffee so I don't buy it,' and waited for Deborah to invite me to her flat instead. Being a girl she'd have everything in, maybe even cake. It would be nice to sit and have a chat. I quite like my own company but sometimes I want someone to talk to. I imagined Deborah and myself watching a DVD together some time, getting a bit drunk, and who knows what else – once we've got past the tea-and-cake stage. It's good with an older woman, according to Clive.

I put my hands in my pockets and waited.

'Oh, well,' Deborah said, her keys coming back out of her handbag. 'Let's do it another time, then.' She looked over her shoulder at me and gave me a lovely, maybe sexy, smile as she let herself into her flat. 'Bye,' she said and I returned to mine, trying to work out what she meant by 'do it'.

Back playing my game, I tried drawing up a revision plan for the afternoon. English then history, or history then English? If I got the next bottle top in the saucepan, I'd go through my Woolf notes. If I missed, it would be totalitarian regimes. If it missed by less than ten centimetres, I'd play computer chess.

I played chess. God, will I be glad when this is over and I can go and join my parents on their hacienda or whatever, in Spain. They planned their big life-altering move for last autumn to coincide with me going to university, not thinking I might fail two-thirds of my exams and have to spend a year retaking. It's their fault, mind you. Physics was easy – I got an A star – and if Mum and Dad had let me do maths and computer studies with it, as I'd wanted, I'd be at Oxford or somewhere now. But no, they were convinced I'd be narrowing my options too much.

But I like having narrow options. What I don't like are English and history. Well, Virginia Woolf's good. And some of history's OK. Especially totalitarian regimes. I could write a whole book about Stalin and collectivisation.

Back indoors, I caught the time on the computer screen. Jessica Fletcher! I found the remote under *Mrs Dalloway* and switched the TV on. I'd missed the first five minutes but it didn't really matter. The victim never gets murdered till they've shown you all the people with a grudge. And anyway, I knew who did it.

* * *

Tim 'Could you spell that, sir?'

'DEB—'

'The surname, if you please.'

'Oh, right.' I spelled out Clinker into the phone. 'Only we're not sure that's her real name. You see, my ex-wife grew up in Shelcombe and she's never heard of her.'

'We do have a population of thirty thousand, sir. Now, when did you last see the missing woman?'

'Yesterday. We had an appointment.'

I listened to a very long sigh before the policeman said, 'In that case I'd better report myself missing, as my wife and kids haven't seen me since then either.' He laughed at his joke, as did a secretary or WPC in his vicinity.

'Look,' I said, 'her clothes were found on the beach this morning.'

'Hundreds of items of clothing are found on the beach each year, sir. People forget about them mainly. But let me make a note of what you've got.'

'Cardigan, trousers and one shoe. I've been back and searched but can't find anything else.' I wasn't sure whether to mention the wig. Or the fact that I'm short-sighted.

'Married?'

'Me or Debbie?'

Another sigh. 'Ms Clinker. Is she married?'

'Yes. No. I don't know. Possibly to someone called Gary.'

'Address?'

'Mine or—'

'Hers, please.'

'I'm afraid I don't know. She didn't ever tell me.'

'I see. Phone number? *Hers.*'

'Er, no. Sorry.'

'A good friend of yours, then?'

'She always called *me*, you see, about appointments and things. From a call box. I was . . .' I braced myself, '. . . her life coach.'

A hand must have gone over the receiver, for all I could hear were muffled noises. When the copper came back he was clearly suppressing laughter. 'Now let me get this straight, sir. The woman you've been so-called *life* coaching had an appointment with you yesterday then went and walked into the sea?'

'Actually, our session was cancelled. She arrived but had stomach ache, so went home. Well, we thought she was going home.'

'We?'

'Me and my ex-wife. I'm using her house to see clients while mine's being refurbished.'

'If you wouldn't mind telling me that address then, sir. As the last place the probably-not-missing person was sighted, for the time being.'

'Yes, of course. It's twenty-four Drake Street.'

I heard an intake of breath. 'Erica's place?' I was asked quietly. 'I mean . . . Miss Jones-Downer's?'

'You know her?'

'Yes,' the policeman said, his voice almost a whisper.

'We're acquainted. Well, were.' He cleared his throat and, back to normal volume, said, 'May I suggest you wait a few days, sir, and if she doesn't turn up, come in, bring this note you mentioned and we'll take more details. I expect Ms Clinker simply mislaid her clothes. I've done that myself.'

I bet you have, I thought. Erica worked her way through several boyfriends after we split up, me included on occasion. I can't remember a policeman, but then she'd probably keep quiet about a married copper. 'OK,' I said. 'I'll do that.' If only to check this guy out. 'And your name is?'

'Sergeant Lillywhite,' the man said, and at last it was my turn to laugh.

Later, I met Erica from her train, told her about Debbie, hurried her home to change, then bought us both fish and chips, which we ate as we walked along the beach. Erica's always been good at finding things – missing keys and so on – and I was hoping she'd spot something vital. Or not, preferably.

'Anyway, I phoned the police station,' I said, when I had a good view of her face, 'and Sergeant Lillywhite told me to come in if she doesn't turn up soon.'

She flinched, but only slightly. 'Sergeant Lillywhite, you say?'

'Yes.'

'Huh.'

'What?'

58

She picked up a stone and hurled it into the sea. 'Funny name.'

'Yes.'

'Anyway, I'm sure Debbie's fine,' she said. 'I expect she came and had a bit of a sit on the beach, took her wig off and, before she knew it, some dog was running away with it. That forced her to give up the whole disguise thing and go back to whoever she really was.'

I had a sudden surge of love for my ex-wife for being so reassuring. How like the old days it felt, walking along the beach together, nattering away.

'Yeah,' I said, casually placing an arm around her shoulders. 'She's probably up there somewhere –' I pointed towards the prom – 'watching us right now.'

Erica stopped dead and ducked down, leaving me with my arm in the air. Was my touching her so repellent these days? 'Or maybe not,' she said, hooking a pair of dark tortoiseshell glasses from the sand and giving them a shake. 'Aren't these . . . ?'

'Oh, bloody hell.' I took them from her and had a good look, first at them, then through them. Everything appeared a bit clearer to me, so they were definitely prescription glasses. Weak, though.

'We'd better take them to Chris,' said Erica. 'I mean . . .'

Erica It was nice this evening, the three of us sitting round the table, chatting. If Alice had only shut up about the state of the beach, it would have been even nicer.

'Chill,' I wanted to say, but you can't actually tell Alice anything these days.

'So,' she continued, 'I phoned the *Bugle* and they said they'll send a reporter and photographer along, but we'll believe that when we see it. You'd better bring your camera, Mum.'

'Camera?' I'd been thinking about Chris Lillywhite. Not exactly an oil painting, but a demon in the sack. Lots of attention to detail, I remember. Maybe that's policemen for you.

'Those things that take pictures?' Alice said, pulling a face. 'Anyway, that district councillor, you know, the Lib Dem, vaguely green guy, says he'll come. I put notices up at school and in the post office and on all the lamp-posts along the front, so we might get a few turning up. There'll be a petition, of course.'

'It could be she doesn't actually need those glasses?' I whispered to Tim, who'd been chewing on a thumb since we sat down.

'You mean she's got another, more attractive pair?' he said, bucking up a bit. 'Or wears lenses?'

'Maybe.'

'Ex*cuse* me,' Alice said with a sharp rap on the table. 'I know this might sound callous, but there's not much we can do about your client, Dad, whereas a lot can be done about the beach if we all pull together.'

Tim sighed. 'Yes, of course.'

It was getting late. I wanted to go to bed and phone Kurt, so made exaggerated yawning noises and told them what a long day I'd had. Tim took the hint and left.

'Night, Alice,' I said at the kitchen door. 'I'll be catching an early train tomorrow, so might not see you.'

She looked up and smiled at me. Such a lovely smile – she should try it more often. 'We'll see you at the scout hut at seven then?' she said. 'I'll prepare something for you to say, don't worry.'

'Pardon?'

'I thought you could speak. I mean, no one's going to listen to an eighteen-year-old.'

'Well . . .' I said wearily. Oh hell, I'd sort this out with her tomorrow. Phone from London with some excuse. 'Night.'

'No cleavage, though, Mum.'

'Yeah, yeah.'

Deborah I had a productive couple of hours this afternoon, eventually packing it in around three o'clock. It was then, after I'd shut down the computer and tidied all my papers away, that I started feeling bad about the kid next door. I really should have invited him into my flat for tea when he said he didn't have any. However, there had been things I hadn't wanted him to see. Tim's brochure, lots of printed-out info on life coaches, my part-written article on screen. I'd only popped out for bread.

I decided to make up for my rudeness. With all references to Tim and life coaching out the way, I went and knocked on Jonathan's door again. I knew he was in because I'd been listening to his TV for the past hour. I made a nice smiley face and waited. And waited. Once more I knocked, but yet again he didn't come to the door. There must be some reasonable explanation, I decided, letting myself back into my flat. Someone he's avoiding. Me, perhaps?

This evening I wandered around town for a while, picked up a bottle of wine and a ready meal for later, then walked along the front. It was pretty dead and a bit blowy, but the fresh air was nice. And the space too. You forget what it's like to see a long way, when you live in London. There was a lighthouse on the horizon and distant tiny boats. Nearer, were the remains of Shelcombe pier; half its original length and blocked off to the public. A huge board announced the council's Shelcombe Pier Project, with an architect's vision of the finished article, complete with happy people walking its length, heading for the theatre, pool room, bar and amusement arcade; some of them eating ice cream, none of them pale and plump. I wondered whether Debbie Clinker would have got a job on the posh new pier, and pictured her all happy in a brand-new booth. But then I stopped in my tracks and shook my head. Maybe I was spending too much time on my own.

THURSDAY

Tim How easy it was! On the spur of the moment, I went into the optician's for an eye test and to choose frames, but, once there, was talked into trying out a pair of daily throwaway contact lenses. 'You won't feel a thing,' the young woman promised, and to my astonishment she was right. Oh joy, I thought, on leaving the building with a month's trial supply, minus the two in my eyes. I could read signs and bus numbers again! I could see the time without lifting my arm to my face!

The downside came on arriving home, where I stood frozen for a while, astounded by the wall-to-wall canopy of cobwebs above my head, the stains all down the side of the cooker, the dead insects on the windowsill. How crisp my vision of these atrocities was, and how tempting to remove the lenses and go back to blurdom. But I didn't take them out. Instead, I went to the mirror, where an unshaven, hairy man with a smoker's pallor and a face like a road map greeted me. Had all those lines etched themselves in since I broke my glasses? While I wasn't looking? Twenty-odd years of smoking must have suddenly caught up with me.

There's only one thing for it, I decided, and that is to give up the revolting face-wrinkling habit. But how? Going cold turkey has never worked, so perhaps I should try patches or gum or something. What, though?

I sat down at the kitchen table, pulled the full ashtray towards me and delved into my pocket. There's nothing like a cigarette to help concentrate the mind.

Halfway through my third smoke, Shelcombe Scrubbers arrived. I took the small wiry woman and her wiry twenty-something son into the kitchen and announced that this was the room I'd like them to begin with. 'It being the worst, probably. Then the sitting room. And then, let me think . . .'

'I'm sorry,' the woman said, hands on her slim hips, 'but did you book us for two hours or two weeks?'

The son was scanning the kitchen and shaking his head in a sod-this-for-a-lark way, while his mother was busy opening up some kind of toolbox. She took out a cloth and what could have been a blowtorch, and waved them at the cooker. 'We might just get this corner here sorted in two hours.'

'What?' I cried. 'I was hoping you'd clean the whole house, have a bit of a clear-out too. I'm guessing that would cost me a fortune?'

'You want us to give you a quote?' the son asked keenly.

'Er . . . yeah, OK.'

It took them a while to tour my tall house, giving me a chance to fill the dishwasher and hide my final demands. When they returned the woman said, 'About two hundred,' which pretty much stunned me. 'We could do it today and tomorrow,' she went on with an enthusiasm I sensed could be catching. 'Have the place cleared, cleaned and organised by the weekend, top to bottom. What do you reckon?'

I wasn't sure what I reckoned. Two hundred would make a big hole in Debbie's money, but perhaps a big difference to my quality of life. 'One fifty for cash?' I suggested.

'Right you are,' she said, already squirting my cooker. 'Best if you keep out the way, though. Have you got a job to go to?'

It was an innocent question but one that filled me with self-disappointment. 'Yes, of course,' I said, and for credibility went upstairs to get my old briefcase. While in the study, I gathered all the papers off the desk, chair and floor, then dropped them in the filing cabinet I'd bought a year ago but not yet used. Luckily, the keys were still in it. Having locked anything incriminating or embarrassing away, I left my house in the hands of Shelcombe Scrubbers and headed for the bar of the Lobster Pot, stopping en route to buy a *Bugle*.

The place was packed with lunchtime boozers and people waiting for tables in the restaurant. I've often wondered what these folk do, in their suits, their blouses, their shiny shoes. There's that new business park, of course, just on the edge of town, full of soulless buildings that I can't picture anything happening in, no matter how hard I try. I took Alice there for our first and last driving lesson, my car having died shortly afterwards. They all looked happy and buzzy, though, these office workers. Just pleased to be away from their netherworlds, perhaps.

I got a pint and made a beeline for the one spare seat I could see. 'Is anyone sitting here?' I asked a young red-haired woman working on a laptop. In her little leather jacket, I guessed she wasn't from the business park.

She looked up and quietly gasped. 'You gave me a fright,' she said, hand on her chest.

'I'm so sorry.' That was it, no more cigarettes.

She moved her computer bag from the chair. 'Yes, it's free.'

'Thanks,' I said, sitting down.

Deborah Having got over the initial shock, I sat typing rubbish while I peered over my laptop at Tim circling jobs in the local paper. Although I was having to read upside down, I could see he was aiming low: *Warehouse Operative, Off-Licence Cash Operative, Fresh Food Operative.*

It was too painful to witness in someone who's been to public school, got a degree, been a teacher. And surely he'd have to be presentable to handle fresh food? No, no, this was all wrong. I slowly lowered my screen and he looked up at me.

'Job hunting,' he said with shrug.

'Ah.' I held my breath. If he didn't recognise me in the next couple of minutes, I'd be safe. 'What kind of thing are you looking for?'

'Actually, anything.'

I smiled at him. 'You're multitalented then?'

'No,' he said. 'That's why I'll consider anything.'

'May I have a look?' I asked, closing the laptop.

'Er . . . yeah,' he said, sliding the newspaper towards me. 'Are you job hunting too?'

'No, but I might be soon.' I turned the newspaper round and ran a finger down the first then the second column of jobs. Lots of seasonal workers were needed: waiting staff, chambermaids. 'Bingo caller?' I asked as a joke, then spotted the faint circle around it.

'Yes,' he said. 'I've had some experience, you see. Holiday job, a long time ago.'

'I bet that was fun. What else have you done, if you don't mind me asking?'

'Oh . . . teacher, office worker, estate agent for a while. And you?' he asked, nodding at the laptop. 'What do you do?'

'Features writer for a magazine. But, as I said, maybe not for much longer. It hasn't been doing too well lately.'

'Will I have heard of it?'

'It's called *Zip!*. Mostly lifestyle stuff.'

'Ah. So many magazines on the market, that's the

trouble. But anyway, you're young and you've got a skill. You'll be OK.'

'I hope so.'

He said, 'I'm Tim, by the way,' and held out a hand.

'Deborah,' I told him.

His eyebrows shot up. 'How funny.'

'I'm sorry?'

'Oh, nothing.'

I wondered why he hadn't mentioned life coaching in his list of careers. Could Debbie have been his one and only client? I carried on scanning the jobs, trying to imagine Tim packing, filling, stacking or van driving for a living. But then I saw an ad for 'Care and Support Workers'. Surely that was just life coaching for poor folks?

I pointed it out to him and he pulled a face. 'Isn't that helping old people on the toilet?'

'Sometimes,' I said laughing. 'But a friend of mine works with young adults with learning difficulties and loves it.'

'Really?' He turned the paper back round. 'Seems to be through an agency.'

'Yes.'

Tim looked up and started making long and unsettling eye contact with me, his lips pursed. Had the penny dropped? I casually reopened my laptop and pretended to get on with some work, head bowed. Now I desperately wanted to leave, but standing up would give him more of me to recognise.

'Do you know something?' he said.

Shit. I kept my eyes down and gave him a distracted, 'Mm?'

'I might just investigate this support worker thing.'

'Good,' I said, breathing out and looking him full in the face.

He gave me a big smile. 'Thanks for your help.'

'My pleasure.'

Erica When the train pulled into Shelcombe station this evening, I spotted Alice and Rupert and tried to slide down in my seat but bumped knees with the elderly man opposite. I apologised and he said, 'Not at all,' in a way that implied I could play kneesy with him anytime.

I'd forgotten about the meeting, that was the problem, plus I didn't want to go. I took my mobile out and switched it back on. Yes, Alice had been trying to get hold of me. Left a message even. 'Just to remind you about the meeting about the beach, Mum. You've got to come, yeah? I don't know why, but people listen to you.' No one does back-handed compliments quite like Alice.

They'd seen me and were waving. Damn. All I wanted was a bath and a gin and tonic. I waved back. Did I care about the state of the beach? It's improved, if anything, now families holiday abroad instead of bringing Granddad and the dog and nasty hard-boiled eggs to Shelcombe. And anyway, who'd want to venture into a sea that three years ago was deemed unfit for swimming by Europe? They've sorted out the sewage problem now, but all the same . . .

'Come on,' said Alice, once I was on the platform. She hooked an arm through mine and steered me towards the exit, Rupert trailing behind us. 'It starts in half an hour and I need to brief you on your speech.'

'Do I really have—'

'*Mum*, the beach is a mess and the council does nothing about it. I can't believe you don't give a shit. Talking of which, dogs have *really* got to be banned if we're ever going to get a Blue Flag. Rupert, go and get Mum some fish and chips.'

I didn't want fish and chips, not again. I wanted that gin and a bath. As far as I could recall, I'd never agreed to all this. And anyway, no dogs on the beach? They're the only ones who get pleasure from it these days. 'I'm not hungry,' I said, but Alice was already handing money over to Rupert and saying, 'Not too much vinegar this time.'

'Alice!' I snapped. 'I don't want fish and chips and I don't want to speak at your bloody meeting. I'm sorry, I just want to go home.'

'Fine!' said Alice, taking the money back from Rupert. 'Fine!' It obviously wasn't, but I let her flounce off.

'I'll try and get along in about an hour,' I called limply after the two of them.

Rupert said, 'Laters then, man', Alice said, 'Don't bother!' and I said, 'Oh, fuck' under my breath.

'What are you wearing?' I asked.

'Dark blue suit.'

'Take it off.'

'Both bits?'

'Uh-huh.'

'But Tilly's outside at her desk,' he whispered. 'She's sixty-three. The excitement could kill her.'

'Then close the door, but be quick.'

'Well, OK.'

He clonked the phone down and was soon back. 'Jacket's off, now for the pants,' he said, puffing. 'OK, hun . . . I'm sitting behind my desk in shirt, tie and shorts. Tell me your wildest fantasy.'

'Boxers off first.'

'Jeez, Erica, what if—'

'Off!'

He put the phone down for a while, then said, 'Yeah, they're off.'

'Swear?'

'On my doggie's life.'

'OK . . . we're at the Royal Opera House.'

'Again?'

'Didn't you like it?'

'No, it was great. But listen, how about this time I get a bit of the action? Ask me, this Stefan guy kinda monopolised you.'

'Mmm, I know, he's terrible.'

'So what are you wearing? At the opera, I mean.'

'High-heeled shoes, fur coat.'

'Period?'

'Yeuch, no. Oh . . . you mean full stop?'

'Sure.'

'Yeah, full stop.'

'Sounds good.'

'Anyway . . . where was I? Oh yeah, Stefan, the usher, takes us to our box. The house lights have dimmed, the orchestra's striking up, and in a small dark nook to one side of our seats, he offers to take my coat.'

'OK, but how about I—'

'Hmm, it is awfully warm in there . . . Do you think I should let him?'

'Tell you what, why don't I—'

'Oh! There he goes, sliding my coat off from behind, running a finger down my back as he does so . . . mmmm . . .'

'Pastrami on rye. Oh, and get me a latte.'

My eyes popped open. 'Kurt?'

'Sorry, hon. Tilly's going for lunch.'

'You're fully dressed, aren't you?'

'Well . . .'

'God, you're no fun,' I said. 'And come to think of it, you don't have a dog.'

'Used to.'

I turned the hot tap on with my foot and sipped from my glass. I really had to look for a man in the same time zone. 'I suppose we can carry on with you dressed. It's not the same, though. I like to feel I'm wielding power over you.'

'I like that too, hun. Only at work . . . you know . . .'

'Yeah, yeah, I understand. So, Stefan's running a finger down my bare back. All the way down . . . down . . .'

'Shall I let you know when my sandwich arrives?'

'Yes, Kurt. You do that.'

Tim The woman at the agency said there were a few jobs going, one at a small home for people who couldn't quite cope with the world, which she thought might be just up my street. I tried not to take that as an insult.

'Oh, no,' she told me, 'that one's been filled. How do you feel about working with the elderly?'

'Actually—'

'They can be absolute dears, some of them.'

'Hmm.'

'Full of interesting stories about the old days.'

I could imagine. 'Don't you have anything else?' I asked. 'Support worker in a home for supermodels. That kind of thing.'

She sucked air through her teeth and said, 'We wouldn't normally take on someone who was last employed two years ago.'

'I've been self-employed.'

She gave me an 'I've heard that one before' look and wondered out loud if they should do a police check.

'I haven't been in prison!' I protested.

'It's fairly routine. In the meantime, you'll hear from Social Services, tomorrow or Monday, I'd imagine. If they like you, I expect they'll want you to start quite soon.'

'Really?' This was happening a bit too quickly. And

with old people? Still, there was nothing to stop me changing my mind.

So stunned was I at the prospect of possibly having a job again that I'd quite forgotten about Shelcombe Scrubbers.

'Stone the . . . What the . . . ? Bloody hell,' I said, standing in my kitchen. Where were all my things? Where was all my stuff? I couldn't quite remember what the stuff consisted of but I knew it was there when I left five hours ago. The bastards had cleaned me out. Stolen everything. Why had I been so trusting? Not asked for references?

Jesus, what an idiot, I was telling myself, when I saw a note, all alone on the completely bare wall-length counter.

Back at 9 tomorrow. Most things got chucked,
but rest boxed in shed. We found this fifty quid
in the oven. If you've got money to burn, you
can always pay us more!
     Damon

Under the note was the fifty pounds my father sent me for my birthday last October. After a night on the town – six pints at the Anchor – I'd put the money in a safe place. And, as is often the way with safe places and with doing something like that when you're drunk, I'd forgotten where. How I could have done with that fifty pounds at Christmas, or for Alice's birthday in March. But no, it has to turn up the minute I've been paid a nice lump sum and probably got myself a job. I raised my eyes to the cobweb-free ceiling. Someone up there was definitely having a laugh.

When I finally tore myself away from my half-transformed house and hurtled to the scout hut, I found Alice and Rupert on a small platform, facing an elderly woman drinking from a flask, and a fed-up-looking man leaning on a broom.

'I don't suppose I gave people enough notice,' Alice sighed, while I tried to decide which of the hundred empty seats to take. 'What we need is an organised, co-ordinated campaign.'

I nodded. 'Good idea.'

'With leaflets, posters, lots of petitions. We could bus people in from around the region to demonstrate or pick up litter.'

'I'll run a little tea and cake stall,' said the elderly lady, screwing her cup back on.

'Wiv laak burgers and French fraas?' asked Rupert.

'Pardon?' she said.

Alice came down from the platform and started stacking chairs. 'Of course, Dad, it's all going to cost. The printing and everything.'

'Right.' I got up and helped her.

'It might be an idea,' she went on, 'to have a bit of a whip-round now. Just to get us started.' She put two chairs on top of two others then delved into her jeans pocket. 'I've got a fiver. Rupert?'

'Uh . . .' He too rummaged in a pocket, then counted his change. 'Free pands fir-ee.'

'Why can't they talk properly?' the flask lady asked me. 'You can take some of my pension,' she told Alice in a wobbly voice, 'but I doubt you'd want to.'

'Oh, I'm sure you can spare a few pounds,' Alice said. 'I mean, compared to the elderly in Third World countries you live like a queen.'

'Well, when you put it like that . . .' The woman unclipped her handbag and took out a very large purse for someone with little money.

'And you, Dad?' I was asked at close quarters.

I stopped stacking, found my wallet, removed the fifty-pound note, then checked all the compartments. 'Ah. Sorry, I've only got this—'

'Great,' said Alice, whipping it from my fingers. 'That's *really* generous. Isn't it, Rupert?'

Deborah I called Mel, who was home from her fruitarian experience and making her way through a chicken and bacon sandwich as we spoke. She was packing, she told me, bringing home to me that I had under two weeks to find somewhere to live.

'Rumour has it,' Mel said, 'that we'll all be served our redundancy notices tomorrow.'

'Great.' No job, no home, and all this time spent on two features that won't get published. 'What's Stefan going to do?' I asked. 'This must be the third magazine he's seen die.'

'Work on his novel, I suppose. He does have rent coming in from two properties, remember.'

'So he does. Has anyone seen this so-called novel?' I asked.

'Er, yeah. I have.'

'And you kept quiet?'

'He asked me to.'

I was shocked. 'You're going to tell me you've slept with him too.'

She didn't say anything.

'Mel!'

'It was just the once, during the Christmas party.'

'But how could you keep that from me?'

'I don't know. It all felt a bit predictable and grubby, I suppose. I was pissed and he was dishy . . . you know.'

'No, not really.' Personally, I've never been drawn to the handsome-and-knows-it Stefan. 'So what's the novel like?'

'OK, but a bit—'

'Hang on,' I said at the sound of a knock. 'Someone at my door.' I crossed the room gingerly, mobile still in hand, praying it wasn't Timothy Cash tracking me down. But it was the boy next door.

'I bought tea,' he said, looking older and really quite nice in the dimming light of the hallway. 'It's called Yorkshire tea, but they can't grow tea in Yorkshire, so I was confused. Then I checked the packet and it said blended in Yorkshire.'

'Ah,' I said, laughing. He was taller than I remembered.

Slim, but not lanky. His hands were self-consciously dug into the pockets of his low-slung jeans. He didn't say anything, so I asked if he was inviting me round now.

'Yes.'

'Great,' I said. 'I'll be there in a minute.'

'Did I hear a man?' asked Mel, after he'd gone.

'No, more of a boy. About eighteen or nineteen, I guess. I'm having tea with him.'

'Yeah, right . . . You know, they can go on all night at that age.'

'Don't be disgusting,' I said, and because Jonathan hadn't mentioned milk, I grabbed some from the fridge. 'Gotta go.'

SATURDAY

Stefan I've absolutely got to get this novel published. Get myself a nice advance, now the salary's disappearing. I'm almost, but not quite, there. As soon as I got up this morning, I printed out the three hundred-odd pages and took them to the sofa, where I pretended to be an agent or editor, reading the manuscript for the first time. This was tricky, as any agent or editor wouldn't know it off by heart, the way I do. But I carried on trying to see it with fresh eyes until I got to the dreaded page 12 and Zara's appearance. I skipped a whole chunk – full of 'More' or 'Describe' or 'Flesh out' instructions to myself – then by page 14 was back in safe territory again: Saul Sanders, private detective, territory.

Several friends have read the first draft of *Deception Row*, and although feedback has been pretty positive, the one female reader, Mel, thought that Zara, Saul Sanders's beautiful, blonde, sophisticated and sex-craving assistant, was totally unconvincing. Mel wasn't kind about my bed scenes either: 'Honestly, Stefan, you'll lose half your readership with all this wham-bam stuff.'

I tried taking the sex out, but that didn't work. Saul and Zara are having an illicit relationship, both deceiving their partners. There has to be sex. What I don't understand is how I can't write about something I'm so practised and, I'm told, good at. I went back to Mel to find out where I was going wrong and she said, 'I think you need to research your character more. Once you've really grasped her, it'll probably all fall into place.'

I took her advice and spent a week reading chicklit, but didn't find Zara there. She wasn't in the top-shelf books aimed at women either; they were all either passive or too domineering, and never well drawn. I'd been about to give up and change Zara altogether – to a sensible Sarah, perhaps – but then, when discussing it with my friend George over a pint, Erica's name came up.

'She could be your pneumatic blonde,' George said. 'Was when I knew her. Very imaginative, if you know what I mean. Late thirties, is that OK? I know you like them younger in real life.'

Not in a position to be choosy, I'd said, 'Go on.'

Some time ago George inherited a seafront flat in Shelcombe and had been weekending there when Erica Jones-Downer was 'what you might call full on' at a blues night in a pub. She and George had a casual thing for a couple of months. 'Until Erica met some Yank she was mad about. Anyway, she's quite a goer, and an astute businesswoman too. Why not look her up?' He wrote down the name of a London dating agency, which I then hurried home to find online.

So now I'm signed up with Opposites, hoping to get to know Erica better. She actually invited me down to Shelcombe the other day. I thought once Deborah had left the flat, I might just go.

As I tried reading my oh-so-familiar manuscript, I wondered if Deborah had been told she'll be out of a job in two weeks. Such a shame her article won't be used. She was full of praise for this Tim guy when we last spoke, and the section she emailed through made interesting reading. I decided to give her a call. The manuscript could wait.

She knew about the redundancies, she said. 'I heard from Mel. A bit of a downer, but not exactly unexpected.'

'No. Talking of Downers, ho ho, I'm sorry your life coach piece has been a waste of time.'

'That's OK. I've quite enjoyed it. Shelcombe's not such a bad place.'

'So I've heard. In fact, I was thinking of coming down for a few days.'

'Really? You know, it's actually not that special.'

'It would make a change, though. I thought maybe if you were going to be vacating George's flat . . . say later today . . . ?' The idea of going now suddenly appealed.

'What!' she cried. 'I can't go today. I need to . . . um, I dunno . . . look for a job.'

'Chambermaiding?' I asked jokily, but then got the impression from her silence that she was serious. 'Haven't you got a place in Peckham?'

'The lease is about to run out, so I was kind of hoping George might let me stay on here. I'd pay him the market rent, of course.'

This was scuppering my spur-of-the-moment plan, although I guessed there'd be hotels and guesthouses. 'I suppose I can ask him. I know he was looking for a tenant.'

'Oh, would you?' she said, sounding quite chipper. Either she's discovered this little seaside town is her spiritual home, or she's met someone.

'I'll do it now,' I told her, then hung up and called George.

'The agents have just found someone to take it,' he said. 'But surely she doesn't want to stay in Shelcombe?'

'She seems to like it,' I told him. 'Maybe I'll find out why later. I'm thinking of going down today.'

George broke into a leery laugh. 'Doing a bit of horizontal research?'

'I wasn't going to take it that far. Not sure she's my type.'

'You mean she's over twenty-two?'

I suddenly remembered Abbie, so cut short my conversation with George and wandered into the bedroom. 'Abbie?' I whispered, gently shaking her beautiful bare shoulder.

She rolled towards me and said, 'Aggie. What?'

'I'm afraid you're going to have to leave, sweetheart. I'm going away for the weekend.'

She rubbed her eyes with her knuckles. 'Can't I come?'

Why do they always ask that? 'Sorry. Family event.'

'So?'

Christ. 'Do you need taxi fare?'

'I am your girlfriend, after all.'

In her dreams. 'Will twenty cover it to . . . er . . .' Where was she from?

'Hounslow.'

It had to be. 'It'll get you to a station, anyway.' I pulled the duvet off. 'Come on then, young lady,' I said, taking in her naked rear. 'Up you get.'

The raven-haired Abbie, or Aggie, rolled on to her back, stretched her arms above her head and smiled far too nicely at me.

'But,' I said, untying my robe and pulling my stomach in, 'maybe not just yet.'

Alice I can barely speak to my mother. While *she* totally opted out of my beach meeting, Dad gave us fifty quid he can't really spare, despite his windfall. I know, because I saw his credit card statement the other day.

Just now I said, 'Mum, I don't suppose you'd like to come and help clear the coastal path this afternoon? To like make up for letting us down the other evening?'

You'd think I'd asked her to come and nurse AIDS victims in a war-torn country from the look on her face and the number of things she *really* had to do. The front garden pots being the most pressing. I don't know what's wrong with everyone. Rupert says he wants to go into Bournemouth and buy CDs. No way. When I phoned Dad about helping, he wanted me to believe someone had thrown all his clothes away: 'Got to go shopping, sorry.' I'm not saying I'm the late Mother Teresa or anything, but I don't know how the world would get by without people like her and myself.

Tim I'd been expecting a young Clint Eastwood type when I wandered into the station this morning, but Sergeant Lillywhite is greying, fairly stocky and has a longish, protruding chin that makes him look bad-tempered and possibly a bit dim. I slid the rough drawing I'd done of Debbie Clinker across the counter and said, 'She looks something like this. Only the hair was a wig and we found it on the beach, and she wouldn't be wearing those glasses because we found those on the beach too.'

The sergeant picked up the drawing and held it at arm's length. 'Very helpful, I'm sure.'

'I'm not much of an artist.'

'No.' He handed the drawing to a young WPC sitting at a desk, who snorted hysterically and passed it back. 'Well,' Sergeant Lillywhite said, 'we'll *see* if we can get a E-fit done, based on this. Put it out with a description of the, er . . . individual. Sort of half woman, half pig, would you say?'

I guessed he was referring to the two nostrils with brackets either side. I've never been able to draw noses from the front. I was tempted to snatch my artistry from the man's hand and say, 'Forget it, you wanker', but the thought of Debbie, stranded and naked somewhere, stopped me.

Sergeant Lillywhite dragged a notepad towards him and took a pen from his top pocket. 'Right. Missing Person's Report it is, then. Name?'

'Mine or . . . ?'

Deborah Making my way up off the beach and towards the headland, I thought about my neighbour. Such a lovely-looking boy: an almost pretty face, surrounded by longish black curls; beautiful blue eyes; a squarish chin. But Jonathan is an odd one.

Two days in a row we've had tea together – yesterday in my flat, where he talked a lot about totalitarian regimes. 'You know the fascist regimes of the last century and the protofascist regimes of today have strikingly similar *modus operandi*,' he'd say – or something like that. And I'd reply, 'Is that right?' and ask if he wanted topping up. Then he'd be off again. Mel was right, he probably could go on all night.

One problem with our studio flats is that when you have a guest, someone usually ends up on the bed. Jonathan's is a single, so it's a bit like sitting on a sofa. But mine's a double, and no matter how I arranged myself on it yesterday, I could see in the mirror how come-and-get-me it looked.

But he didn't come and get me, thank goodness. In fact, he barely made eye contact. We parted at my door without so much as touching, but did arrange to go to a pub in Shelcombe tonight. 'My friend Clive's playing there,' he said.

I was pleased to hear he had a friend but I wasn't sure I wanted to meet this Clive. Jonathan probably thinks I'm younger than I am, but his friends might not. 'Great,' I said. 'Will we be dancing?' I waved my hands around and wiggled my hips. 'I love to dance, don't you?' He stared at me – all of me – said no he didn't, and made a dive for his flat.

At the headland I sat on a small rock for a while, and looked out to sea. It was a windy day and the waves were choppy and frothy in places. It was all quite uplifting and a nice antidote to Jonathan's mini-lectures. From my little rucksack, I took one of the flapjacks I'd packed for slow-release energy, just in case I got carried away and had to walk back from Lyme Regis or some-where. As I sat quietly chewing and contemplating my future, I heard a vaguely familiar voice say, 'Not *there*, Rupert! *Here.*'

I got up, hoisted my bag on to my back and carried on eating while I walked towards the voice. At the top of the incline was a group of people, and as I approached I saw Alice doing lots of pointing and shouting. Would she be any better at recognising faces than her father? Our only meeting had been brief, so I guessed I was safe.

'Good morning,' I called out. Most in the group were bent over, scraping at the path, moving stones or tugging at grass.

Alice swung round and said, 'Out the way, everybody!'

'That's OK,' I told them. 'I can go round.'

'Fanks,' said the guy right in front of me. Rupert, I

guessed, from Tim's description of his daughter's boyfriend.

Just as I was veering to one side of him and popping the last bit of flapjack in my mouth, the wind caught my wrapper and swept it off in the direction I'd just come. 'Oops,' I said.

'Rupert!' cried Alice. 'Fetch!'

While Rupert charged off, Alice took a long step and blocked my way. 'It's litterbugs like you who ruin our beautiful beach, you know.'

'I'm sorry, but the wind—'

'If I wasn't such a nice person,' she went on with her nose very close to mine, 'I'd report you or make a citizen's arrest.'

I wasn't convinced Alice was a nice person, or that she wouldn't recognise me at such close quarters, so I apologised abjectly, then did a quick footballer's zigzag around her.

Once back on the path, I heard Alice shout, 'Rupert, you're hopeless!'

Kill her, I willed him.

'Surely you can run faster than that!'

Tim Again I went, 'Agh!' when I walked into my sitting room, still being taken by surprise each time.

'The one thing we can't wash are the walls,' Damon the Scrubber had said. 'But I'll come and give them a lick of paint if you like.' I decided I would like, and we agreed on a price for the downstairs to be painted a colour of Damon's choosing. Magnolia would be safest, apparently.

I sat on the three-seater sofa I haven't seen in quite a while. It felt odd, and even a bit lonely, not to be surrounded by jumpers and newspapers and used plates, so I picked up one of the freshly washed cushions and cuddled it as I jotted down the things I should spend the afternoon doing. 'Buy new shoes, shirt, trousers, jacket – x 2 or maybe 3.' I'd searched the shed and everywhere for my clothes, and was having to rewear yesterday's things. 'Haircut.' Long overdue and what with the new job . . . 'Shaver.'

I checked the time and realised I'd have to get the next train to Bournemouth if I was going to accomplish everything in an afternoon. How lucky we are still to have our little branch line. Without it, I'd never leave Shelcombe these days. I wrote, 'Monday – take car to garage?' but then remembered I might have an interview on Monday and crossed it out.

In fact, did I really need the list? I thought not, crumpled the sheet of paper into a ball and, forgetting, chucked it at the fireplace. It landed on the pretty fern now sitting in the buffed-up grate.

I went and retrieved it, took a whole load of cash from the Jiffy bag I'd stuffed up the chimney breast – relieved Scrubbers hadn't made a nice fire for me to come home to – and set off for the station.

Erica It isn't every day you open your front door and

find the man, literally, of your fantasies there. 'Stefan?' I asked stupidly.

'Well, you did say to look you up.' He wore a brown leather jacket that matched his hair, a pair of black jeans and a lascivious smile, or maybe just a friendly one. From behind his back came a bouquet of flowers that no way had he found in Shelcombe.

'Wow,' I said, taking them, then kissing both his cheeks. 'They're amazing. Gosh, what have I done to deserve these?'

While he shrugged and cocked an eyebrow, my head raced up the stairs two at a time, zoomed along the landing, turned into the master bedroom and inspected the sheets. Clean on yesterday. 'Well, come in,' I told him.

'I hope this isn't a bad time. Are you in the middle of something, or about to go out?'

'No, not at all,' I said, leading him down to the kitchen.

'Nice pots of tulips out the front.'

'Thanks.'

'And a lovely house,' he said, looking around. 'So, do you live here alone?'

I've never mentioned an eighteen-year-old daughter in any of our chats. 'With my little girl,' I told him. 'But she's out having fun on the beach.'

'That's nice.'

I wondered about double-locking the front door, phoning Tim and asking him to abduct Alice. After filling

a vase from the tap, I unwrapped the stylish arrangement and slipped it in the water without moving a single
stem. What fabulous taste this adorable man had. I then
turned, and in a bit of fantasy role reversal, asked if I
could take his coat.

'I'm fine,' he said. 'Thanks.'

Oh, well. 'Would you like a drink?'

'Tea would be nice.'

I'd meant something more exciting, of course. 'OK.
Why don't you sit down and I'll put the kettle on.'

'How old's your daughter?' he asked, taking a seat that
faced me.

'Eight . . .'

'Ah, lovely age.'

'. . . teen.'

He laughed and from inside his jacket pulled out a
small notebook. He unhooked a tiny pen or pencil, wrote
something down, then put both things back.

After making a pot of tea and giving it a stir, I carried
the tray to the table just as Stefan was slipping his notebook away a second time. It was both odd and exhilarating to see him sitting in the corner of my kitchen.
Mostly exhilarating. 'Are you working on an article?' I
asked.

'No, no. Just got made redundant, in fact.'

'Oh dear. What are you going to do?'

'Well, I'll try and get something else, but will also take
the opportunity to finish the novel. Meanwhile, I've got
rent coming in from a couple of places in London.'

Propertied, as well as hunky and creative. It just got better and better. 'Milk?'

'Please.'

My hand shook slightly as I poured. 'Fuck it,' I said, putting the jug down. 'I'm going to have a glass of wine. You'll join me, won't you?'

'Um. Oh, why not?'

I crossed the room again and felt his eyes on my rear. I said, 'You're not driving back to London, then?'

'Not today, no. I'll probably book myself into one of those B & Bs up the street.'

The hell he would. 'Oh, don't do that. There's a guest room here, now Alice has got the attic.'

'Well . . .'

'I insist,' I said, popping a cork out. I took the bottle and two glasses back to the table, pushed the tea things aside, sat down and crossed my legs towards him, wishing I'd put a skirt on. I'd wear one later, I decided, when we went out. What a brilliant stroke of luck it was, Stefan turning up in time for the Gay City Rollers.

Jonathan I can't make out if Deborah wants us to have sex, or if she thinks of me as a bit of a younger brother; someone to chat with and go to the pub with because she doesn't know anyone else in Shelcombe. I wish I was better at reading people, especially women.

Deborah's here to write some article about Shelcombe. I can't remember what exactly. Anyway, it sounded dull. But then my head is full of loftier things, like the intersection of time and timelessness in *Mrs Dalloway*. That's the good thing about studying – you don't have to think about the mundane.

It was exactly eight o'clock, so I knocked on Deborah's door and said, 'Ready?'

She said, 'Just a tick.' Then she hurried across her room in a really hot outfit with lots of bare middle and I remembered that sexy little dance she did for me yesterday and decided she does want to have sex with me. She came back with a bag over her shoulder and a biggish jacket I hoped she wasn't going to put on.

'By the way,' I said, when we were out of the building and she was wrapped up in her jacket, 'my friend Clive is just standing in for the drummer as a favour. He isn't in any way a member of Gay City Rollers, right?'

'OK, but why so serious about it?'

'Well . . .' I didn't want her thinking I knew someone who'd play with such a joke outfit, because she might change her mind about having sex with me. Clive belongs to a cool R and B band that has a big local following but is too good to ever get a recording contract. He's an electrician by day and a musician and drug dealer the rest of the time. I told Deborah this, but not the drug dealer bit, and she said, 'You mean this band we're going to see is crap?'

'According to Clive. But we don't have to stay long.' We could go back to hers and discuss history and politics again. Then maybe go to bed.

'No,' she said, smiling beautifully at me. 'We don't.'

I couldn't help thinking, tonight's definitely the night. When we got to the pub it was packed and noisy. I don't know how people can enjoy themselves with so much noise going on. I waved Clive over and he introduced himself to Deborah and the three of us grabbed the last table going, in the corner by the Gents. Clive said he'd learned from experience that if you put your hand over your nose every time a bloke went in or out, that spot was bearable.

'Can I get you a drink?' I asked Deborah, who had her hand over her nose even though no one was coming and going.

'A pint of bitter,' she said through her fingers, but when I came back from the bar it turned out she'd said vodka and tonic. She insisted on keeping it, but I don't think she likes bitter. Every time she took a sip, she pulled a face then put her hand back over her nose. It wasn't the best start to the evening, but I thought lively conversation might save the situation, so said – well, shouted – 'Did you know Il Duce once worked as an elementary school teacher, and that he later wrote a novel?'

'I can't hear a word you're saying!' Deborah shouted back, and I think that's when I felt my black cloud coming on.

Tim It felt all wrong, sitting alone with my smart new haircut and brand-new clothes. Like a waste. At nine-thirty I switched the TV off, took some more money from the chimney breast and headed for Erica's house, hoping I could entice someone, preferably Erica, out for a drink. But I found the place in darkness. I banged the knocker twice, then read the poster in the window. Ah.

It was a job squeezing into the Anchor and an even harder job reaching the bar. 'A pint of that, please,' I shouted, pointing at a pump. 'And some crisps. Plain.' Shelcombe Scrubbers had left my kitchen almost devoid of food. 'Don't you ever check sell-by dates?' the mother had asked.

For want of a space anywhere else, I chose to prop up the bar, while my eyes scanned all the faces for Erica, Alice and Rupert. I nodded at several people I knew, then saw Erica above the crowd. She must have been standing on a chair or something. Her arms were waving around in the air and her head was bobbing from side to side. She was clearly enjoying herself and possibly pissed.

I'm pretty tall, but I still had to stand on tiptoe to catch sight of the band. They were all blokes, of a sort, dressed in kilts and heavily made up. Apart from the drummer, that was, who wore a black jacket with the hood up, so that all you could see was the tip of his nose. They were singing 'Bye Bye Baby', as was Erica. Hence the waving, I supposed. There's the odd occasion when I'm quite pleased not to be married to her.

'Tim?' someone shouted behind me. I spun round and saw the woman I'd met in the Lobster Pot.

'Hi!' I said. Name, name, name . . . of course, it was Deborah. 'How are you, Deborah?'

'Fine. You?'

'Good, yeah. Are you trying to get to the bar?'

She nodded and I let her in. 'Thanks,' she said.

It was obvious she was going to have a long wait and that we should try to make conversation. 'I got a job,' I kicked off loudly, right by her ear.

'Hey!' she shouted into mine.

'Well, maybe,' I yelled back. It was hard work. 'Support worker. I've still got to be interviewed, I think. It's all a bit vague. But the woman at the agency gave me the impression they'd want me.'

'That's brilliant. Well done!'

'It's thanks to you, of course.'

She shrugged and shouted, 'I like the haircut, by the way. Suits you.'

'It's not too short?'

'Not at all.' She waved a twenty-pound note at the staff. 'Funny thing is, *I'm* out of a job now.'

'Oh dear!'

'A double vodka and tonic and a pint of Fosters!' she told the barman.

I wondered who she was with and wanted to ask. I said, laughing, 'You know they're desperate for care and support workers.'

'I'm not sure I'd have the patience.' She paid for the drinks, took a sip of hers and said, 'Ah, that's better.' After gathering up change and the pint, she asked if I'd like to join them. 'We're by the loos, I'm afraid.'

I looked over to where Erica was still go-going. 'Yeah, OK.'

It was only as I followed her through the bodies that I noticed the lightly tanned bareness around Deborah's middle. Nice. When we got to her table there was a twelve-year-old sitting there. 'This is Jonathan,' she shouted. 'Jonathan, this is Tim. He's coming to join us, is that OK?'

I took a seat, even though Jonathan didn't look at all OK about it. We were further from the band now, but it was still hard to make conversation, so I just sat and took swigs of lager and tapped my foot to the whole pub singing 'Shang-A-Lang'. All the while, young Jonathan seemed to be slowly murdering me with his eyes.

Stefan It's not easy, taking notes in the hubbub and general excitement of a Gay City Rollers night, but I forced myself, not wanting to forget any useful details. Erica is certainly a find. She oozes sexuality, litters conversation with double entrendres and now, bless her, was standing on two chairs, showing off her stockinged legs – I'd caught sight of bare thigh earlier – and wiggling her arse at me.

Since we'd been on the wine from four onwards, she was 'drunk as a skunk' as her daughter, the delightfully attractive Alice, had just put it. The girl was beside me now, rolling her eyes at her mother's behaviour and shouting something in my ear about shagging on the beach. It wasn't an invitation, I realised in time, but a bit of a rant about used condoms.

Because I'm viewing my stay in Shelcombe as work, I'd tried to moderate my alcohol intake, surreptitiously pouring wine down the sink or into Erica's glass when she was out of the room. I had four pages of notes now, to which I added, 'As she danced, her buttocks swayed and rolled like two plump puppies trying to switch sides in a sack.' I was using shorthand, luckily, as Alice had grabbed the notebook from me earlier and tried reading it. Naughty girl.

'Where are the toilets?' I asked, and she pointed to the back of the crowded bar. I tucked my notebook away and said, 'Don't let anyone take my seat, will you?'

'I wouldn't dream of it,' she told me, placing her hand where I'd just been sitting. Something about the way she did that made me wonder, just briefly . . . But, no, she had that brain-dead boyfriend in tow.

I made my way past a group of people who were waving tartan scarves above their heads at the band, then past a bunch of tattooed fairground types, then past Deborah.

Deborah!

'Hey,' I said, turning and letting the door to the Gents slam shut again.

Her eyes were out on stalks. She was staring in a hard and penetrating way at me. There was some kind of message in that stare but I wasn't receiving it. I may have gone easy on the wine but that didn't mean I was sober. The band's song came to an end and I just stood there giving her a big smile until, after an age, she said, 'Stefan! What are you doing here?'

I bent and kissed her cheek and nodded at the two guys she was sitting with. One very young, the other in his forties. I waited to be introduced, but would have waited for ever. 'I'm Stefan,' I told them.

The older guy said hello, while the young kid chewed the inside of his mouth. Deborah introduced the boy as Jonathan. 'Hi,' I said, but he just glowered.

'And this is Tim,' Deborah told me. Again, she was giving me the scary stare.

'Nice to meet you, Tim,' I said. I pointed at the toilet. 'Excuse me. Back in a minute.'

While I peed, aware I was swaying and aiming badly, I managed to put two and two together. I splashed my face with cold water, keen to get back and find out what Erica was up to and wanting to be alert enough to take notes. Outside again, I stopped at Deborah's table.

'I've just realised who you are,' I said to Tim. 'Heard great things about your life coaching from Deborah.'

'I'm sorry?' Tim's eyes darted to Deborah, then to me, then back to Deborah. 'What's going on?' he asked. 'I don't think I've told you I'm a life coach?'

Deborah slumped down in her seat with her glass and threw her spare hand in the air. 'I ain't got no excuses,' she said in the most peculiar voice, and it was Tim-the-life-coach's eyes that were now on stalks. 'At the end of the day,' she went on in a dire sort of West Country cockney, 'it's a fair cop. Know what I mean?'

I pushed my way back to my seat, wondering if I was more drunk than I thought, and whether darling Alice still had her hand on it.

MONDAY

Tim The funny thing is, looking back, that when this total stranger, i.e., Debbie Clinker, was helping me find a job in the Lobster Pot last week, I thought: I know those teeth. It was a brief *déjà vu* moment that quickly faded when she started asking me what I'd done in the past. I also remember, now, that it seemed a bit odd the way she asked to have a look at the newspaper I was reading. You'd do that with someone you knew, not someone you'd met seconds ago.

The other thing was Debbie's farewell note. My first reaction wasn't to the content, I remember now, but to the way it was punctuated. I couldn't believe that someone who uses 'we was' in conversation would know where to put apostrophes. When I told Deborah, she laughed and said she'd remember next time.

If that Stefan guy hadn't put his foot in it, I'd probably never have sussed that Deborah was Debbie. However, I'm not sure anyone could accuse me of being blind, deaf and imbecilic for not realising. Although Alice came close. All the same, I did feel a bit stupid when it came out.

Confused and in shock, despite Deborah's careful and apologetic explanation, I had to get away from all that shang-a-lang racket and incessant chatter. I said I was going to the bar, but slipped out of the pub and went down to the front, where I smoked two cigarettes in a row and looked at the sea. Actually, I couldn't see it, there being no moon and half the bulbs along the prom blown, but I could hear it and smell it.

With the cigarettes having changed my pH balance, I found myself chuckling away in a semi-churlish manner. *I* was supposed to be the life coach but, between them, Debbie and Deborah had sorted out my home, my appearance and maybe even my livelihood. I suppose it was then, leaning against the railings, feeling duped but at the same time grateful, and also being a magnanimous kind of chap, that I decided to forgive Debbie. Deborah.

'Still looking for her, then?' a familiar voice boomed from behind. It was Sergeant Lillywhite, in civvies and walking a dog with a beard that gave it a similar long-chinned profile to its owner. The sergeant nodded towards the black water and I waited for a derisory remark that didn't come.

All the same, I couldn't bring myself to tell him Debbie Clinker had turned up, guessing he'd be all smug-bastard about it. So I said, 'Yes. Although we've more or less given up hope.'

He scratched at his chin. 'Look, I'm sorry if I was a bit, you know, funny with you.'

Hilarious, yes. 'It was understandable, don't worry.'

'We'll be doing our best to find her, you know.'

'Great,' I said, although I was now worrying about wasting police resources, and whether it was a punishable crime. 'But it might not be worth spending too much time on it. You know, she'll either turn up, or she's . . .' I nodded towards the sea.

'True,' he said, 'but we'll pull out all the stops, nevertheless.'

'I . . . well, thanks.' I'd have to go into the station next week. Announce I'd found her.

We discussed the weather, then he wished me good night, tugged at the lead and said, 'Come along then, Watson.' As I watched them trot off, I tried to picture Sergeant Lillywhite having sex with my ex-wife. All I could think was that Erica had been trying out her opposites idea.

Without realising it, I'd become frozen to the core, so I strode at a pace through the Saturday night yobs and the drunk girls with bare legs, to the second biggest surprise of the night. On my doorstep sat Deborah, her tummy covered by a large jacket, I was pleased to see. A woman could catch her death trying to be fashionable in Shelcombe.

'Erica told me your address,' she said.

Deborah It was nice coming across Tim at the bar, after days of weird Jonathan. Suddenly I was talking to a grown-up, who, in the strange pub light and with his hair trimmed, although still a bit eighties, and his face shaved, didn't look at all bad. He wasn't going on about fascists either. I don't think I fancy Tim but I do like his company.

I like his house too. *Love* his house. It's all seventeenth-century thick wonky walls and beams and nooks and window seats, and incongruous Victorian fireplaces. Used to be two fishermen's cottages, apparently. Tim sleeps in the attic. 'I moved in there when we split up,' he said. 'Couldn't bear to stay in our bedroom.' He showed me their old room and it had the most beautiful brass bed in it. 'Erica didn't want it, for some reason. I suppose beds are full of . . . And, anyway, she's gone quite modern.' He went over to the window. 'There's a great view from here. Can't see it now, of course. We used to open the curtains at weekends and look at the sea while we drank our tea. It was . . .' His voice caught and he blinked hard. 'It was . . .'

'It's a lovely room,' I told him, not helping.

'I don't come in often,' he said. 'Not now. Alice used to sleep here when she stayed, but she doesn't do that any more. She came for a whole, frankly difficult, month last year while her mother let her house and went to New York. Hasn't been to stay since. I just get the occasional brief visit.'

'Oh, I'm sorry.'

'Don't be. I'm quite glad, to be honest. It's a terrible thing to say, but she's very, well, you know.'

'Yes,' I said, as know I did.

There were just four beers and some butter in his fridge. Tim explained that, what with preparing for the job, he hadn't got round to food shopping. We took the beers and went and sat in his big square sitting room in front of another Victorian fireplace, where we nattered away easily about this and that. Shelcombe, London, family, our respective homes. 'I adore yours,' I told him, and pointed at the chimney breast. 'I wonder if there's an inglenook behind there?'

'Oh, almost certainly. I keep meaning to get it all opened up, but it's a big job. I'm not sure I want the mess.'

'I've noticed you're very tidy.'

'Yes,' he said chuckling. 'I am now. Another beer?'

I told him I should really go and get some sleep. 'But thanks, anyway.'

Tim walked me home, as he said I was bound to get a guy with sick down his front lurching into me. In fact, it was the girls we ended up giving the widest berth to, in their big boots and terrifyingly tiny skirts, screeching at one another and into their phones.

When we approached the flats, I saw the silhouette of my neighbour standing on his balcony and realised I owed him an apology, even though he'd been the one to disappear from the pub. After Tim said good night, I went up the two flights and knocked on Jonathan's door.

'I'm really sorry,' I said. 'It's just that—'

To my horror, he stepped forward, put an arm around my waist and yanked me towards him. I could smell the Anchor. 'Did you sleep with him?' he asked roughly.

'No,' I said, wanting to be outraged but feeling too stunned.

'So we can do it, then?' he said, his soft nineteen-year-old lips flicking across my cheek towards my mouth.

'Mhhmm,' I said when they got there. I told myself that I'd soon wake up. That Stefan hadn't come to Shelcombe, Tim hadn't discovered I was Debbie and Jonathan hadn't given me a clumsy kiss with a thumb digging into my upper arm.

'No,' I said, pulling away. He took a step back and looked hurt and a bit baffled. What could I say? 'Jonathan, you're too weird,' wouldn't be nice. I began to feel very uneasy. I was pretty sure he wasn't capable of violence – that thumb in my arm was just clumsiness – but I didn't know him well enough to be certain.

'You're a nice-looking boy,' I said, deciding to keep things friendly. 'And I'm very flattered. But, you know, you really ought to be concentrating on your exams right now.'

He smiled at me, just briefly, and I realised how expressionless Jonathan usually is. 'OK,' he said, and shut the door on me.

I didn't see him for the rest of the weekend, but he's just knocked on my door and asked, slightly awkwardly, if I'd like to come and have a cup of tea and watch *Columbo*. Harmless, I'd say.

Stefan I made an appearance at the office today, for fear of losing the paltry compensation I've been promised, then rushed home to do a bit more polyfilling, as I call it. Plugging up the gaps in the novel with lively descriptions of Zara. Each time I finish a section, I thank George for sending me Erica.

When she really came up trumps was after Alice and I helped her to bed on Saturday night. Not immediately, about half an hour later, when I was in the very girlie bedroom that was once Alice's, wide awake with the coffee I'd drunk at midnight and going through my manuscript. All of a sudden, Erica was talking and giggling through the wall. Although our heads were a matter of inches apart, I couldn't catch what she was saying, so I pushed the pink duvet aside, got up and crept along the landing to her slightly ajar door.

'And while he gently eases his large swelling into me,' I heard quite plainly. I wasn't sure if she had someone in there, was on the phone, or was just thinking out loud, but it didn't matter. I had to get it down.

Not wanting to waste time dressing, I just grabbed my pen and notebook and returned to her door, where I wrote furiously in only underpants, aware that Alice was downstairs, also on the phone. '*Look*, Rupert,' or 'For Christ's *sake*, Rupert,' I kept catching. Rupert had left the pub early with some mates, saying if he listened to any more he'd go mental. Whether it was the music he'd meant, or Alice, wasn't clear. She can go on a bit.

After ten minutes or so, when I may have had enough filthy escapades for the entire Saul Sanders series I'm planning, Alice went quiet downstairs and I heard the click, click of light switches. I hurried back to bed, my head whirring, my body zinging with the things I'd just heard. When I reread my notes things whirred and zinged more fiercely. The combination of caffeine and the bonfire going on in my loins left me in no doubt I wouldn't sleep. I thought about a cold shower, I thought about quickly pleasuring myself. I even considered offering to pleasure the drunken Erica.

I was about to go for the middle option, when the lovely Alice suddenly stuck her top half round my door saying, 'Is there anything you need?' with a generous anything-at-all-just-ask-me smile. I . . . well, it was just bad timing, really.

Alice The thing about Mum is she thinks she's middle class and a yuppie businesswoman and all that, but she's actually quite common. She also thinks just because she was once a stunner, any man she flirts with will automatically start worshipping at her size sevens. If she'd turned around when she was gyrating stupidly on those chairs, she would have seen Stefan staring down my top.

Oh God, just thinking about it makes me go hot. I *can't* think about it, I've got exams to do and a beach to get cleared up. I can't think about him lying under my favourite, aged nine, duvet cover. I can't think about me asking if he needed anything and him pulling back my favourite, aged nine, duvet and saying, 'You could give me a hand with this.' Because if I do think about it, about his thing – not that different from Rupert's – and what his thing and his mouth got up to on my old candy-stripe carpet – 'Does your boyfriend do this?' *No!* 'Or

106

this?' *Never!* – then I won't get any work done and I'll fail my exams and I'll end up working for Mum, or worse.

I might call the campaign 'Let's Fly the Flag' – hoping people will realise it means the Blue Flag given to clean beaches. Come to think of it, 'Let's Fly the Blue Flag' might be better, since I don't suppose the average IQ in Shelcombe is that high. And we do want to get all sorts involved, not just the same people in hiking clothes who turn up all the time.

'God, you're passionate,' he whispered. I could hear Mum rambling on through the wall. The floor was hard but better than my squeaky bed.

I know, I'll put posters about the next meeting in that Bargainbuys, or whatever it's called, supermarket, where they practically give away food to damage your family with. They're the people who have to be educated, beach-wise and every otherwise.

He sent me a text today, telling me I had breasts like two halves of an avocado. 'Do you mean peeled?' I replied, but I haven't heard back. I expect he's writing.

Jonathan Deborah came round this afternoon and we watched *Columbo* together, then had a disagreement about it. I said I thought it was a brilliant, perhaps Dostoevsky-inspired, format, displaying Lieutenant Columbo's psychological hold over the perp.

Deborah said, 'Basically, they show you the murder, Columbo guesses who did it, then there's another hour and a half to sit through.'

I carried on insisting it was clever and compelling. 'In *Crime and Punishment*, remember, you know from the beginning who committed the murder.' She said she hadn't read it. Anyway, I decided never to let her watch *Murder, She Wrote* with me, then asked if she wanted to have sex. I told her I'd done lots of revision since Saturday, so she needn't worry about my exams.

She sort of groaned, and instead we went for a walk along the beach and discussed *To the Lighthouse*. Well, I did. Deborah told me she'd never read Virginia Woolf. 'I'm reading a gripping Grisham,' she said, but I didn't want to hear about that, so I talked about the symbolism in *To the Lighthouse*. For example, how the destructive nature of the sea is a reminder of the impermanence and delicacy of human life.

Deborah said, didn't I think they did a really good job on Nicole Kidman's nose when she played Virginia Woolf in that film? 'Yes,' I agreed. It was a bit of a lie and normally I can't see the point of lying. But this time I could. I haven't seen the film or Nicole's fake nose, but I do want to keep things friendly between us, because it's good to have someone to practise my revision on, and because, *re* sex, it will probably help.

Deborah When I spotted a girl and boy ahead of us, picking things off the sand and putting them in black bags, I tried to steer Jonathan away. But he's tall and not very steerable, and after several more paces, he said, 'Ugh, I can't stand her.'

'You know Alice?'

'From school.' He stopped and stared at me. 'For someone who's only been here a week you know a lot of people.'

I shrugged. 'That happens when you're a journalist. You have to put yourself about, strike up friendships with all sorts.'

As we approached, Alice put her black sack down. 'Oh, it's you. Debbie, Deborah, whatever it is.' Tim had introduced us in the pub on Saturday, then went on to explain that I was also Debbie Clinker but he hadn't realised. Alice had laughed and said, 'Zero out of ten for observation, Dad.'

Now she was giving me a withering look. 'Here to drop more litter?'

'It was just a flapjack wrapper,' I protested, 'and the wind—'

'Wig, clothes, dangerous glass spectacles . . .'

'Oh,' I said, 'those. You know, I did come back to look for them but there was just one shoe left. I had a good hunt.'

'Not that good.'

'I'll try to be more careful in future. What more can I say or do?'

Alice pushed her sleeves up her arms and for a moment I thought she might hit me, but it was just a sign she was getting back to business. She snatched up her bag. 'You could put your name on the litter-duty list. Rupert! List!'

While Rupert rummaged in his trousers, I asked Alice

if Stefan was still staying with them, and, here's the strange thing, she turned bright red, right up to her hairline. 'No,' she said. 'Why?'

'We were going to get together,' I told her.

'What?' The bin bag fell from her hand. 'What do you mean?'

'Er . . . he's my boss. We thought while he was here we'd have lunch or something.'

Jonathan said, 'What do you mean, "or something"?'

'Jesus,' I said, 'talk about the Spanish Inquisition.' I took the list from Rupert and saw that only his name was on it, and for every day of the coming week. 'You're going to be busy,' I told him, putting myself down for Wednesday 5 till 7. What else do I have to do, apart from find a job and a home?

Rupert bobbed his head at Alice. 'Ah dint have no choice, man. Specially as Alice has gotta go to London for laak free days.'

'Oh?'

'Field trip,' Alice said, though why that would make her blush, I don't know.

Tim This morning a social worker called Kay rang. Could I come into the office for a chat? I went, we chatted, then some higher-up person came and joined in. After a while, I was told I'd got the job, subject to references, but, in the meantime, would I be able to start now? 'We're quite desperate.'

Before I could ask what my official title was, Kay and

I had arrived at a surprisingly large red-brick house where I was to meet Elspeth. 'Will she need help going to the toilet?' I asked nervously, and Kay said it might be worth offering.

'This is Tim!' shouted Kay when we arrived. 'He's going to be keeping an eye on you!'

I'd been told Elspeth was eighty-one, widowed, mobile but prone to depression and suicidal thoughts, and sometimes tricky. She absolutely refused to go into a home. Her grey, slightly receding hair was in a bun, her green gemstone jewellery exactly matched her thick woollen cardigan. She wore a checked pleated skirt, beige tights and enormous fluffy slippers. After settling in an armchair that dwarfed her, she looked up at me with her rheumy eyes and said, 'You're not going to be another shouter, are you, dear? I honestly don't think I could bear it.'

'Well, I'll be off!' announced Kay. 'Leave you two to get acquainted! I'll just show Tim where the kettle is, Elspeth! I expect you'd like a NICE CUP OF TEA!'

Kay wheeled me into the kitchen and said, 'See what I mean? Difficult from the outset. She insists on lemon not milk, by the way. Come and see me later?'

By the time I got back with a tray of tea things and a wrinkled half lemon, Elspeth was fast asleep; worn out, I guessed, by a lifetime of motherhood, grandmotherhood, daytime TV . . . I sat myself opposite her in another armchair and for fifteen minutes did nothing but drink tea and read the nearest book: *A Practical Guide to Marine Biology*. It was hard to believe I was being paid for this.

If I'd known social work meant just hanging out, I'd have signed up long ago.

'Remember to secure tools, instruments and other essential equipment, as the sea can suddenly turn choppy and send everything flying. Many a vital item has been damaged through complacency,' I learned.

The large room, I began to notice, had a maritime theme: shells and bits of driftwood in the hearth, a painting of a magnificent whale above the fireplace, pen-and-ink drawings of ships along the wall behind me. I quickly came to the conclusion that Elspeth's husband must have worked at sea in some capacity. A marine biologist, even. 'Test all life jackets . . .'

Every now and then I looked over at Elspeth's chest to make sure she was still breathing. I wondered how long I should let her sleep, for the room was becoming increasingly chilly. If Elspeth didn't get hypothermia, I might. I could see fire-lighting items – logs, coal, news-paper – but thought it would be rude to get one going. And maybe in her woollen items, she was quite snug. 'Ensure each person involved in deck operations has a hard hat.'

Elspeth shuffled in her armchair and I looked up to see she'd woken. 'Ah, you're reading my book,' she said.

'Oh, sorry.' I held it out to her. 'Did you want to—'

'Goodness, no. How rude of me to drop orf, but you know it peps me up terrifically. Is there still tea, dear?'

I made another pot, took it back through, and, with her bladder in mind, poured her only half a cup.

'My, you're stingy,' she chuckled. 'Top me up, there's a good chap.'

I can't say I found Elspeth in the least tricky. Just a delightful old lady who wanted to know if I was married, had children, the usual things. I asked if she had photos of her family and she said, 'William and I didn't have children, didn't they tell you?'

'No,' I said, feeling cross with the scatty Kay. Overworked Kay, perhaps.

'But be honest, Timothy, would you want to look at photos of them, even if we had?'

'Well . . .'

'If it's photographs you want, I might have something interesting to show you. Bring me the plum-coloured album,' she said, pointing. 'Beside the tantalus.'

I wouldn't know a tantalus if it bit me on the ankle, but I did spot a plum-coloured album beside a row of decanters. I went and picked it up. 'This?'

'Yes. Now fetch the carver from the dining room and come and sit here.'

I assumed she meant a chair not a knife, and soon I was settled beside her in an ancient mahogany job with shiny arms. Behind us, a tasselled standard lamp threw extra light on to an album she first stroked, then carefully opened. '1953' was written in beautiful italics, then 'Southern Pacific'.

'My husband and I adored being at sea,' she said. 'Luckily, as we were both marine biologists.'

My arm slipped off the chair in shock, and while she

113

carefully turned a page, I leaned across to the book I'd been reading and spun it round with the tips of my fingers. *A Practical Guide to Marine Biology* was written by Elspeth Fitzgibbon.

'Look at me in this one,' she said in her wobbly voice. 'So tanned. We were there studying the whales' winter breeding grounds. Have you ever been to French Polynesia, Timothy?'

I shook my head and felt ashamed. Not because I haven't been to French Polynesia, but because I'd seen Elspeth as old and ailing, and only that.

'Oh, you must go. Do you scuba dive?'

'No, er, not really. Well, never tried.'

'Oh, it's frightfully easy. And you'll get to see the manta rays and pygmy orcas. We had such fun there, William and I.'

Half an hour rushed by, full of tales of discovery and daring, and photographs of the pretty and athletic-looking Elspeth: swimming, diving, hanging over the sides of ships, working at a tiny desk in a cabin, enjoying a drink with a ship's crew. It was uplifting, but at the same time depressing, to see what she'd packed into 1953. I had the sudden realisation that I'd wasted forty years, and wondered if it wasn't too late to become a marine biologist.

When Elspeth finally closed the album she said, 'I'm awfully sorry, dear, but I have to powder my nose.'

What did she mean, she was sorry? My heart sank. 'Would you like me to come and help?' I asked.

'Don't be ridiculous,' she cried, fairly springing from her chair and laughing. 'You're not a pervert, are you, Timothy?'

Erica So Stefan's turned out to be quite the gentleman. Who'd have guessed. Could be shyness, of course. If I hadn't been legless on Saturday night, perhaps I might have taken the initiative. That's what we Aries do, after all. God, what a state I was in. When I was in bed and on the phone to Kurt, he kept saying, 'Hey, this is *really* good. Are you blotto, Erica?'

I tried calling Stefan today, on the pretext of telling him the flowers were looking even more fabulous. He wasn't at work, and didn't answer his home number or mobile. I assumed he was out networking, or at interviews, or maybe just holed up with his novel.

Meanwhile, life goes on. Alice and I are back on speaking terms, following my non-attendance at her meeting. In fact, she was absolutely adorable yesterday, making me a concoction for my hangover and saying why didn't I go back to bed while she looked after Stefan. As I napped, she cooked him Sunday lunch, which was quite something as she roasted the non-free-range chicken I'd rushed out for late Saturday afternoon. Whenever *I* cook non-free-range chicken, she says she hopes I'm reincarnated as an anaemic pecked-to-death battery hen.

She'd taken Stefan off to the beach by the time I woke up, around three. Alice can be such a love when she tries.

TUESDAY

Tim After work – how strange that sounds – I called for Deborah and we went together to the police station. Unfortunately, Sergeant Lillywhite was still on desk duty. I'd phoned this morning to tell him Debbie Clinker had turned up and to close the case, but he'd insisted I bring her in. I rather hoped that if I left it long enough, he'd have gone home. But there he was, resting on his elbows and doing the crossword in the *Bugle*.

'One Debbie Clinker,' I told him, with a twirl of my hand. 'In the flesh. Alive and well.'

He stood upright, put his pen down, slowly closed the newspaper and stared at Deborah. He scratched his chin, frowned, then bent down and retrieved something from below the counter. My drawing. 'Now, sir,' he said, holding it at arm's length for us all to see, 'call me a sceptic, but . . .'

'What's that?' Deborah screeched.

'You, apparently,' said Sergeant Lillywhite.

'But it's—'

'I can't draw noses from the front,' I explained.

'No,' said the sergeant. 'You can't. Of course, the rest is pure Da Vinci.'

'*You* did this?' Deborah asked between hoots. 'Oh, I'm sorry.'

When things calmed down, Sergeant Lillywhite got his paperwork out. 'Now, if you could just provide us with proof of identity . . .' he told Deborah.

She showed him her driving licence, but he wasn't at all happy with the name on it. When she explained about her disguise, he remained unhappy. 'What's to say you two haven't done away with this Debbie Clinker, for whatever reason? Who knows, perhaps she had a million under the mattress . . .' I heard Deborah quietly choke, '. . . and you're now wanting me to believe this very attractive, clearly not fortysomething, ginger-haired—'

'Auburn,' said Deborah.

'Excuse me. *Auburn*-haired lady, with what I might say is a perfect nose, is *her*.' Again he held up the drawing; again Deborah hooted. A WPC came through from the back and I knew I was doomed. 'Ah,' Sergeant Lillywhite said, 'Fiona. Now, come and tell me what you think about this.'

Deborah I'd been hoping never to see that wig again. But there I was, in the police station, wearing the damn thing, along with the ghastly glasses.

'Yes, we're getting a better likeness,' said the policeman,

pulling a shoe from the plastic bag containing Debbie Clinker items. 'But now for the final, what you might call Cinderella, test.'

When the shoe fitted perfectly, he let us go. 'Unless you'd like to stay and write up the blessed report I've now got to do?'

We declined, apologised as much as two people ever have, then walked along the prom towards a much-needed glass of wine in the Lobster Pot, where Tim talked about his new job, looking after Elspeth.

'She sounds fascinating,' I said. 'I'd love to interview her. Maybe sell the piece to one of those magazines for older people, or a boating mag.'

'Why don't you come with me tomorrow?'

'Shall I? No, no I can't. I've *got* to find somewhere to live. The flat's only free for another week and a half, then I really will be homeless. I'm, er, sort of hoping to find somewhere in Shelcombe.' I held my breath and waited.

'You could always come and stay with me,' he said. 'You know, if you got desperate. Sleep in the—'

'Lovely front bedroom?'

'Is it lovely?'

'Very,' I said, breathing out. 'Listen, are you sure it's all right?'

'What?'

'Me coming and staying?'

'Oh, you want to?'

'I'd pay you rent.'

'What, be like a lodger? Wouldn't it be dreary for you?

I mean, wouldn't you rather find a nice lively house full of young people?'

'I think I've had my share of lively houses, thanks.'

I offered to get us both another drink, leaving him to mull things over, and when I got back, he said, 'Actually, it would help me a lot, having a lodger. You see I can't sign on, now I'm working properly. And, to be honest, the hourly rate's not great.'

I laughed. 'You mean you were a life coach on the dole?'

'Yes, why . . . oh, I see what you mean. Anyway, the rent would be useful, but perhaps we should make it a trial.'

'Good idea. Three months?'

'OK.'

We drank a toast, then Tim asked if I knew what a tantalus was.

I thought about it. 'Poisonous spider?'

'Mm, that's what I would have said.'

Jonathan I'd seen them leave earlier, all chatty. Although I had a new-to-me *CSI Miami* to watch, I also kept an ear and an eye open for Deborah's return. Which didn't happen till quite late, annoyingly. I could have concentrated so much better on the crime scene investigation if I'd known she'd be out till eight.

When I eventually heard her voice approach the building, I slipped behind the curtain and took a look. There he was again. I know I shouldn't be threatened by someone so old, but some girls go for that. You couldn't call him handsome, but he's not ugly, either. He's got money, I bet. You probably make a fortune being a life coach.

'Well,' I heard him say, 'good night, then.'

He wasn't coming up. Good. Unless she was about to invite him.

'Night,' she said, kissing his cheek.

I was feeling more and more relieved, and thought about meeting her halfway down the stairs to ask her in for a drink and, with a bit of luck, sex. Afterwards, we could watch *CSI*, and this time I'd be able to follow it better.

I heard him call out, 'At least you'll have a garden when you move in with me!' and my world came to a halt. Then it started up again, and I ran out the room and down the stairs, just as Deborah was letting herself into the building.

'You're moving in with that . . . that . . . *Tim?*' I said.

'Have you been eavesdropping?' she asked. She hooked her bag over her shoulder and passed me on the bottom stair. 'You hear things you don't want to that way, you know. *Or . . .*' she turned and sort of smiled, '. . . you get the wrong end of the stick.'

'But I heard him say—'

'Got any alcohol?' she asked, which was a bit of a surprise. 'I feel like completely unwinding.'

I didn't have alcohol. If I buy beer I drink it all in one go, whether it's a six pack, or two six packs. I can't help it. I play chess on the computer and drink beer and then, when I go to bed, all the beer's gone. I thought about running over to the off-licence to get some, but by the time I got back, Deborah might have gone off the idea of spending time with me; be engrossed in the TV or something. I didn't know what to tell her.

She said, 'You haven't got any, have you?'

I said, 'I've got Yorkshire tea.'

'No,' she said. 'Thanks. Maybe I'll have a bath and an early night.'

'Water?'

She laughed and said, 'Another time, Jonathan. Night.'

Then she was gone, but I still raced to the off-licence, got some beers and, just in case, some wine. I ran back home and rang her doorbell. There was no answer, so I went out on my balcony and listened. I could hear water running. 'Deborah!' I said. I knocked on her glass door, then again louder. 'Deborah! I've got some alcohol! Deb*raaahh*!' There was no response. Well, only from the guy above telling me to shut the fuck up. I don't know why people have to be so nasty. In fact, I wish everyone would die and leave just me and Deborah. And maybe Jessica.

Erica I can't help wishing Stefan had visited three days later. With Alice off studying the Thames Barrier, we'd have had the house to ourselves. And perhaps he'd be more up for sex without a teenager around. I'm sure they can be off-putting for some men.

I tried both of his phones again this evening, with no luck. I suppose if he's busy writing, it might be easier if I visit him. After work one day. Dressed to seduce. Tomorrow? I'll pull the manuscript from his hands, throw it on the bed and we'll do it on the scattered pages, getting ink all over our bodies . . . I tried calling Kurt to discuss the scenario but, surprise, he was in a meeting.

It's actually a bit quiet here without Alice. Almost too quiet. She seems to be having a good time, though. When I called her earlier, she was babbling away about flood defences, talking excitedly. It was hard to sound interested but I think I managed it. When I was Alice's age I spent a week in London with friends and we did normal things: clubbing, getting drunk, picking up boys and shopping ourselves to death. I don't know, I suppose I'm quite glad Alice isn't doing that.

Stefan 'Aggie,' I whispered, half awake. I kissed her bare shoulder.

'*Alice*. What?'

'I have to go out.'

'Where to?'

'A sort of party.'

'Can't I come?'

'It'll be tedious, you'd hate it.'

'No, I wouldn't.'

'Lots of up-themselves journalists and authors.'

She rolled over to face me, her eyes all lit up. 'Authors?'

Shit. 'Oh, only minor ones. Of course, I'd love to take

you and show you off, only we're not allowed to bring guests.'

'Not even your girlfriend?'

'It's a bore, isn't it?'

'Do you have to go?'

'Afraid so, sweetie. Networking and all that.' I kissed her forehead and pulled the sheet off us. But before you could say Jack Robinson, or even John Thomas, young Alice had whipped the sheet back and was diving beneath it towards my exhausted and doggedly limp tackle.

Not that exhausted or dogged, it turned out.

'You're twenty-five,' I told her in the taxi. 'Remember?'

'Yeah, yeah. Will I meet Salman Rushdie?'

'No, it'll be very Z list.'

'But you're invited.'

'Quite.'

I put a hand on her cheek and turned her face to mine. 'You're a features writer, OK? You're *not* at school.'

'Can't I be an academic?'

'What sort?'

'Environmental studies.'

I looked her up and down. We'd had to go and buy her clothes and shoes, as she'd only brought field-study garments with her. Her dress was black and clingy and added several years to her. The bits and pieces of makeup I'd found around my flat added more. All in all, she was looking mid-twenties under her wild hair. 'Do you know anything about environmental issues?'

'Loads.'

'Well . . . all right, then. Just don't say too much, that's all. You'll come across people, journalists, who do know stuff.'

She told me not to worry, but I did. I was there, after all, to find a job and flog a book.

WEDNESDAY

Tim 'I do miss him terribly,' Elspeth told me, a small tear forming in each eye. 'It's been fifteen years now, but I still find myself thinking, William won't want chipolatas in his baked beans, when I'm at the corner shop. Or, I must get William to prune the lavateria. We spent almost all our adult life in each other's company, working together as we did and not having children to take up our attention. It's funny, we were always finishing each other's sentences. Did you and your wife do that?'

'Not that I remember.'

'I don't suppose I shall ever recover from the loss.'

'It'll take time,' I said, wishing I could be more original.

'Oh, and the sea, Timothy. I do so miss being at sea.'

'Really?' Now this I found hard to relate to, being a bit waterphobic. No, more than a bit. The idea of all that ocean beneath a boat or ship quite terrifies me. Even in the swimming pool I make sure I'm near the side if

I swim a length, so I can stop and cling on to something firm. I told Elspeth and soon she was crying tears of laughter instead of the other kind, asking if I called myself a man.

'Maybe not in the traditional sense,' I said. 'I mean, I don't strip car engines or even know how they—'

'Would you be awfully kind, Timothy, and walk me down to the sea?'

'Now?'

'Please. Is it raining?'

'Er, no.' I pointed to the window. 'It's a lovely day, look.'

'Only I adore walking in the rain, don't you?'

'Well, I didn't used to mind it,' I told her, 'before my car packed up and I was forced to walk in horizontal rain in mid-winter along Shelcombe's seafront, with the wind blasting up my trouser legs.'

'Oh, Timothy,' she sighed, 'you're not terribly hardy, are you? Now be a dear and fetch me my tam-o'-shanter. You'll find it at the bottom of the tallboy, in the vestibule.'

Following further instructions, this time in English, I managed to find a tartan hat in a big chest of drawers in the entrance hall. We then set off for the beach, not at a yard an hour as I'd expected, but at a surprisingly brisk pace. At the bowling green we had a little sit-down, more for my benefit, then hurried on to the beach, where Elspeth filled her lungs with the sea air and said, 'Aahhh, yes.'

When she started removing shoes and socks, I

panicked. But nothing I could say – 'You'll get pneumonia! Or be bitten by a jellyfish!' – stopped Elspeth wading in the waves to her knees, trousers hitched up.

'Lovely!' she called out.

'Good!' I replied from where I sat well back, having a sneaky cigarette.

Elspeth disapproves of my smoking and has offered to hypnotise me out of the habit. 'I discovered I had this ability,' she told me. 'You see, William suffered dreadfully from seasickness. Then one time, whilst I held the bowl and mopped his brow, I tried to reassure him; telling him he'd never feel nauseous at sea again. To our astonishment, he never did. William went around boasting about my achievement and, well, I got a bit of a reputation. Sometimes the deckhands and scientists would be queuing to be cured. Goodness, if only I'd charged!'

Anyway, I told Elspeth I'd think about it. What worries me most is that she might drop off, or even pop off, mid-hypnotism, leaving me in a permanent trance.

'Timothy!' she was shouting, looking far from popping off. 'Come on in! The water's lovely!'

There are moments when you feel you're the dullest person alive. Actually, I've had quite a few of those moments, mostly in Erica's company. I took a drag and thought about Elspeth's request. When had I last paddled in Shelcombe's waves? It was with Alice, years ago.

Oh, why not? I put my cigarette out in the sand and buried it deeply, then pulled my shoes and socks off, got up and padded down to where Elspeth, in her funny tartan hat, was kicking water in the air. En route, several sharp shells cut into my soles and I was quite dreading the cold waves, but I kept in mind, as I rolled my trousers up to my knees, that I was being paid for this.

Deborah It was only coming back to London to pack up my stuff that made me question what I'm actually doing. Shelcombe instead of London, moving in with someone I hardly know, befriending a decidedly weird nineteen-year-old. Was I mad? And what on earth was I going to do for money down on the coast? Tim's asked for a ludicrously low rent, but I still have to live.

Overcome with indecision, I sat surrounded by boxes from the local supermarket, where you can sometimes feel you're in Jamaica or Karachi or Khartoum. Had I seen even one black face in Shelcombe?

Oh God, the high spot of every week would be 'music' night at the Anchor. I'd probably end up being a waitress for the rest of my life. Either that or I'd go down the arty and reclusive route. End up with leathery skin and a wardrobe of fisherman's smocks.

I decided to phone Tim on his new mobile. I wasn't sure why, I just thought talking to someone in that other world might clarify my feelings.

'There's no need to shout,' I told him.

'Sorry! I'm in the sea and the waves are a bit noisy!'

'*Why* are you in the sea?' I asked. 'Isn't it freezing?'

'Elspeth enticed me in. Once you lose all feeling it's OK. How's the packing going?'

'Slowly,' I shouted back. 'Look, I might be having second thoughts. It suddenly seems like a crazy idea, moving to Shelcombe.'

'Can you afford to stay in London, with no job?'

'No.'

'Well, then.'

'Yeah, you're right.' It was Shelcombe or back to my parents, again. I toyed with the idea of mentioning the piano to Tim. It was my grandmother's and goes everywhere with me. Later, perhaps. He could barely hear me anyway. 'See you Friday!' I yelled.

I got up and slammed the window shut against the traffic roar. Of course, moving to Shelcombe was a good idea. All that fresh air . . . the slower pace of life . . . the beach to walk along . . . Oh *shit*, the beach. Wasn't I supposed to be on litter duty this evening? I started hyperventilating, then remembered Alice was in London and relaxed.

Alice I popped into the office to tell Mum the field trip was going well, and that the youth hostel was great, fingers crossed behind my back all the while. What's good, when you and your friends get to eighteen, is that none of your parents are in touch any more. None are in touch with Mum, anyway. Partly because she's in London a lot, and partly because she's not like my friends' parents. Younger for a start. Tartier, definitely. Today she was in a low-cut top and short skirt, and was tottering around on these mad high heels. How she manages the rush hour without being molested or breaking an ankle is a miracle.

I said, 'I probably won't be home on Friday, after all.'

'Oh?'

'Some of us thought we might stay on for the weekend. Go shopping.'

'Shopping?' she said, throwing her head back with laughter and exposing more breast. 'You?'

'I don't mean Oxford Street, dummy. Camden Market, that sort of thing.'

'Do you need money?'

'Well . . .' I still had Dad's ten per cent, but if I spent that I'd worry about karma. And the people in Africa, of course. I'm not exactly going to go hungry, though. Stefan's being generous and I ate enough canapés last night to see me through the week.

It was a fantastic party, well, book launch. I talked to loads of interesting people, including the author himself, Dominic something. He's the latest big thing, everyone kept telling me. He was nice but a bit gropey. Stefan was odd, though. Always hovering nearby, watching, but sort of pretending I wasn't with him.

I wanted to tell Mum about the party, but instead said, 'I do need to buy some wellies. We're going to study the estuary at close quarters tomorrow.' Sometimes, the way I can just make things up makes me think I should be a novelist too.

Mum said, 'That sounds fun,' but I could tell she was

miles away. She opened the petty cash tin and handed me five twenty-pound notes.

'Are you sure?' I said. 'Not even designer wellies cost this much.'

'Stay as long as you like. Let your hair down. You don't do that often enough.'

Stefan thinks I should always wear my hair down. He likes its wildness. Says he's tired of women with sleek, snipped-to-perfection hairstyles. I think I love him.

'OK,' I said, tucking the money in a rucksack pocket. 'Thanks. Better go. We're doing the Thames boat trip today.'

'That sounds fun,' she said again. 'So you won't be back till Sunday, then?'

'Probably not.'

She gave my cheek a kiss and said she'd miss me; though, obviously, I wasn't convinced.

Because I had to kill the afternoon – Stefan wanted some space to write – and because I don't *really* like lying, I did the boat trip to the Thames Barrier and back. It was raining so we all sat inside. We were given a running commentary from someone who fancied himself as a comedian, but I didn't catch that much of it, my mind being on Stefan and sex, and how I was going to tell Rupert I've got a new boyfriend. We've been together for eight months, which isn't that long, so he should be all right. I like Rupert because he's so easygoing and thoughtful, but that can be infuriating too, and sometimes makes me want to slap him about the face. Actually, I did once.

I wouldn't call Stefan easygoing. In fact, I'd call him difficult and self-absorbed, but that goes with being creative, I suppose. He keeps getting my name wrong, which is irritating, but I haven't made a big thing of it.

He's touchy too. This morning, I criticised him for driving round London instead of catching buses, and he told me not to tell him how to live his life and didn't speak to me for almost an hour. Then he said he was going into work, and that when he got back he'd like the place to himself all afternoon.

'OK,' I agreed with my best smile. Obviously, you don't want to be distracted when you're writing a novel. I shouldn't think Mrs Tolstoy was always playing the balalaika in the next room, or asking Leo if he wanted more cabbage soup.

I bought Stefan a glass Millennium Dome snowstorm thing. I hope he realises it's a joke present.

Erica After work, I made my way to Islington through light drizzle, found the street and the house easily, then rang the bell for Flat 3.

'Yes?' said Stefan, through the intercom.

'It's me, Erica . . .' I announced. 'Just thought I'd come and say hello. Of course, if you're busy, I'll leave you to your work, only . . . Hello? . . . Stefan?'

The door opened and there he was, breathless and carrying a brolly. He grabbed my elbow and led me down the short path, then along to the end of the street where, on the main road, he flagged down a taxi.

'Anywhere you like,' he told the driver, as he eased me in.

The man looked over his shoulder. 'John O' Groats, then?'

'Um . . . um . . .' dithered Stefan. 'The West End. Covent Garden. No, not Covent Garden. Somewhere tourists wouldn't go.'

'Elephant and Castle?'

'Perfect.'

I tried to work out what was going on. Stefan clearly had a need to be away from his flat: cabin fever, perhaps. And away from busy spots – fairly understandable. But why was he perspiring and slumped so very low in the back of the taxi?

We'd gone a good half-mile before he sat completely upright, breathed out noisily and said, 'Lovely to see you, Erica.' He kissed my cheek. 'How are you?'

Tim I asked Damon the Scrubber if he'd give the front bedroom a lick of paint. He's only halfway through the downstairs, but I thought it might be nice for Deborah to have magnolia walls, instead of that cerise Erica chose in the eighties. Fine at the time but now scuffed and chipped in places. Also, it clashes with Deborah's hair.

Damon can paint a room in a flash; no ground sheet or masking tape and, magically, no drips on the floor. 'Brush not roller' was the secret, he told me. After he left at six with, 'Don't touch them window frames,' I put a vase of flowers on the little pine dressing table, with a Happy New Home card I'd found in town.

What Deborah and I hadn't discussed was meals. Were we to eat together, like a couple, or divide up the fridge and take it in turns to cook, like students? I tend to go for microwaved ready-made these days, but having someone to feed might encourage me to eat healthily. I always used to enjoy cooking, before I was on my own. Of course, if we did eat together, there'd be expectations. Having to get home for meals, for a start. But, then again, maybe I was giving it too much thought.

Around nine, I called Alice to see how her field trip was going. 'Great, yeah,' she said sniffing.

'Are you crying?' I asked.

'Of course not,' she said in a thick voice. 'Got a bit of a cold. You know, from being in the estuary all the time.'

'Ah. Well, make sure you wrap up.'

'Will do.'

'And come home if the cold gets worse?'

'OK.'

'Promise?'

'Yeah,' she said, this time with a loud sob. 'Bye.'

'Alice?'

Stefan How was I to know the silly girl hadn't taken the spare key with her.

'What spare key?' she said, wet, shivering and extremely

upset. 'You didn't tell me about a spare key. The people in the other two flats weren't in either. It was awful. I went and had a coffee, then came back and still no one was in and then it got dark and frightening. I could have been raped or anything. I tried your mobile a hundred times – why weren't you answering?'

'I, er . . . look, I'm sorry. Something came up. Something important. I didn't want to be interrupted.'

'But where have you *been* till half ten?'

I wouldn't normally put up with this degree of interrogation, but she'd looked such a sorry sight on the doorstep. I went to the bedroom and got my robe. 'Here, take those clothes off and put this on. I'll make you a hot toddy and run you a nice warm bath.'

'Good,' she said. Her frown ironed itself out and I sensed she was calming down.

In the kitchen, I warmed milk and added brandy, then took the mug through. She was sitting on the edge of the sofa in my dressing gown, arms wrapped around her middle, teeth still chattering, hair still wet.

'I was having dinner with a potential agent,' I told her. Untrue, of course. I'd had a particularly constructive evening with her mother, discussing the possibility of collaborating on a wickedly erotic book.

I went to the bathroom and called out, 'She read the first rough draft of my novel and loved it. Wants me to sign up with her. But I don't know, maybe I'll shop around.' I poured bubble bath into the water, gave it a swish, had a quick shave ready for sex, and wandered back to the sitting room. 'There's no great hurry, particularly as the book's not quite . . . Oh.'

She was all curled up on the sofa, eyes closed, a hand cupping one of those glass snowstorm things. As I approached, I saw the Millennium Dome in the middle. Was she asleep or not quite asleep? I couldn't tell. She looked adorable, though, with her dark tendrils all damp and spread over a crimson cushion. She shouldn't fall asleep with wet hair, I decided, so, kneeling beside the sofa, I pulled the robe back and kissed her shoulder.

'Aggie,' I whispered, but didn't have time to correct myself before the Dome came up and smacked my cheekbone.

THURSDAY

Tim 'We married in 1948,' said Elspeth. 'At Shelcombe Register Office. My father disapproved of the venue, but then he disapproved of most things. Daddy was a Royal Naval Captain. Terribly dashing, but away from home far too much to ever understand his children. My brother went into the theatre, to Daddy's undisguised horror. Daddy thought acting made one a homosexual and created a dreadful fuss about it over a rare family dinner. Douglas said, "But, Father, isn't it the Navy that does that to a chap?" and they didn't speak for months.'

'Oh dear. Can I top you up?'

'Thank you. During the war Douglas moved into films. He always seemed to be a plucky young pilot, spinning to his death in a Spitfire. Then back into rep after 1945. He never shot to stardom, but made a steady living at what he loved doing. We were both lucky in that respect.'

'Yes.'

'Lucky in our relationships too. Douglas had thirty

terribly happy years with Simon, whom he met when they were doing *An Ideal Husband*. Douglas saw it as fate, Simon turning out to be his ideal husband.'

'I'm guessing your father objected to their relationship?'

'Oh golly, no one dared tell Daddy. He'd have shot them both in their sleep.'

'Really?'

'One could go to prison for it in those days.'

'Yes, I know.'

'And then . . . in 1976 . . . Well, they were on holiday, motoring through Italy, when . . . it was a nasty bend . . . an accident hotspot, we learned later. That was it, my adorable older brother, and dear Simon, gone in a flash.'

'How dreadful,' I said. She was sitting bolt upright in her big armchair, staring into the past with eyes that were slowly welling up. I put a hand on her slender arm. 'Would you like another custard cream, Elspeth?'

'No, thank you, dear. But don't let that stop you. I can tell you're partial.'

'Yes,' I said, taking two.

She blinked away the tears and perked up. 'My early childhood was spent in Portsmouth, but then Mummy got a hankering for a smaller seaside town, so we left married quarters and rented this house. When Daddy left the Navy, he and Mummy bought it with the help of his retirement lump sum. Do tell me if I'm boring you, Timothy.'

'No, you're not. Not at all.'

'Shortly after we moved here, I was packed orf to boarding school, as one was. The Navy paid a fair chunk of the fees, you see. I loved being a boarder but, stuck in the middle of Worcestershire, I did miss the sea.'

'Ah.'

'That was when I decided to become a marine biologist. You know how one just has a moment, a sort of epiphany, when one absolutely *knows* where one's headed. Tell me, Timothy, when did you decide on social work?'

'Er . . . last Thursday.'

'Oh, you're such a wag,' she chortled. 'Now, how about a stroll down to the beach again? You'll find my costume on the clothes horse in the utility room. It was a little musty so I gave it a rinse through, in case we had another super day.'

Although the rain had stopped, it was barely sixteen degrees outside. 'I really don't think,' I began, but could see such excitement and expectation in Elspeth's now dry eyes that I simply got up and did as I was told.

'Now,' she announced when I returned, 'I'm going to put my costume on under my clothes. And *no*, I don't need any help, Timothy. Shall we take the windbreaker and a flask of soup?'

Only if you carry them, I felt like saying, but then she most likely would.

Jonathan Deborah's in London. This afternoon, when I called her for the fourth time, she said, 'I think we need to talk, Jonathan.' I asked what about. 'Us.' I asked what about us. 'I think you're waiting for me to fall into bed with you, and . . . well, you're great, and very handsome, but I'm far too old for you.' I told her she wasn't. 'I'm thirty-five in July,' she said, and, to be honest, I was shocked. When I told her she didn't look it, she said, 'That's beside the point.' I asked if she was sleeping with Tim. '*No*,' she said, 'and I probably never will.' When I asked what she meant by probably, she said there was someone at the door and she had to go.

I skipped the revision I'd planned and had a long slow think on the sofa. Does Deborah find me attractive? Yes, she said so. Does she like me? Yes, she said so. Does she find me knowledgeable and interesting? I don't know how you can tell these things. Usually, she listens to me and says, 'Mm,' a lot like she's really fascinated. I honestly don't care that she's just six years younger than my mother. I'm a mature nineteen, and she's a youthful thirty-four. If you added the right number of years on to me, and took them off her, I calculate we'd meet at twenty-six. I made a sandwich and phoned her.

'Are you drunk?' she asked, after my suggestion that we're both twenty-six in spirit and looks, so should think of ourselves as that age. I'd thought she'd be more gracious, thank me for the compliment, even. 'Look, I'm really busy,' she said. 'I'll talk to you when I get back, yeah? How's the revision going?'

I said I couldn't revise when my life was in turmoil, and she told me not to be a drama queen and asked what the weather was like. 'Showery,' I told her.

'Same here. Listen, you don't know anyone who might be able to house a piano, do you?'

'Whose piano?'

'Mine.'

'Do you play?'

'A bit.'

I looked around the flat. If I moved the bed over to the window . . . 'I've got room,' I said, but she told me not to be ridiculous and, anyway, it might fit into Tim's house.

'Right.' A garden, a piano . . . she'll never come and see me. 'So where's his house?' I asked, and she told me there was someone else at her door.

'I'll call you back in a tick,' she said, but it was a lie because that was four hours ago.

Tim Elspeth's amazing. Not only does she have boundless energy – when she's not napping, that is – but, thanks to her, I haven't had a fag since four o'clock.

After she'd been swimming in the choppy waves for a good long while, and I'd got through three cigarettes, due to the stress of thinking I might be called upon to save her life at any point, she finally emerged from the water and picked up her towel. Incredibly, I couldn't see a single goosebump on her papery skin. In fact, she was glowing.

'Terribly good for the circulation,' she puffed as she rubbed the towel up and down one leg, then the other. She's got a bit of a tummy and not much of a bottom, but I've seen fifty-year-olds with worse figures. 'And feel those negative ions, Timothy.'

'Sorry?'

'The sea. It gives orf negative ions. That's why we all feel so much better beside it.'

'We do?' I said, laughing.

She flipped the corner of her towel against my head. '*Yes*,' she insisted, 'you do. You just counteract the ions with your silly smoking. Now, turn your head, while I dress under the towel, then we'll go home and I'll hypnotise you.'

'Hmm,' I said.

Actually, it went very smoothly. I sat in a big comfy chair and Elspeth just sort of talked. No pendulum or 'You feel sleepy'. She got me to relax different bits of my body and at no point, as far as I know, did I lose consciousness. She talked a lot about breathing in fresh air, about how I no longer needed cigarettes to get me going or calm me down. That whenever it felt like cigarette time, I should do or have something else I like. She repeated over and over I was no longer a smoker. And then, after she'd brought me round, she opened the packet of cigarettes she'd made me hand over, and offered me one.

'No, thanks,' I said, easy as anything. 'I don't smoke.'

When I got home, without a single cigarette on my person, I found a rucksack in the hall and Alice stretched out on the sofa. 'You've cleared up the house,' she said weakly. 'It looks really good.'

'Thanks. Are you all right?'

She sniffed and beckoned me over.

'What?' I asked when I got to her.

'I just want to give you a hug.'

'Really?' I knelt on the floor and she put her arms around me. 'Are you ill?' I asked. It was the only explanation.

'Er, yeah, something like that.'

She sounded very down and I offered to make her a drink. Luckily, I'd done a big shop to fill my naked cupboards and fridge. 'Hot chocolate?'

'I don't know. How old is it?'

'Bought yesterday.'

'All right, then.'

As I heated milk, I began to see my role in life as making hot drinks for people. Obviously, there are worse roles: traffic warden, hated dictator. Just as I was whisking away the lumps, the doorbell rang and there was Rupert.

'Got Alice's text. She awight, man?'

'I'm not sure,' I said, and showed him into the sitting room, where Alice jumped from the sofa and into his arms.

'I really missed you,' she sobbed, showering the boy with kisses. I could see he was taken aback. 'Listen, I'm going to be *much* nicer to you from now on, Rupe. I *promise*.'

While she squeezed him hard, Rupert was making faces at me over her shoulder. 'Quali-ee,' he said rather romantically.

I pulled a face back, gave him a thumbs-up and left them to it, but not before hearing him say, 'So how come yous was the only person at school what went on a laak environmental studies field trip?'

'Oh,' she said. 'I, er . . . it's because . . . I know, it's because I'm the only one doing the Thames Barrier for my extended essay.'

Had she told me she was going alone? I thought not. I stood in the hall wondering what to do. With all these extra hours that not smoking's going to leave me, I'd have to take up a hobby. Like gardening, maybe.

'Right,' I said, once out in my private jungle. I looked around, not too sure where to start, and if I could actually get to the shed for the necessary tools. Normally, at this point, I'd have had a quick fag and a think. 'Right,' I repeated then, remembering Alice's drink, went back in, got the custard creams out, sat at the kitchen table and dunked my biscuit in the mug of hot chocolate. Lovely.

Erica In quiet moments at work today, I made a start on our erotic novella in my head.

'Something tells me you'd be good at writing that kind of stuff,' Stefan said in the restaurant last night. 'We could make a fortune if it took off, you know. People love smutty books involving cultured and outwardly respectable characters.'

'Trouble is,' I told him 'I haven't written an essay since I left school.'

'But I bet you like making up stories? In fact, I know you do.'

He was giving me a twinkly-eyed, crinkly-browed smile, and that was when everything fell into place. Stefan must have overheard me on the phone to Kurt the other night. So, one, he knows I've got a man and is therefore holding back, and two, he knows I've got a vivid imagination and wants to cash in on it. One thing's for sure, you don't need a Ph.D. in Men to work them out.

'Well,' I said, 'I suppose I could have a go. I should have the time now. You see –' I looked him straight in the eye – 'me and my American boyfriend have decided to call it a day.' A slight fib, but obviously Kurt and I aren't going anywhere.

Stefan said, 'Oh, I'm sorry to hear that,' but he didn't look it.

We drank a toast and at the end of the evening I fully expected to be invited back for the night, not bundled into a taxi and whisked to Waterloo station. He came with me. 'Just want to see you safely to your train,' he said. Chivalrous but a bit baffling, I decided on the journey.

God, I spend so much time on expensive rail travel. Coming home this evening, I wondered, not for the first time, if I wouldn't be better off just getting an office job in Shelcombe. I jotted down figures in the back of my diary and discovered I was right. Time to wind down the business, perhaps. I doodled while I thought about it, then something came into my head and the doodles turned to words. There was a deserted beach, a man who looked like Stefan; I called him Steven. There were large boulder-type rocks. Steven was draped over one, naked. A woman – Eleanor? – fully dressed, was gently lashing his buttocks with long shiny strands of seaweed. No, long wet strands of seaweed. I crossed it out. Long wet strands of shiny seaweed. I was ruining the 28 December to 3 January page, but couldn't stop.

Alice I asked Dad if I could move in with him, now the house is decent. Only I said emptier, not decent. Anyway, it seems Deborah, of all people, is moving in.

'Are you, you know, together?' I asked and he did this sort of guffawing thing, which made me realise he'd quite like them to be, even though he said, 'Don't be daft, she'll just be a lodger. Deborah's got nowhere to live and I could do with the rent.' He took another biscuit from a packet. 'It's only for three months . . . well, to begin with.'

'Right.' I was still clinging on to Rupert. It's funny how two days with a cold uncaring bastard can make you appreciate what you've got.

'Deborah's laak really hot, man,' Rupert said, and for the first time in our relationship, I felt a bit jealous. Actually, very jealous. My boyfriend and my dad *both* fancy her. What's she got that I haven't? Apart from sleek hair.

'Shall we go?' I asked Rupert. 'To my room? We could watch a DVD?' That was a euphemism, of course.

'Ah can't, man. I ain't cleaned up da beach yet.'

'Oohh,' I said, rubbing his back, 'let's forget the beach for a day.'

After fetching my things we went to say goodbye to Dad, but he decided to walk some of the way with us. Something about needing more biscuits.

Erica Alice's rucksack was in the hall when I got home.

'Hi, Mum,' she shouted from the kitchen. I could smell garlic.

'Hi,' I called back wearily and a bit disappointed. In the restaurant, I'd invited Stefan down for the weekend to discuss our novella and possibly try out some scenarios. Not quite how I'd put it. Although he didn't give a definite yes — something about his mother expecting him — I felt there was a slim chance he'd turn up, being a Gemini.

'Women usually run a mile when I tell them my star sign,' he'd said. 'I like to think of myself as excitingly Mercurial, but girlfriends say I'm just unreliable and hard to pin down. Sometimes I lie and say I'm a Pisces, then they usually go, "Aahh", and put a protective arm around me.'

Last night, I looked up the Aries woman, Gemini man combination. 'Always be your usual sparkling self,' I was told, if I wanted to hold my Gemini's attention, 'both out of bed and in.' First step, of course, is to get him in. Having my daughter around wasn't going to help.

'Are you OK?' I asked Alice. She was stir-frying. Her

eyes were red and puffy and she was hanging on to Rupert, as though she couldn't quite stand up properly. She put the spatula down, let go of her boyfriend and came and gave me a cuddle.

'I'm just *really* pleased to be home,' she said, planting a kiss on my cheek, while I steadied myself on the table. What on earth had come over her? 'London's the pits,' she added.

'Oh, I don't know,' I said, hugging her back. 'It can be full of surprises. Last night, for example, Stefan and I found a fabulous little restaurant in—'

I stopped because Alice had sort of slipped from me and was heading for the floor. Rupert dashed over and caught her. We helped her on to a chair, where Rupert stroked her hand and some colour came back to her face.

'So are you and Stefan an item?' she asked quietly.

'Sort of business partners,' I said. 'I'm working with him on a book.'

'But you're not a literary agent?'

I laughed. 'Not as far as I know.'

'Hey, am ah gonna be a father?' asked Rupert.

'Don't be ridiculous,' Alice snapped. 'Oh, sorry. Didn't mean to be rude, Rupert. Look, people faint for all sorts of reasons. I think I just got overtired.'

'Only, if you was expectin', we'd have to laak get married and that.'

Now I felt like fainting. 'Anyone for a glass of wine?' I asked, fairly desperate for one myself.

MAY

SATURDAY

Tim I usually take Deborah a cup of tea on Saturday morning, then she brings me one on Sunday. When I knocked and went in this morning, she was sitting up in bed bashing away furiously on her laptop.

'Thanks,' she said, and I asked what she was writing. 'It's a piece on gambling. Working-class gambling. Before I started at the arcade I had no idea it was such a problem.'

She picked up her mug and blew on it, then took a graceful sip. Deborah's very graceful, I've noticed. Especially on the piano. While I tend to plonk and jerk my way through the things I play, Deborah taps and flows, her body swaying one way, her head the other. It's quite lovely to watch. When we duet, I'm even more aware of my lack of a delicate touch. It's nice sitting buttock by buttock on the piano stool, though.

'It's serious then?' I asked, propping myself on the very edge of the brass bed. She moved a foot to make space.

'God, yeah. It's not just the machines. There's the

Bingo, Lotto, scratch cards. And those stupid TV phone-in things. You know, "Who wrote Romeo and Juliet? a) Kevin Shakespeare, b) Gordon Shakespeare . . ." It's not surgeons and top lawyers making pound-a-minute calls to win a holiday in Verona.'

'No.' I wasn't sure I'd ever seen Deborah this worked up, and so early in the day. 'Would you like a biscuit with that?'

'No, thanks,' she said, her eyes darting to my waist, then back to her screen. 'I'm trying to watch what I eat.'

A hint, I could tell. Deborah would never come out and say, 'Tim, you're getting a bit of a paunch.' I'm glad, really. Too much honesty between housemates could be damaging. For instance, if I'd said, 'Deborah, this spaghetti carbonara looks and possibly tastes like baby sick,' last night, I wouldn't have been able to perch myself so readily on the end of her bed this morning. No, we're very polite with each other and I'm tactful about her cooking. 'Mmm, carbonara sauce. Maybe needs a bit of salt?'

'The people who can least afford to gamble,' she continued, 'are the ones being ripped off all the time.'

'True,' I agreed, while Deborah's phone did a little twiddle-de-dee to tell her she had a text. She picked it up and worked it with her thumb, then groaned.

'Jonathan?' I asked.

'Yeah. Says he can't face Monday's history exam without seeing me and sorting things out.'

'Is there anything to sort out?'

Deborah claims this is a one-sided crush and that nothing's happened between herself and this boy, but I sometimes wonder if she's stringing him along.

'It's tricky,' she said, shaking her head, as if it wasn't a huge ego boost having a cute nineteen-year-old chasing you. 'He's . . . well, difficult. I'll meet him, though. Wouldn't want to be responsible for him failing.'

She put her computer to one side and pulled back the duvet. For a moment, I imagined being invited to come and join her under it. About as likely as Shelcombe FC getting to Wembley, but still . . . 'I could murder some scrambled egg,' Deborah said, and before she had a chance to do just that, I was back in the kitchen and warming the pan.

It was a day off for me, but as Elspeth has become a supporter, benefactor and fan of my daughter's, she was keen to come along to the fourth big clear-up.

'William and I hated sitting in front of our beach hut,' Elspeth said when I called for her, 'looking at those wretched polyester containers.'

'Polystyrene.'

'What a dismal experience it must be, eating orf something like that, and with a chubby little plastic fork! Mummy used to pack her second-best silver in our beach hamper, and everything was fresh and made from scratch, even the lemonade. None of these fluorescent Hush Puppies.'

'Slush Puppies.'

'Don't you despair, Timothy?'

'Yes,' I said, because I do.

Down on the beach we found the usual suspects, plus one or two unfamiliar faces. About twenty people, all being allocated different areas to scour. Some were in gardening gloves, some rubber gloves. One woman wore a mask. Everyone looked eager, which was nice for Alice.

Elspeth put her hand up.

'Yes?' said Alice.

'Could I have the beach hut area, dear?' She pointed at it. 'Only I'd like a jolly thorough job done around there.'

'Of course,' said Alice, looking dubious. 'Maybe you could help Elspeth, Dad?'

'OK.'

Off we went with our black bags, and while Elspeth zoomed in on anything polystyrene, I picked up bits of burst beach ball, newspaper, hair slides, sandwich wrappers, a zillion cigarette ends and around a pound in coins. When we stopped for a little rest, I asked Elspeth which beach hut was hers. There were nine in all, in sets of three; some neat, others flaking paint. One looked particularly sorry for itself.

'Oh, second from the right,' she said, waving a hand but barely turning her head. Not surprisingly, as second from the right was the decrepit one. 'Awfully embarrassing, I know, but it's so full of memories, I can't bear to go in, let alone maintain it.'

'I've never seen inside one of these huts,' I told her. Not strictly true, as I've had glimpses over the years when walking past. I just wanted to encourage Elspeth to open hers up, face her demons, or whatever. After all, she cared about the beach surrounding it. 'Have you got the key with you?'

'Oh golly, no. You see . . .'

'Yes?'

'Well, we were here . . . I was here, when William . . . The last time I . . . He took the dinghy out.' She pointed to sea. 'Sometimes we both went, but . . . Oh Lord, if only I *had* gone. A beautiful July evening, it was, although breezy. We'd brought a lovely picnic. Fois gras, a bottle of bubbly . . .'

I felt myself coming over cold. I'd never asked Elspeth what her husband died of, assuming it was an illness of some sort. 'Are you saying he . . . ?'

'The body was never found,' she said. 'Just the dinghy.'

I took my jacket off and put it round her. 'Oh, Elspeth, nobody told me.'

'Not many people know, and I certainly haven't told those ghastly social workers. Such a long time ago now. There was a bit of a splash in the *Bugle* at the time, but he was just seen as another silly fool, washed out to sea in a small vessel he couldn't control. William was actually marvellous with boats. You've seen his trophies?'

'Yes.'

'I've always thought it must have been a heart attack or something.'

'Ah.'

'Someone deflated the dinghy and put it back in the hut. I haven't been in since. How could I? It was the last place I ever spoke to my husband. The trouble is, I can't bear the idea of selling the hut, either.'

'Oh, Elspeth,' I said again. I patted her hand and for the first time understood her regular lapses into melancholia. 'And you wanted to clear this bit of beach because . . . ?'

'Out of respect for William. This was where he took his last steps on terra firma.' She sniffed, then rummaged in her pocket for a tissue. 'It shouldn't be covered in rubber johnnies and cheesy whotnots,' she said, dabbing at her tears, then blowing her nose.

'Wotsits.'

'Still . . .' She straightened her back, lifted her chin and managed a wan smile. 'Better than a long and painful illness, don't you think?'

'Yes. But such a dreadful shock for you.'

'It was. The two men I've loved the most, first my brother then William, plucked from me in an instant.' She squeezed my hand, the tissue still in hers. 'Now don't you go crashing your car, Timothy, and make it a hat trick!'

'A chance would be a fine thing,' I told her, surprised that she should feel so attached to me. The son she never had? 'It needs a new clutch, four tyres and an MOT before I can crash it.'

'Good,' she said, laughing and easing herself up off

the sand. 'Because I'm hoping, this time, *I'll* be the first to go.'

It's a terrible thing to say, but I'm hoping she will too.

Jonathan My sister called me obsessive/compulsive the other day. She's studying psychology and thinks she knows everything. My parents have told her she has to come and check on me once a month. She only comes for the day because there's nowhere for her to sleep, and besides, I'd go mad if she stayed.

Anyway, it was when we were watching a *Columbo* together. She'd wanted to go for a walk, but I told her it was a particularly good episode that she'd regret not seeing. 'Look,' I said, 'if I *were* obsessive/compulsive, wouldn't I be doing revision all day long and live in a very tidy flat?' But she just said it didn't work that way and started describing the 'disorder' at length, so I turned the TV volume up.

I think everyone's got a disorder. My sister, for example, has nymphomania. I read that the average person has something like seven sexual partners in their lifetime, whereas my sister gets through that many in a year. And they're only the ones I know about.

The other day, when I asked Deborah, not for the first time – in fact, maybe for about the tenth – how many men she'd slept with, she asked if anyone had done any personality disorder tests on me. That word again. Women! I've got a theory that they feel the need to label men – womaniser, nerd, wimp, manic depressive – in order to feel a bit more in control in a phallocentric world. When I met Deborah at the Anchor for lunch today, I told her my theory and she asked if I'd got it from Virginia Woolf.

'No!' I said, insulted. 'Why would I say it's my theory, if I stole it?' She laughed at me and said I shouldn't take her so seriously. She's always saying that. Then she asked if I was ready for my history exam.

'I'm not sure,' I said. 'The thing is, there are the bits I'm interested in and know really well, like—'

'Totalitarian regimes.'

'Totalitarian regimes. Then there's liberal democracies and stuff, which I have a low boredom threshold for and can't be bothered with. It's the same with English. I really like—'

'Virginia Woolf.'

'Virginia Woolf. But can't get into the contemporary stuff or poetry. I wish I'd taken maths and chemistry.'

Deborah nodded and gave me one of her sighs. 'So you've said. Many times.'

Anyway, we had a nice cuddle outside the pub and she wished me good luck and said I was to tell her how it went. Deborah always leaves a door open like that. I'm convinced that once all my exams are over and I'm no longer officially a schoolboy, our relationship will move into a different gear. I'll have to cancel my flight to Spain.

'Will do,' I said.

Deborah looked at her watch and told me she had to get to work or she'd be sacked.

'You've got a job?' I asked.

Then she was shaking her head at me for some reason and saying, 'Oh, Jonathan.'

'What?'

'I've *told* you. Lots of times.'

It's not that I haven't tried listening to people, it's just that I don't find most of what they have to say exactly gripping. Especially when I've got something really interesting to tell *them*. I stood there, trying to remember what Deborah's job was, but she had to help.

'Slotsa Fun, remember? The arcade?'

I made a note in my head to remember the name, then she was gone.

Deborah I've got used to the new black wig now. It does the trick, that's for sure. When I first started giving out change, I'd say, 'How would you like it?' and found myself getting the same old replies – 'From behind', 'You on top, darlin'.' Now I'm doing the Debbie Clinker thing, only without the padding in my cheeks. I have sunglasses, which make the arcade even darker, so I only put them on when I see a group of Neanderthals approach. Most days I wear big beige tops, and most days I don't get sexually harassed.

What I like about the job, now that the noise isn't bothering me so much, is that I can do my other work too. There's a small shelf in the booth, just the right size for my laptop and out of sight of customers. The manager doesn't mind; just told me to get it insured because Slotsa Fun 'didn't give a flying fuck' when his mobile got nicked.

But, today being a busy Saturday, I didn't even bother taking the computer in. I gave out change non-stop until eight, when big burly Steve, who can only just fit in the booth, came and took over. They're not keen on women doing the Friday and Saturday night shifts, luckily for me. It's not a bad job. And it's only part time, which makes it even more bearable and means I can work at home on my freelance stuff. All I need is for someone to take my freelance stuff.

After leaving the arcade, I went straight to the Anchor, where Tim had a double vodka and tonic waiting for me. 'So what's for dinner?' I asked. 'I'm starving.' I'd meant to eat when I met up with Jonathan, but Jonathan has a strange relationship with food, sometimes going a whole day without even thinking of eating. Anyway, lunch sort of slipped my mind too, and there's nothing but junk along the front.

'Thai,' Tim said. 'Just needs heating up.'

I did a mock swoon. There's something about having a man cook for you, especially when it's not exactly your forte. Tim always eats what I dish up, but I can see it's sometimes a struggle.

'Shall we go?' I asked, knocking back my drink. I nodded to where the bluegrass band from Gosport were testing the mikes.

Tim pulled a face. 'Good idea. Anything on telly tonight?'

'Nothing. I had a look.'

'Game of Boggle?'

'OK.'

Over dinner, Tim told me about Elspeth's husband, drowning in an inflatable dinghy after a lifetime at sea. 'How awful,' I said. 'And a bit embarrassing too.'

'Not if you're dead.'

'I meant Elspeth must have felt embarrassment on her husband's part. That's why she hasn't told you before, I suppose. You'd think she would have done. You're very close.'

'Are we?'

'I'm sure she'd marry you, if you asked. Has she got money?'

'Yes, I think so.'

'Might be worth thinking about, then.'

Tim grinned. 'Imagine the headlines. "Gold Digger Marries Pensioner!"'

'"From Social Service to Wedding Service!"'

'Very good. You're such a wordsmith, Deborah. No wonder you always beat me at Boggle.'

After dinner, I did indeed thrash him at Boggle, then we went to the DVD shop and hired *Titanic*, a film I've managed to avoid for years – wisely, it turned out – but which had poor Tim in tears. His mind on Elspeth, no doubt.

Stefan I wish Erica would stop inviting me down to

Shelcombe for weekends. So far I've used my mother, a car problem, a job interview I needed to prepare for and, in desperation this weekend, gastric flu. She wants to discuss the book, she says, but from the erotic episodes she emails me through, it's evident she has designs on my body. Or, at least, a guy my height, shape and appearance, called Steven. The other thing is her glorious daughter. Would I be able to keep my hands off her? Would she assault me again?

And besides, I don't need to discuss the book. It's taking shape very nicely under our current arrangement. Erica sends me the sex scenes, all in the first person and written from the perspective of a hot-blooded and experienced blonde woman called Eleanor, and I change it to third person and make the central character a twenty-three-year-old post-grad – for the moment called Alicia, though obviously I'll change that before Erica reads it. It just helps to have young Alice in mind as I write. We're about two-thirds of the way through and I'm determined to get to the end without ever having to visit the south coast.

Must be careful, though, as I can't have Erica going off me. There was a bit of a close shave this afternoon, when Aggie rolled over and picked up the phone before I could stop her. I had to think *very* quickly when she said, 'Someone called Erica,' and handed it to me.

'Who's that?' Erica asked.

'My niece.' Not very original, I know.

'I thought you had gastric flu. Won't she catch it?'

'She's already had it, so she's come to look after her poor old uncle.'

'But didn't you say you were an only child?'

Fuck. 'I'm . . . a sort of honorary uncle to her, aren't I, Aggie?' Aggie was looking none too pleased, but I'd deal with that later. 'Her father and I grew up together. In St Albans. He married young and I visited them a lot.' Too much information, but the storyteller in me couldn't stop. 'He's called John, his wife's Clarissa and they've got three children. All girls.' On I went. 'Aggie's the oldest, aren't you, Aggie?'

At this point dear Aggie got up off the sofa and said, 'Bullshit!' as she passed me on her way to the kitchen.

'Ah, ha ha,' I said to Erica. 'Got to that awkward age.' There was a deathly silence on the other end of the line. 'Erica?' I asked. 'Are you still there? Hello?'

'Yes,' she said, after a while. 'I'm still here.'

SUNDAY

Erica 'The time is right to thrash things out with a partner, Aries. Meetings and discussions will prove constructive, but may throw up one or two surprises!'

Well, that decided it. I showered, dressed and headed to London in the car. There were things I wasn't happy about. For a start, all that juicy material I'd come up with, and I still hadn't seen his, or rather *our*, manuscript. And who the hell was this Aggie person? True, Stefan isn't accountable to me for what he does, but he's being far too slippery – Geminian, you might say – for my liking. Flirtatious on the phone and in emails, but then irritatingly elusive. I can't bear things not to be open and straight, and I was on my way to tell him so.

Outside his flat, I waited in the car, thinking about how to get in. If I rang his buzzer, I might end up at the Elephant and Castle. I decided to try one of the other buttons.

'Hi, it's me,' I said to *Ms K. Powell*.

'Who?' she asked.

I mumbled something.

'Sorry?'

I mumbled again.

'Oh . . . come on up,' she said, and when the door buzzed, I let myself in.

I climbed the stairs to Stefan's top flat, apologising to Ms Powell on the middle landing for pressing the wrong bell, then took a deep breath and knocked twice.

'How the hell did you get in?' he asked. I'd got him out of bed by the look of it. He was in a short, short robe and I couldn't help staring at the fabulous brown legs I hadn't seen before but had imagined many times. It wasn't the nicest of greetings.

'I'm sorry,' I said, a bit thrown by his rudeness. 'But I wanted to come and clear up a few things.' I managed to take a step inside the flat, making it impossible for him to shut me out. 'I'd like to see our novel so far, for a start. You have been keeping up your end of the deal, I take it?' Something had got me on the attack; the look on Stefan's face perhaps. I felt my chances of ever bedding him slipping away but was beginning not to care. 'And a coffee would be nice. I've had a long drive.'

'Well, come on through,' he said and I followed. On the way, he quickly closed a door, then showed me into a messy sitting room. There was a horribly stale atmosphere and I was relieved when he flung open the window. 'Have a seat. Milk? Sugar?'

'Just milk, thanks.'

I couldn't believe the clutter. What might at one time have been an attractive, tastefully furnished room, was now just a dumping ground for books, clothes, magazines, letters, ink cartridges, endless carrier bags and a million other items. What stood out though, amid the chaos, were an empty bottle of wine, two glasses and several takeaway Indian food cartons. So much for gastric flu.

I cleared a space on one of the sofas and heard kitchen noises, then splashing and brushing from the bathroom, then a door opening and shutting, and opening and shutting again. Finally, Stefan appeared, dressed, with two mugs of coffee and the old familiar smile. 'Sorry about that. Not good first thing in the morning.'

I looked at my watch.

'OK, afternoon.' He went over to the computer in the corner and switched it on. 'I'll print out a copy of what I've done so far. I just thought it might be better if you read the whole thing through at the end, that's all.'

'Right. Nice place,' I said.

He spun his office chair to face me. 'Thanks. Bit of a mess, though. Sorry.'

'This is what I could do with. A little one-bedroom flat in London.'

'There are plenty for sale or rent.'

'At a price.'

'That's true.'

While the printer chugged away, my anger waned. I'd been a bit forceful and abrasive and wanted to make up for it, so asked how his tummy was – 'Better' – how the job hunting was going – 'One or two possibilities'. I was about to ask if he'd had any luck with his proper novel when I heard the clunk of a door knob and the sound of feet on floorboards.

Stefan said, far too brightly, 'Aggie, you're up at last!'

I turned and saw a black-haired waif in the doorway. She was wrapped in Stefan's robe and her pale and beautiful face was scowling at him.

'This is a business associate of mine,' he told her. 'Erica.'

'Hi,' she croaked. 'Is there any coffee going, *Uncle* Stefan?'

'In the pot.' He jumped up and turned his back on both of us, busying himself with the printing. 'Help yourself.'

When she'd gone, I said, 'So this is actually a two-bedroom flat?'

'Absolutely. More coffee?'

'No, thanks.'

I asked if I could use the bathroom and he dropped the printed pages and ran ahead of me, closing a door en route, then opening another. 'In here,' he said.

I stopped and looked around. Sitting room, bedroom, bathroom, kitchen. Where the second bedroom was, I couldn't make out.

When I emerged I heard mutterings in the kitchen so went back to the sitting room, where I had a bit of a nose around and happened upon a copy of Stefan's other manuscript, *Deception Row*. I had a flick through, as quietly as I could and with regular peeks over my shoulder. Would he mind me reading it?

It seemed fairly typical private dick stuff, set in London and sharply written. The hero was Saul Sanders, early middle-age, slightly world-weary. There was a character called Zara, Saul's assistant. Blonde, attractive and quite a bit younger than him. I flicked, and flicked some more, stopping at a bedroom scene. I turned back a page to where things had started hotting up. Zara was dancing on two chairs, in a pub. A band was playing . . . she was in a short skirt and stockings . . . and . . . it was all beginning to feel horribly familiar . . . singing along to 'Bye Bye Baby'. 'As she danced, her buttocks swayed and rolled like two plump puppies trying to switch sides in a sack.'

If only I'd stopped at that point, I might have felt flattered that Stefan had modelled his raunchy character on me. I wasn't sure I liked the 'plump', but it was probably intended as a compliment. Unfortunately, or perhaps fortunately, I read on, to discover Saul Sander's thoughts on the breasts of the young, dark-haired beauty sitting beside him, and what he might do if he got access to them. I felt confused, to put it mildly.

When Stefan returned I made my excuses. Another friend to see in London. Hadn't realised it was so late. I grabbed the pages lying in front of the printer, saying, 'This is plenty to be getting on with', and left a slightly stunned Stefan and his 'niece' to it.

I didn't go far. Just a couple of streets. I bought a

two-hour ticket and stuck it on the windscreen, found a café, ordered a coffee and got out the thirty-odd pages, dying to see how Stefan had crafted a tale around Eleanor, and her antics. But it didn't take me long to realise there wasn't going to be an Eleanor.

Our book, it turns out, features a twenty-three-year-old called Alicia. She's dark-haired, long-limbed and has breasts like two halves of an avocado. I got a pen out and wrote, 'You mean green and bumpy?' beside his unappealing description. I added, 'If you touch my daughter, I'll kill you!' – underlining 'kill' twice. I paid for my coffee, drove back to Stefan's flat and shoved just that one sheet of A4 in his mailbox.

Alice Getting a Seaside Award is like halfway to getting a Blue Flag, so that's what we're aiming for first. Now that we're going to have a dog-free main beach area between May and September, we just need a few more litter bins and the lifesaving equipment specified. Plus daily cleaning of the loos on the prom. We've got to meet all twenty-nine criteria, and I think we're almost there. Every councillor standing for re-election the other week made getting a Seaside Award a priority, thanks to all the front-page *Bugle* articles showing me and the gang cleaning up, dumping stuff on doorsteps and so on. I kept getting quoted saying what a 'total disgrace' it was. My fifteen minutes of fame, Dad called it. He thinks I should go into politics, but I said I could never be corrupt and self-serving enough.

Now I've got to channel my energies into my exams, which start tomorrow. Although I've got a retentive mind, I thought I'd do some revision today. Practice essays, mostly. I called Rupert to see if he wanted to come and help, since his exams don't start for another week, but his dad said he'd gone for his elocution lesson. When I laughed, Mr Gerrard told me it wasn't funny. 'Rupert will never get into my chambers speaking that way.'

Poor Rupert. He should just tell his dad he wants to work in a music shop.

I sat and did a couple of past-paper questions, all on my own, wondering if Mum was ever going to get back to cook lunch. Then, when it got to three, I packed it in and went round to Dad's and ate their leftovers. Dad's taken to doing a full roast every Sunday and, because Deborah's like me and cares about the welfare of animals, I know it's safe to eat.

We played a game of Boggle, which was fun, even though I came second. Then we all went for a walk along the coastal path and back. Afterwards we had scones in a new place called Cakes and Ale, which is a bit misleading as the only ale is ginger.

When I got home around eight, Mum was halfway through a bottle of wine and looking really low, which isn't like her. She asked what kind of a day I'd had, which isn't like her either.

'Good,' I said. 'I've been at Dad's. We all played Boggle and went for a walk.'

'All?'

'Me, Dad and Deborah.'

'Ah. Are he and Deborah a couple now?'

'I don't think they can be,' I said. 'They get on too well.'

That cheered her up for some reason. 'Fancy some dinner?' she asked. 'I picked up a free-range chicken on the way back from London.'

'Sorry. Way too full.'

'That's a shame,' she said miserably. She poured herself another glass of wine. Something had happened.

'Did you have a good day?' I asked.

'No, I wouldn't call it good. I went to see Stefan.'

'Ah,' I said, feeling a blush coming on. I jumped out the chair and headed for the door. 'Maybe I am hungry. Shall I put the oven on?'

'Bastard,' she said. I don't think it was to me.

MONDAY

Tim 'Now,' I said, handing the large patterned bowl to Elspeth, 'tell me which key is which in here, then I'll be able to get into the shed for the mower.' It was a bit of trickery on my part. I'd already worked out which was the shed key and, indeed, had already used it when she was dozing one day and I was bored and feeling nosy. No, it wasn't the shed key I was after. 'Tell you what, why don't we label them?'

Elspeth nodded. 'If you feel it will help, Timothy. Let me see . . .' Her pale wrinkled fingers raked through the dozen or more keys. 'Spare front door,' she said, picking one out. 'You'll need to fetch string and the pack of labels we used to use for specimens. You'll find both in the Davenport.'

'OK, tell me when I'm warm,' I said, wandering off in the direction she'd indicated.

'Beside the occasional chair,' she told me helpfully.

'That?' I said, pointing at a lovely old red satiny affair

with wooden arms. Next to it was a walnut desk. It was only beginning to dawn on me that every piece of Elspeth's furniture was valuable. 'So what is it when it's not being a chair?' I asked. 'A dining table?'

'Ah, ha ha,' cried Elspeth. 'Old joke, Timothy. But lovely to hear it again. Now, try the drawer on the left. Oh, wait a moment, you'll need the key.' She rummaged in the pretty little bowl – another antique? – and picked out the dinkiest little thing. 'Here.'

We sat and labelled, using a code in order to confuse an intruder. 'BD' – back door. 'B2' – bedroom two. 'SH' – shed. He wouldn't be confused for long. It took a while, because I had to go and try each key out. There was one for the pantry, one for each of the five bedrooms, three for the outhouses. With only two identical mortise keys to go, Elspeth suddenly said, 'Well, that's a job well done. Thank you, Timothy. Shall I make us elevenses?' She piled the other keys back in and handed the bowl to me.

'Good idea,' I said, and while she was gone, I fished out one of the unlabelled ones and slipped it into my pocket. Yes, a job well done.

'Evaporated milk in your coffee?' she called out from the kitchen.

'I don't think so, Elspeth.'

Stefan On opening my letter box this morning, I first felt baffled at the crumpled page with hand-written comments on it. Then gradually, starting with my head, I went icy all over at my mistake. I'd printed out the wrong version for Erica. Last week, almost as though I'd sensed her imminent visit, I made a universal change – Alicia to Letitia – but had, oh so stupidly, kept the original file, just in case I couldn't actually work with a character called Letitia.

I screwed the page up, then screwed it some more . . . But *wait*, I told myself. Wasn't this a death threat? What if I'm found beneath an Underground train? I unscrewed the sheet, held it against the door and flattened it with my palm.

Back upstairs, I wrote 'Received from Erica Jones-Downer', together with the date and her address, then tucked it in the folder that held my will and insurance policies. Nobody's going to kill me and get away with it.

I set off for the shops again, downhearted to say the least. The other letter in the box had been a rejection of *Deception Row* from an agent. The third in a week. With both writing projects now pretty much dead in the water, I decided I may as well flog a flat or two and live off the proceeds in a remote part of Italy or Portugal or somewhere. A place in which the young women are bronzed and bored, and where Erica Jones-Downer and a sharp knife aren't likely to find me.

I popped into three estate agents, all inordinately pleased to see me, and all promising the speediest of sales, what with it being the spring. The only thing to choose between the three agents was gender. Two blokes, then in the third office, a tall and attractive brunette of around twenty-five. We got a good bit of rapport going and agreed on Wednesday for her to come and measure me up. I don't think she'll be disappointed.

Tim I wanted an accomplice, so I waited for Deborah to finish her shift at five. We went straight down to the beach hut, where I turned the key in the lock and Deborah stood as lookout. We weren't breaking and entering but we were trespassing, I guess. The lock was rusty but worked. The door creaked open and I held my breath and shut my eyes. What if Elspeth's story had been a lie and William's skeleton was lying with a noose around it, or a knife in its midst?

I opened one eye and saw a mass of rubber – the deflated dinghy – taking up most of the hut's space, which was only about eight foot by ten in all. I breathed out, then inhaled the aroma of dust and mildew and rubber. Around the edge of the hut were deck chairs and paddles, a camping stove, a kettle, towels, sandals, a beach brolly, cups, and lots of cobwebs.

'No dead body,' I told Deborah.

She joined me inside the hut and we had a gentle poke around. All I wanted was to get an idea of what Elspeth can't face, but at the same time can't get rid of. She told me she still pays the couple of hundred the council demands from her every year, despite the fact that the hut is privately owned. She's regularly asked to keep the place in better order but ignores their requests.

'Have you got a plan?' asked Deborah. She held up a

large pair of maroon bathing trunks, shivered, then put them down again.

'Not yet.'

'It's a bit of a museum, isn't it? There's a newspaper here with Princess Di on the front, at some function.'

'Do you think we should do something with all this stuff?' I asked.

'We?'

'OK, me. Elspeth never will.'

'But maybe she just wants it left this way till she dies.'

I wasn't so sure. She loves being on the beach and in the water – it's only the hut that gives her the creeps. 'I think I should clear everything out and put it in my garage. It'll be empty next week, when my car's back on the road. Then I'll secretly paint the place for Elspeth and if she wants her things back, I'll still have them. I'm sure she'll love the surprise.'

Deborah looked sceptical. 'But Elspeth might like to come and help.' She bent down and picked up an ice bucket with an open champagne bottle still in it.

'No,' I said, remembering *Titanic* and suddenly wanting to get out. 'I don't think so.'

Jonathan I couldn't be bothered with the question on liberal democracies, so I wrote the essay on Stalin I've practised and practised because, incredibly, he didn't come up anywhere in the paper. I hate being thrown like that.

After the exam, I went and found Slotsa Fun to tell Deborah I've probably failed, but when I approached I saw her and her so-called landlord walking out together, so I hung back for a while, then followed them. They went down on the beach, along to that row of huts that sell for tens of thousands of pounds. I saw an estate agent on TV saying they've got nostalgic value, but a lot of sheds in Shelcombe are even older and much more useful.

Tim opened up the worst-looking one, then they both went in. I wondered if they were having sex, so, even though the door wasn't quite shut, I went over and walked around the hut, hoping to find an open window, but there was just a boarded-up one at the back. However, I could tell from the way Deborah and Tim were talking that they weren't having sex, so before they spotted me I got off the beach and sat on a bench on the promenade and timed them until they reappeared. Four minutes forty-one seconds, from the time I sat down. I wondered if that was long enough for a quickie. I'll ask Clive.

Deborah I spotted Jonathan on a bench, watching us, but didn't mention it to Tim, who was happily rabbiting on about the hut and Elspeth's stuff. The thing to do, I decided a couple of weeks ago, is just wait. Jonathan's due to fly to Spain in a couple of weeks' time, to join his parents. He's definitely odd, and I fear I've become one of his obsessions, but I'm convinced now that he's harmless. I was tempted to wave at him, but didn't. He probably wanted to tell me how his exam went. I did ask him to, after all.

At the top of the steps off the beach, I said to Tim,

'Listen, I just need to pick up a few things in town. See you back at the house?' We went in opposite directions and I crossed the road and pretended to be engrossed in a tacky gift shop.

Within seconds Jonathan said, 'Hello, Deborah,' behind me.

'Hey,' I replied, turning. 'How did it go?'

We walked along the prom, chatting. Well, Jonathan chatted; not even stopping when a guy appeared from the blue and took a photo of us. The man handed me a ticket and pointed to a booth, where we could collect the picture in an hour. 'Thanks,' I said, slightly pissed off. I just knew I'd go and pay some rip-off price for it.

By the time we got to Jonathan's flat, he'd moved on to his second exam answer, the one there wasn't actually a question about. I blame his parents. If you have a child like Jonathan you can't steamroller them into doing anything they're not interested in. It's so obvious he should be studying science or maths or computing.

'I recorded a *Murder, She Wrote* yesterday,' he said at the downstairs door. 'Do you want to watch it?'

'Um . . .'

'It's a good one.'

'How many times have you watched it?'

'Nine, I think. But I haven't seen it for a while.'

I suddenly felt so sorry for Jonathan, that I agreed.

When I got home, having picked up the really-not-bad photo, Tim was almost cross with me, wanting to know where I'd been. 'I was worried,' he said, hands on hips like a cross parent. 'I tried your mobile but heard it upstairs.'

'I've stopped taking it to work,' I said. 'I can never hear it ringing and it might get nicked. I was at Jonathan's.'

Tim ran fingers through his hair, shaking his head. 'I don't get it. This Jonathan thing.'

I took a deep breath and explained, from the beginning. How Jonathan and I struck up a friendship, being neighbours. How Jonathan didn't seem to have friends or go out much, then before I knew it he had a crush on me. 'Jonathan has a few problems,' I said. 'His brain is wired differently from yours and mine.'

'Where's his family?'

'Spain. He's flying out there after his exams, so I'm just sort of being there for him till then. He was very wound up about today's history paper. Deliberately wrote an answer to a question he thought should have been in it, but wasn't. He knows he's failed and when I left he was in one of his bleak moods.'

'I'm sorry,' Tim said. 'Of course you don't have to inform me of your every move. I was being ridiculous. I cooked, by the way. Lasagne. But maybe you ate at Jonathan's?'

'He doesn't eat,' I said. 'Not as far as I can make out. No wonder he's so nice and slim.'

Tim's arms quickly wrapped themselves round his stomach to hide the mound that's built up since he stopped smoking and took up biscuits. I'm tempted to suggest more hypnosis, this time to get him off the custard creams.

Erica 'Hi, Kurt,' I said. 'What are you wearing? Take it all off.'

'Hey, Erica. Long time no phone sex.'

'Been busy, sorry.'

'I, er . . . me too. Actually, hun, I've been meaning to call you and . . .'

'What?'

'It's just that . . .'

'Who is she?'

'Oh. Er, someone from the firm. Listen, I'm real sorry—'

'How old?'

'Let me see . . . uh, twenny uh . . .'

'Twenty what?'

'Five. Four.'

'Are you stopping at four?'

'Soon. She'll soon be twenty-four. But you know, Erica, she's not a patch on—'

'Bye, Kurt,' I said, and put the phone down.

I lay stunned on the sofa for a while, then got up and went to the mirror. I looked more or less as I always look, but I felt ancient. No longer an attractive being; suddenly devalued. Like all those Hollywood actresses hitting the forty wall. This was terrible. First Stefan, then Kurt. Was God trying to tell me I was past it? It comes to us all, I suppose.

But wait a minute . . . without men and sex, what was I going to do for the next fifty years? And there won't be men because all they want are little girls, like Alice. I put my hands on my cheeks and pulled the skin back. My face was flatter, brighter, younger. But could I be bothered with surgery? The money, the pain. Wouldn't it just be a ridiculous and sad route to take?

I sighed, let my face drop and felt the garden beckoning. There was still an hour or so of light left and some bindweed to clear. This is my future, I thought miserably, taking my padded gloves from a drawer. I'll be a woman who gardens.

FRIDAY

Alice All week Mum's been moping around, not going to London but not working at home either, just gardening. Every day she's asked how my exams are going, and even listened when I told her. Every evening she's cooked us both a nice meal *with a pudding*. But, most amazingly, she's been to see Gran *three times*. I wondered if it was hormones, and when I said, 'It's not the menopause, is it?' she burst into tears and ran out the kitchen. So maybe it is.

With no exams today, I went to see Rupert and blurted out my concerns about Mum. 'Perhaps she's having a bit of a mid-lifer,' he said. 'Having to come to terms with her fading looks, not that they are fading.'

I said, 'Rupert, you're talking normally!'

'Yes, I know. Couldn't stand my elocution teacher, and making me go on Sundays was plain cruel. My parents think she's a miracle worker.'

He sounded so different, so mature. And posh, just

like his parents. It was exciting. Like having a whole new boyfriend. 'Shall we go to bed?' I asked, and we did.

Afterwards, while we pillow-talked, Rupert said, 'So does your mother still have her American boyfriend?'

'I think that's over.'

'Is she seeing that other bloke? The one she was with in the Anchor.'

'Stefan? Oh . . . um, I don't know. No. No, no. Definitely not. They've just got some book project going.'

Rupert reared his head back and looked at me. 'Why are you blushing?'

'I'm not,' I told him, kicking his duvet off. 'It's really hot, that's all.'

'Is it? Anyway,' he continued, wrapping his arms round me again, 'maybe what your mother needs is a toy boy to boost her confidence. She could easily get a guy half her age.'

I wasn't liking the sound of this. Now Rupert could talk properly, Mum might go for him.

'Come to think of it,' I said after a bit of a pause, 'maybe she is having a thing with Stefan. Yes, I'm pretty sure she is.'

'You're blushing again.'

'Look, I'm *not*,' I said. 'OK?'

I walked back from Rupert's via the beach. It was half eight and the sky was turning an interesting swirly pink, which is supposed to mean it's going to be nice tomorrow, but that doesn't always work. Sometimes I think I never want to see the sea or another shell or grain of sand again; that I could happily go and live in a huge city and never leave. But this evening, with the beach looking so much nicer now the council's pulled its finger out, I wondered how I was going to wrench myself away. But I have to.

I'm going to have a gap year, maybe even two, because I'm not that sure I know what I want to do with my life. What to study. There's nothing worse than getting on the wrong track, like Dad did. So, last week, I kind of signed up to go and help build latrines for remote communities in Ghana. I haven't told Mum yet because I know I'll have to get inside her frame of reference for her to even remotely understand why I want to do it: 'OK, Mum. Well, you know that get-me-out-the-jungle thing you watched, yeah . . . ?'

Rupert's given up on the music shop idea and is going to apply to do law at Cambridge, spending a thrilling gap year working for his dad. I expect that'll be the end of us. For a start, we'll be thousands of miles apart. Plus, I don't want to watch him turn into his dad, who's so blatant about his mistress, while Mrs Gerrard turns a blind eye and runs the Shelcombe History Society. Rupert says he'd never work on behalf of huge companies, like his father, but would use his legal knowledge to help the oppressed and underprivileged.

'Yeah, right,' I said. Fat chance.

When I got home, I heard Mum say, 'Bye then, Rupert. Yes, nice talking to you too. Thanks for calling.' I hurried to the sitting room, just as she was putting the receiver down.

'Does he want me to call him back?' I asked.

'I don't think so. He just phoned to see how I was. He's got a lovely voice when he speaks English, don't you think?'

'Yes, I do.'

She got up out of the armchair in her scraggy old gardening clothes, fluffed up her hair and said, 'I've always liked Rupert.'

No she hasn't.

SATURDAY

Tim When Elspeth told me she hadn't been in a pub for fifteen years, I assured her she wasn't missing much. 'It's all football on huge screens these days.'

'William drank draught bitter but I was always a stout person, myself.'

I said, 'Well you're very slim now,' and she curled up laughing. I love it that Elspeth's so easily amused. While I cut her lawn this morning – yes, it's my day off, but the grass was so long – she sat in a deep malaise on the patio. So I made myself a little Hitler moustache from the cuttings, did the salute and a bit of goose-stepping and soon she was giggling and saluting me back. I can't think of a single other person who'd have found it funny.

I suggested a lunchtime drink, but Elspeth thought sitting in a dingy pub drinking alcohol on a beautiful day was 'a rather unwholesome activity' and I couldn't disagree.

'How about this evening, then?' I said. 'Deborah and

I thought we'd check out the music at the Anchor. Why not join us?'

'That's terribly kind of you, dear, but I haven't a thing to wear!'

'Now, you know that's not true.' Elspeth's clothing fills four wardrobes. She seems to have hung on to every article since peace was declared. 'And anyway, nobody dresses up to go to the Anchor.'

But Elspeth wasn't listening. 'There's always my trusty old taffeta cocktail dress,' she said. 'I had it made in Hong Kong. It's the shade of aquamarine William absolutely adored me in. Said it matched my eyes. Have you been to Hong Kong, Timothy?'

'Not yet, no.'

'Why don't we take a look at it?'

'Hong Kong?'

She laughed and gave my knee a playful tap. 'Funny boy. Now help me out of the chair. Gosh, a Saturday night painting the town red. How terribly exciting.'

It wasn't yet one o'clock, far too early to be getting ready, but I went along with it. In the master bedroom – 'MB' – we decided against the taffeta dress; someone was bound to spill beer on it. Elspeth opted instead for a dark blue, what she called 'poodle' skirt in a thinnish material. It could have been cotton, but what do I know? She proved it was completely circular by laying it out on her bed.

'I've always had a twenty-three-inch waist,' she said proudly, when buttoning herself in. 'There! Goodness,

it used to be knee length, now it's down to mid-calf.
You'll have this to come, Timothy. Beware.'

I told her I liked my skirts mid-calf, but this time
didn't get so much as a chuckle. 'Now,' she said, totally
absorbed in her task, 'what shall I wear with it? Yes I
know, the cashmere bolero. No, no, the fuchsia blouse.
Could you fetch it from the rosewood wardrobe?' She
was very excited, I could tell. If only we were taking her
to the theatre or opera, not Cousin Jed's Rockabilly Nite.

Eventually, I was forced to leave her to it, in order to
get my car to the garage before they closed at five. My
next-door neighbour, Ken, who always knows someone
who can do or get something for you, had a mate with
a proper tow bar, who took me for a tenner. The people
at the garage scratched their cheeks and shook their heads.
They told me my old Citroën wasn't worth repairing and
before I knew it I was buying a ten-year-old Ford with
a suspiciously low 54,000 on the clock. It was just under
three hundred and had a full MOT. 'One careful lady
owner,' they promised in time-honoured fashion. They
were keen to take my rustbucket in part exchange, which
worried me slightly. If I see it out on their forecourt for
a grand next week, I'm informing trading standards.

It felt peculiar driving again, and in a new car, so I only
took it down to the car park by the front, where I looked
out to sea for a while, feeling I should have an elderly wife
beside me. In my pocket I fiddled with the key to the hut,
and thought about taking some of Elspeth's things to my
garage. Only what if a beach hut neighbour saw me? They

might have Sergeant Lillywhite down here before he could say, 'Not you again!' Best to do it at night, perhaps.

But I was eager to get the place cleaned and painted – although not keen on carrying out the practicalities myself. I rang Shelcombe Scrubbers from my mobile. Business must be slow because Damon arrived in their van within minutes and said, 'Let's take a shufti, then.'

By four-thirty the hut was empty and my garage was full. I really wanted to tell Elspeth, but knew I had to wait. Tomorrow, Damon and I are going to make a start on what he calls 'the fun part'.

Stefan I said, 'Hi, Erica,' fairly relieved. I was going to hang up if the daughter answered.

'Hello,' Erica said, not exactly friendly.

'I got your note,' I told her.

'Good.'

'Thing is . . . well, I'm a bit confused. Is it because I've called the character Alicia? Only that was my first girlfriend's name and, you know, first love and all that. It took me a while to work out what you meant. Alice. Alicia.' I managed a weak laugh.

'Your first girlfriend?' she said, surprise in her voice. 'Oh.' While Erica went quiet, I bit my lip. 'Oh, Stefan, I'm so sorry. God, you must think I'm mad.'

'Not at all.' I laughed properly this time, and with some relief. Alice hadn't spilled the beans then.

I'd been planning this call all week, aware that I didn't really want to give up on our joint project, and that it needed just four or five more scenes from Erica. I had to get her back on board. I was pleased with the first-girlfriend idea, even more so now it had worked. It was time to charm her.

'So, how have you been, Erica? I've missed hearing from you.'

'Really?'

'Yes, really. I'm sorry about last Sunday: the chaos, my niece.'

'Your niece,' she snorted. 'Right.'

Don't react, I told myself. 'Her parents are quite worried about her being in London with hardly any money, trying to get into drama school.'

'What are their names again?'

'Pardon?'

'Her parents. Your friends in St Albans.'

Obviously, I couldn't remember the names I'd given them. 'Actually, they're no longer in St Albans. They're in Devizes now. Beautiful spot. Have you been there?'

'Yes, once. What was it, John and . . . ?'

'Oh! Looks like I've got another call coming through. I'm expecting to hear from an agent.'

'Literary?'

'Er, yes. Better go.'

'Hang on,' Erica said, suddenly forceful. 'If you're serious about finishing this book of ours, why don't you come down to Shelcombe this weekend? Today would be good for me. We can discuss what we've done so far. Add to it, even.'

'Er . . .' I was going to lose her if I said no, I could feel it. 'OK. But I'll find somewhere to stay. Save you going to any trouble.'

'Whatever,' she said. 'Just don't forget to bring our work-in-progress.'

When the call ended, I wasn't sure if it had been a good idea or not. I went to the computer and printed out the Letitia version, all the while wondering how young Alice was going to react to me turning up. Christ. The last thing I wanted was a weekend in bloody Shelcombe-on-Sea, but on the plus side, I wouldn't have to show any more young couples with disappointed expressions around my flat. The estate agent could do it today. I gave Lovely Lara a call. She said that with just a little work, I'd probably get the asking price. We're meeting next week to discuss it over dinner.

Four and a half hours later, I was walking up to Erica's house. I'd booked myself into a hotel on the front, showered and had a quick pint in the bar before setting off on foot with a feeling of unease, to put it mildly.

But Erica was very welcoming. She was dressed more casually than usual. Scruffily, in fact, in a ripped old pair of jeans with mud on the knees and a baggy sports top that could have been her ex's. Her face wore no makeup, her hand held a trowel.

'I'm gardening,' she said, sitting me down in the kitchen. 'Just one little job to do then I'll be with you.'

'Can I help?' I asked, leaping up again.

'Yeah, OK. I'm moving the berberis to a shadier spot. If you could hold it straight while I shovel the soil in . . . ?'

We went out into a lovely garden, about sixty foot long and quite narrow, but very pretty. 'Wow, it looks amazing,' I said.

'Thanks.' She stood a large shrub upright and placed it in a hole. 'OK, so just hold this straight, yeah?'

This I did, all the while trying to work out what was different about Erica. Then I realised everything was different about her. I wondered if I was with a secret twin, the one that didn't get the high-octane gene. 'Like this?' I asked.

'A little to your left . . . that's it. Hold it there.'

She wasn't in any way giving me the come-on. No eyelash was fluttered, no lip licked, while she issued instructions. 'Where's Alice?' I asked bravely.

'At her boyfriend's for the weekend. His parents are away and they're holing up for two days and revising together.'

I thanked God. Although, perversely, I was now wary of being alone with Erica. 'That's nice.'

The shrub got bedded in, then the kettle got put on and Erica went off to clean up. While I made us some tea, I fully expected the other twin to come back down the stairs in vamp mode. But no, Erica returned to the kitchen in the same outfit and with the same unmade-up face. 'I baked a lemon cake,' she said. 'Would you like some?'

'Yeah, OK. Thanks.'

'Alice won't eat it because one of the eggs wasn't

free-range. I didn't have enough and had to go to the corner shop. I'm pleased with it, though. It turned out very light.'

She took her cake from a round tin and cut me far too large a slice. It arrived at the table, complete with tiny fork and serviette. Erica sat opposite with a smaller portion and, once she'd settled, I said, 'So, about our book.'

'Yes?'

'I thought perhaps you could read through it whilst I amuse myself, walk along the beach or something.'

'All right.'

'Then later, or tomorrow morning, you might like to come up with one or two, or even three or four more juicy scenes for me to weave into the climax, as it were.'

'Sure,' she said. The other Erica would have made something of that 'climax'. She had freckles, I noticed. Just a smattering, across her nose and cheeks. Her skin had a pinkish hue, but only in places. Women wear makeup to look younger, but today Erica could have passed for thirty, no problem. 'What do you think?' she asked, eyebrows raised.

'Sorry?'

'The cake.'

'Oh. Delicious.'

'I found the recipe in *Family Circle*.'

I laughed. Couldn't help it.

'At the dentist's,' she said, joining in. Such a lovely laugh. Why had I never noticed?

* * *

Jonathan I sometimes get so depressed that I can't do anything except sit and stare into space. It happened when our cat got run over but there doesn't always have to be a reason. Anyway, most of the week's been like that, though today was worse.

When Deborah called round on her way to work this morning, she kept saying I should see someone. She wanted to phone my GP, but I told her that was pointless. My father took me to him three years ago because he thought I might have something wrong with me. 'He doesn't have friends,' he told Dr Franks. 'Doesn't mix. He's moody and tetchy. He hardly ever leaves his room. He's only got two interests, and when he does emerge, he'll talk non-stop about them. He won't eat with the family. He's rude to people, but doesn't understand how he's upset them. Sometimes he shouts abuse at us all out of the blue. He shows no interest in others and is incapable of empathy.' Dr Franks told my father I was a teenager and sent us on our way. Dad called him a bloody old fool, but not to his face.

My parents have been phoning and phoning my mobile, leaving messages asking how I am and how the exams are going. I don't know what to say so I haven't called them back. I told Deborah and she said that was thoughtless of me. 'Imagine how hurt they must feel.'

I said, 'If they didn't phone *me* back, I wouldn't feel hurt.'

'No,' she said with one of her sighs. She asked me when I'd last eaten and I couldn't remember. Then she made me come part of the way to work with her, so she could buy me something at the sandwich shop. We chose a coronation chicken baguette and I was surprised at how hungry I was. Deborah bought me two more and told me to put them in the fridge for later.

Before she went in Slotsa Fun, she kissed my cheek and said, 'Look after yourself, won't you? I'll come see you some time over the weekend.'

'OK.' I asked her if she was sleeping with Tim yet and she said no, she wasn't, and then she rubbed my arm. Normally, I don't like people touching me like that, unexpectedly. But when it's Deborah it's OK. If it wasn't for Deborah, I probably wouldn't see the point of living. Even with her, I'm not sure.

Deborah I got such a shock when I looked up and saw it was Stefan sliding a fiver under the glass. I said, 'What on earth are you doing here? And don't you realise gambling's a fool's game?'

He just stared for a while, trying to match the voice with the person. I took the wig off and he jumped. 'Deborah! Ha! Well, you found a job then?'

'Just temporary, you understand. So what *are* you doing in Shelcombe?' I thought I might know, actually, having heard from Tim, who'd heard from Alice, that Erica and Stefan were working on a book. I had wondered, briefly, if there was something going on between them, but I'm not sure Erica's nubile or malleable enough.

'Oh, just visiting,' he said.

'Erica?'

He nodded. 'Why the wig?'

'Long story.'

'And you've found somewhere to live?'

'I've got a room at Tim's.'

He found this amusing. 'You're living with the life coach you came to investigate?'

'Not living with as in *living* with.' A queue had formed and I pointed to it.

'Sorry,' Stefan told the bloke behind.

I handed him his change. 'We'll be at the Anchor tonight. Maybe see you there?'

'Maybe. Only Erica and I have planned to work this evening. We're writing a sort of novel together.'

'What's it about?' I asked, as he was beginning to move away.

'Oh . . . men, women, academia.'

'Sounds good. I'll look forward to seeing it in the shops.'

'Er, yeah,' he said, looking uneasy. He added, 'We might use *noms de plumes*, though,' and disappeared.

It's not the hardest job in the world but I'm always glad to finish my shift. I can only take so much 'But *we* don't want to give you *that*', on the Millionaire machine next to the booth. At six, I handed over to Steve and hurried home to soak in the bath, eat, then change for a night at the Anchor.

I love my room. Love the brass bed, the uneven walls,

the view of the sea through the slightly wonky glass of the old multipaned window. I've set up a little office area in one corner: table, chair, laptop, printer, stacked plastic trays. I can go online there, and all-in-all it makes me feel connected to my old world, if only through emails from ex-colleagues telling me they're still job hunting. I haven't told them what I'm doing, but no doubt Stefan will.

While I ran a bath, I checked for messages. Yesterday was busy and I didn't get round to picking up. Unfortunate really, as there was an email from a weekend broadsheet saying they'd be interested in my life coach piece if I could get it down to three thousand words. I went to tell Tim, who was rearranging Elspeth's belongings in his garage.

'If I stack everything against the far wall, I might be able to fit the Ford in,' he said. I get the impression Tim's chuffed with his new car.

'I'll give you a hand,' I said, and as we pressed the deflated dinghy – which I'm convinced Elspeth will never want to see again – against the wall, I told Tim my news.

'Hey!' He let go of the rubber and came and gave me a hug. 'That's great. Well done.'

'It's not signed and sealed,' I said. 'And don't worry, I won't use your name.' I patted his back through his warm, faintly damp shirt. 'I can smell newly cut grass.'

'Elspeth's.'

'Wasn't it a day off?'

'Yes. Listen, I, er, well I've invited her out with us tonight.'

I laughed and tried to ease myself away, but Tim, it

seemed, wasn't having it. I was very aware our cheeks were touching.

'She knows it's rockabilly?'

'Not really, no. I think she just wants to go to a pub again before she dies.'

'Understandable.'

'Yes.'

'Tim,' I said.

'Mm?'

'You can let go of me now.'

'OK.'

Elspeth had gone to some effort. An amazingly full blue skirt, a pink blouse and matching pumps and handbag. Her hair was in a topknot. 'Wow,' I said, when she gave us a twirl, then another. There must have been several miles of material in that skirt. 'Everything was suddenly in abundance,' she said a little breathlessly, 'in the fifties. Material included.'

We got her and her skirt into Tim's new car, which she duly admired, and arrived at the Anchor just as Cousin Jed and his crew broke into 'Mystery Train'.

'Oh, how wonderful,' cried Elspeth, clapping her hands on the barstool we'd propped her on. 'I was sweet on Elvis for years. William was terribly jealous!'

I bought a round of drinks: wine for me, grapefruit juice for the driver, and for Elspeth, a Mackeson, which she knocked back with relish. I got her another while she hand-jived to the song. She leaned my way.

'William was a dreadful snob when it came to music. But give me Elvis over Elgar any day!'

I was only halfway through my first white wine when Elspeth was pouring the remains of her second bottle of stout into her glass. Tim shot me a look and said, 'Steady on now, Elspeth.'

'Oh, I can hold my drink!' she cried. 'One learns how to with sailors. Now help me down, would you, Timothy? I'm going to make a request with that handsome singer. "Kiss Me Quick". Do you know it? One of Elvis's best.' She inched herself forward and began to wobble. 'Goodness, these stools are high.'

'Whooaah,' said Tim. 'Caught you.' He placed Elspeth on the floor, where she tidied her topknot, smoothed her skirt down, then, rather worryingly, got swallowed up by the crowd.

'Do you think I should . . . ?' asked Tim with a nod in her direction.

'I think you should.'

Erica After dinner I took the manuscript up to my bedroom again, and while I heard Stefan pacing around downstairs, listening to a bit of TV, helping himself to drinks and snacks, I concentrated on the task in hand.

Well, tried to. Perhaps it was being horizontal after an energetic day in the garden, at the garden centre, in the garden again. I don't know, it wasn't grabbing me, just as it hadn't this afternoon. In fact, with every page I turned and placed beside me, the heavier my eyes grew.

Letitia was boring me rigid. I wondered if I was missing the Lotto draw. I thought about tomorrow's lunch. Would Stefan stay for it? I hadn't asked.

Every two or three pages there was more frenzied sex, usually with a different man, sometimes two. God, it was tiresome. When Stefan called out, 'Erica, I'm just popping out to the pub for a while!' I think he woke me up.

'OK,' I said croakily. 'But take a key from the dish in the hall!'

As soon as the door slammed, I picked up the remote and put my little portable on. It wasn't quite lottery time. There was a game show going on, so I went through the channels and found nothing of interest.

Back to Letitia. I had to put the character's physical resemblance to Alice out of my head. Letitia was a post-grad student of environmental studies – another strange coincidence – and sometimes presented papers to conferences full of predatory men, or just went along to them with her supervisor, who, naturally, had the hots for her.

I yawned and remembered the cake. Whenever I nap, however briefly, I wake up craving something sweet. As I read on, I kept seeing it; at least a third of it still left in the tin. Should I? No one in the world would care if I got fat, but on the other hand I didn't want to become unhealthy. While Letitia was tied to a bed, having her bottom thwacked by a fellow environmentalist's belt, all I could think about was cake.

Down in the kitchen, I added a dollop of double cream

and took the plate and fork out to the garden, where I surveyed my pretty domain from the old wood-and-wrought-iron bench that needs rubbing down and repainting. There was still so much to do. I bitterly regretted inviting Stefan down, particularly now I'd read his manuscript. He'd turned my please-me-or-else Eleanor, who knows what she wants, into the submissive use-me-and-use-me-again Letitia. The bench would look good painted terracotta, I thought. Or black. I could make a start now . . . but, maybe not. I groaned and got up. I should give Stefan's book – our book – one more go.

With another slice of lemon cake and another dollop of cream, I went back upstairs and picked up where I'd left off: '"*Harder! Harder!*"' While I read and ate, my free hand inched towards the remote.

Alice Rupert said his head was a jumbled maelstrom of confusing images – quite poetic, I thought – so we decided to have a break from the revision and go for a drink. It was a nice sultry evening, so first we took a walk arm in arm along the beach, up to the huts and back. The big red sun was going down over the headland and it was really romantic, even when Rupert said, 'Don't squeeze laak all da blood out my arm, man.' Every now and then he lapses into plonker-speak, as Dad calls it, but only when he's excited or in pain.

'Sorry,' I said, loosening my grip. I stood on tiptoe and kissed his cheek. I do love Rupert. I'm going to miss

Julie Highmore

him when he becomes an arsehole lawyer. 'Shall we go to the Anchor, then?'

'OK.' He pulled his arm away and broke into a trot. 'Last one there buys the drinks?'

I hate doing this, but sometimes you just have to humour them. As we approached the Anchor we were level pegging but I managed to make a last-minute spurt and fell through the door first, out of breath and completely bewildered by what I saw. Either bastard Stefan was jiving with OAP Elspeth, or my head was a jumbled maelstrom of confusing images.

I sort of fell back on to Rupert, elbows first. 'Let's go,' I said, looking up into his contorted face.

He wheezed and wheezed again, but managed to say, 'You just proper winded me, man.'

'Sorry. But let's go. Quick.'

'Why?'

'We, er, need to revise more. Come on.' I took one last look over my shoulder at Stefan, towering over Elspeth; spinning her one way, then back again. I could see she was really enjoying herself. Wait till he leaves you sitting on the doorstep for hours, I wanted to tell her.

'Why have you gone so red?' asked Rupert, still hunched over as we walked out.

'Duh. I've been running, remember?'

Stefan All the lights were out but I sensed a faint glow upstairs somewhere. My legs ached slightly as I climbed, having used muscles I didn't know I owned on the dance

202

floor. I wasn't sure who the woman was – Tim's mother perhaps.

'May I have the honour?' she'd said. 'You're by far the most dashing chap here.'

I hadn't known where to put myself. But because Deborah was the only person in the pub I knew properly, I let go of my ego and jitterbugged, or whatever it was the sweet old lady had me doing. When the band stopped for a break, I hurried out the pub and back to the house. A bit rude, maybe, but I just wanted to be back with Erica. Now she wasn't trying to be a sex bomb, I really enjoyed her company.

'Erica?' I called out on the landing. The light was coming from her bedroom. Should I go in? Would she be in the middle of phone sex? I couldn't hear any noise at all, so I assumed she was still reading our book. But she wasn't, I discovered in the doorway. She was asleep, between two piles of pages.

'Erica?' I whispered again. It was only nine forty and I was hoping to get a bit of collaborative work done this evening. Well, Erica dictating sex scenes to me. 'Erica?' She didn't stir.

I went over to the bed and started gathering up the pages. I noticed her right hand held page 118, where Alicia, or rather Letitia, enjoys a little S & M with Guy, the alternative energy activist. Erica had made her character, Eleanor, the one thrashing the belt against naked male buttocks, but that hadn't felt right, so I'd switched the roles. I was frankly surprised that anyone could fall asleep reading it.

I gently pulled the paper from her fingers, wiped cake crumbs from it and put it on top of page 119. Erica's head lolled sideways on to her pillow and she let out a quiet groan. She looked quite sweet, really. Endearing, even. And almost vulnerable in her big shirt and baggy ripped jeans. Her feet were tanned and a lovely shape, with toenails painted a subdued pink. Beautifully painted, in fact. She looked so peaceful, asleep. Her skin seemed more plumped up; pale and clear. Her soft blonde hair lay flopped across her forehead, then fanned itself adorably on the white cotton pillowcase.

While I gathered more pages, my eyes settled on her mouth. There was a smidgeon of cream on the bottom lip that I had a sudden strong desire to lick off. Could I do it without waking her? I put the pages down, knelt beside the bed and slowly, very slowly, lowered my mouth towards hers and licked. There. Now get up, I told myself. But I couldn't, didn't want to. I licked at the spot again and felt her lips part. Before I knew it we were kissing. Yes, Erica was definitely responding, although possibly in her sleep. I wasn't sure it mattered. She tasted good and felt good, as my hands slid over the shirt, beneath the shirt. Then suddenly, there wasn't a shirt. Erica had pulled it off, over her head. 'Scatter the pages on the bed,' she said, a bit slurry. 'I want us to get ink all over our bodies.'

Jonathan It's past midnight now. Earlier, I watched two *Columbo* episodes, sort of half expecting Deborah to come round. Then I knew she wasn't coming because it was too late. I played computer chess and read *The Waves*, then realised I was hungry. I found the chicken baguettes in the fridge and ate them. Deborah will come tomorrow because she said she was going to visit me over the weekend. At first I felt depressed that she hadn't shown up, but then I realised it would give me something to look forward to tomorrow. People tell me I'm very negative, but I think I'm quite good at seeing the positive side of things. For example, my flat is claustrophobic and hard to keep tidy, and the patterned carpet annoys me because I keep seeing images in it that distract me when I'm trying to watch TV. There's a bit near to where my feet usually are when I'm on the sofa that looks just like Deborah's face from the side. It's like a constant reminder that she's not here. Anyway, the flat is the pits, but I see the positive side to it. At least I've got it all to myself, and don't have to share and put up with other people's germs in the bathroom, and everywhere, like Clive has to.

I thought about sending Deborah a text, but then I discovered my phone had run out of credit and I'd need to top it up at the corner shop, because that's the way I always top it up. First I swore. But then I looked on the positive side. I'll have a reason to go out tomorrow, which means I'll get some fresh air and exercise. Although only a bit. If I run to the shop and back, I might not miss Deborah's visit.

SUNDAY

Deborah 'You know, Deborah,' said Elspeth, 'the fascinating thing about *Inia geoffrensis*, or the pink Amazon river dolphin, is that it's able to move its neck. It's because the neck vertebrae aren't fused together as in other dolphins. You see how her head is at an angle? We photographed this beauty in the Orinoco river.'

'Wow,' I said, trying to place the Orinoco. 'I had no idea dolphins lived in rivers, or that they could be pink. So, which country were you in?'

'Venezuela. And they're terribly gregarious creatures. William and I adored them.'

'Yes?'

Elspeth placed the photograph on the pile we'd looked at. 'How I'd love to go back and see them again. Too late now, of course.'

'Oh, I don't know.'

'Ah, Deborah. One thing you accept as you grow older is that there are things you won't get round to doing. I think it hits one round about the age of seventy.' She laughed. 'So pack everything in now. There must be places you want to see, things you'd like to do. But perhaps one's constricted by finances?'

'Just a bit,' I said. 'Actually, I'd really like . . . no, too embarrassing.'

'Go on.'

'It's just that I never learned to swim.'

Elspeth looked at me with open-mouthed astonishment, as though I'd said I'd never learned to breathe. 'Why ever not?'

'I broke my arm when I was little. While it was in plaster, all my friends had swimming lessons and, well, I just never got round to catching up.'

'Oh, Deborah,' said Elspeth. 'That's so terribly sad.'

'Is it?'

'Never to have enjoyed the thrill of diving from the top board, or simply floating in water on a gloriously hot day.' She seemed genuinely upset. 'How old are you, dear?'

'Thirty-five. Almost.'

'Plenty young enough. Now, why don't you fetch both my costumes and we'll go down to the sea for a swimming lesson.'

She was already getting out of her chair, so I put a hand on her slender arm. For two reasons, I had to not let this happen. One, the cold water. And, two, I was supposed to be keeping Elspeth busy and distracted and well away from the beach today while Tim and

Damon painted her hut. I had to come up with something, and quick. All I could think of was time of the month.

'Personally,' she said when I made my excuse, 'I always found swimming helped. Perhaps another day, then?'

'Sure. Great. But how about at the indoor swimming pool?'

Elspeth grimaced. 'With all that ghastly chlorine, and ten-year-old boys constantly landing on one? Goodness, no. And besides, the salt in the sea helps keep you afloat.'

I could see there'd be no point in my arguing with her. She can be very firm. With me, anyway. Elspeth, I've decided, is a man's woman. Which could be where the Social Services went wrong before Tim, probably sending her a string of female, no-nonsense care workers. Tim can cajole and steer Elspeth – a bit of charm, a dash of humour – in a way I never could. That's not to say I don't like her. She's great fun, particularly after a few Mackesons, and is interesting and, on the whole, quite affable. I just like her better when Tim's around.

'Who's this?' I asked, picking up a photo of a young dark-haired woman, arms draped around a late-middle-aged William. William had been a handsome devil, with playful blue eyes and, in most photos, a good tan and generous smile. In this picture he was grey but still good-looking.

Elspeth peered at the photograph through her reading glasses and I heard a sharp intake of breath. She said, 'How on earth did that get in there?' and went to take the photo from me but changed her mind. 'Be a dear and tear it up, would you?'

'Elspeth, are you sure?'

'Ah!' she cried, the next picture in her hand. '*Odobenus rosmarus divergens*. The Pacific walrus. Haven't seen him for a while. Look at those tusks, Deborah. Aren't they magnificent?'

'Yes.' They certainly were. How lucky Elspeth is to have seen all these creatures in the flesh, in the wild. 'Great moustache,' I said as I tucked the previous photo up my shirt sleeve.

Erica Tim used to accuse me of wanting something only until I'd got it. He'd cite the breadmaker as an example, but I often wondered if he meant himself too.

I'd been the one to do the chasing, after spotting gorgeous lanky Tim on the beach with his mates from university. He already had a girlfriend, he kept telling me, although it was 'a bit rocky'. I saw him as an intellectual, and so sensitive compared to the Shelcombe lads. Only one of our gang, Wanda, had gone off to university. Mostly, we'd all got jobs in local government or insurance offices. I worked at the unemployment benefit office, as it was then called. When Tim told me he was studying sociology, I was so impressed. We made love on the beach, two nights in a row, then kept in touch – mostly my doing – by post.

On impulse one day, I got the train to Nottingham and tracked him down to his shared house. The girlfriend was there and after a bit of a to-do, she left crying. She had no fighting spirit and wouldn't have been right for Tim. Not that I was, in the end.

Anyway, he was mine and he started coming down to Shelcombe regularly, and after a while we got to talking about engagement rings and finding a place together when he graduated. It was all very pragmatic. Tim wasn't as romantic as I'd have wanted, but I liked his company and I liked telling people my boyfriend was at university, so on it went.

I was still living at home and had quite a bit in savings. All my friends were marrying local blokes and setting up home, and it looked like fun. Glamorous even. Eighteen months after I'd spotted him on the beach, we had a Christmas wedding at the register office. I was almost twenty-one, he was twenty-two, and I was already going off him.

So, when I woke up next to Stefan this morning, I expected to think: well, that's another one bagged, time to move on. Kurt and I lasted almost a year, only because of the distance, I'm sure. But when Stefan kissed the back of my head and whispered, 'You've got ink on your shoulder, it's very sexy,' the last thing I wanted was to move on. 'Let's shower together,' he said, and we did. Not in an erotic or romantic way – more a sleepy and helpful way. I soaped his back, he did mine. There was quite a bit of yawning.

We went to the Lobster Pot for breakfast. Stefan ordered waffles and maple syrup, but I had only coffee because of all the lemon cake. Although Stefan seemed far more relaxed than I've ever seen him, every so often he'd have a jittery glance over his shoulder.

'Are you expecting someone?' I asked one time.

'No, no,' he said with a quick smile.

He told me he liked my new look, and I said I didn't know I had one. I'd thrown on some black jeans and a cream hooded top. We were so desperate for caffeine, I didn't have time for makeup. 'I'm just a bit can't-be-bothered at the moment.'

'Well, it suits you,' he said.

'Really?'

'It's hard to believe you've got an eighteen-year-old daughter.' He glanced behind him, then back at me. 'You look lovely.'

You too, I thought. But then he always does. I *can't* fall properly for Stefan, I kept thinking. He'd be such bad news. It was a relief when his food arrived and he stopped hurling compliments my way. He wants something from me, I reminded myself, as he dug into waffles and made me salivate. More sex scenes. Scenes I'm not sure I can come up with, but I'll try. Once he's got those, he'll bugger off. *Don't* fall for him. Remember the niece.

'Will you stay for lunch?' I asked.

He looked behind him again. 'When's Alice back?'

'This evening some time.'

'Love to.'

Tim In the time it took me to paint one inside wall, Damon had scraped and sand-papered the whole of the outside

211

and given it an undercoat. We'd chosen – actually, Damon had chosen – a green the colour of mint ice cream, and a pale pink for the trimmings. Before, the hut had been a flaky and very patchy navy blue, and the door and gables a paler blue. Very nautical.

Round about midday, when I was admiring Damon's work, a man in vest, shorts, sandals and unfortunate socks, waddled over from next-door-but-one and said, 'About bloody time. We've been on to the council for years about this one. Belongs to some old biddy, they told us. Did she kick the bucket?'

'No,' I said. God, I hate the way people talk about the elderly. And, besides, this guy must have been close to sixty himself. 'We're doing it up for her as a surprise. So mum's the word, eh?'

'Cream?'

'No, that's just the undercoat. We're painting it mint green.'

'Oh dear. Mint green. Don't know what the missus'll say about that. But let's see what it's like when it's finished. I'm Brian, by the way.'

'Tim,' I said. 'Nice to meet you.' *Now piss off.* The last thing I wanted was word getting round and then back to Elspeth, via the corner shop or something. I picked up my paintbrush. 'Well, back to work.'

'We've always got a brew on the go, if you're thirsty. And plenty of towels if you fancy a swim.'

'Great.' I could see a substantial woman in a floral outfit approaching, so dived back inside with a, 'Cheers, Brian.'

Halfway through wall three, I got a text from Deborah: 'Help! She wants to go to beach! Dx'. I sent one back, saying I was on my way.

When I told Damon I had to go, he seemed almost pleased. 'I might just stay and tidy up a bit inside.' It was his way of saying he'd go over what I'd done. Still, it's good he's a perfectionist.

We took Elspeth to Bournemouth, to the Oceanarium. The great thing was that, with her as our guide, we didn't have to read a single label. She might not remember where she's left her handbag these days, but she'll never forget the Latin name for a porcupine pufferfish or a mantis shrimp. Every creature came with an interesting detail or two, and sometimes an anecdote, usually beginning with, 'When William and I . . .' It was fascinating and we were the last to be ushered out of the building at closing time.

I fear Elspeth has become a seven-days-a-week job. No, I don't fear it at all. It's just that Deborah tells me that's what Elspeth's become. Officially, I'm with her from ten to five on weekdays, just to make sure she doesn't top herself. Whoever decided Elspeth was a potential suicide victim must have gone to the wrong house, that's all I can say. Yes, she gets low. She's old. All the good stuff's behind her. She's bound to feel a bit pissed off about it. When she does lapse into melancholia, it never lasts for long. A weak gag or a funny walk usually pulls her out of it. But it's good that they got Elspeth wrong because it means I have a job I really enjoy, with no sadistic boss watching over me, or sadistic children walking all over me. And who cares that there's a bit of unpaid overtime involved?

After the Oceanarium, Elspeth fancied a peach melba. 'With fresh raspberries, like they used to serve at the Imperial Hotel in Shelcombe before it began catering for the lowest common, and I mean *very* common, denominator. There wasn't even a choice of desserts last time I went in, only ice cream.'

We didn't find the fresh raspberries. In fact, it took us five restaurants to find a peach melba. It came with a dollop of raspberry jam instead of the real thing, but Elspeth was fairly resigned by then and got stuck in without complaining. She fell asleep in the car going home and I whispered to Deborah that I hoped it wouldn't mean she'd be awake half the night.

'I don't think old people are like babies,' she whispered back. She put her hand on mine on the gear stick, just fleetingly, and said, 'I've got something I'm dying to show you when we get home.'

'Oh?' I said, and for the rest of the journey my imagination was pretty wild.

'Are you sure she told you to rip it up?' I asked. We were passing the photo back and forth across the dinner table.

'Yep.' She took it off me again. 'Who do you think the woman is?' I had formed an opinion but hadn't shared it with Deborah yet, hoping she'd come up with the same idea. 'The similarity is striking,' Deborah continued. 'She could almost be his . . .'

'Daughter?'

'Yes.'

I said, 'That's what I thought,' pleased that we agreed, but still a bit gutted that all she'd wanted to show me was a photo.

'So,' said Deborah, 'what do we have? Elspeth and William married young and didn't have children. But here's a woman of, what, twenty or so, who could be – *has* to be – William's daughter.'

'Plus Elspeth wants photo of said woman torn up. Oh dear. Poor Elspeth.'

Deborah shook her head. 'Men really are the pits, aren't they?'

'Yes.'

'Selfish, hedonistic . . .'

'Uncaring,' I chipped in. 'Dictated to by their willies.'

'Are you?'

'Not all of us.'

We ate in silence for a while, then Deborah said, 'Do you remember what Elspeth was telling us about the male bass? You know, that article she read.'

'Mm, that they're becoming feminised because of all the oestrogen in the Potomac. Producing eggs even. Amazing, eh?'

'Yes.'

'God,' I snorted, 'wouldn't it be awful if that started happening to male humans?'

Deborah nodded. Then, at more or less the same time, we both looked up and said, 'Oh, I don't know.'

Erica Stefan made lunch, while I sat at the computer and tried – and I really did try – to write another raunchy scene for our book. The trouble was, Stefan and I were coming from very different places. Where previously I'd bashed out stuff, oblivious to what my co-author was doing with it, now I knew just what he was turning my scenes into.

'I'm blocked,' I told him back in the kitchen. It was hot and I took my hooded top off.

He said, 'Maybe if I left, you'd—'

'No. I don't think so.'

'So you really can't produce your Eleanor stuff?'

'Nope.' Here goes, I thought. He'll come over moody, say he doesn't want any lunch after all, and leave. 'I have tried, but I really don't like what you turn her into, Stefan. I'm sorry.'

He stood with a slice of cheese in one hand, and a crusty roll in the other, just staring my way. I got the impression he was having a little internal debate about me, about the book, weighing things up on his mental scales. The cheese rose in the air a little and the roll went down. The roll rose, the cheese dropped. He said, 'I, er . . . shall I put spring onion in?'

'OK. Fancy a glass of wine with it?' I realised I hadn't had a drink since Stefan arrived.

'Half a glass only for me. Driving.'

He'd be leaving today, then. At least there wouldn't

be time for me to go off him. I poured one and a half glasses and put them on the table, with a couple of place-mats and serviettes. I thought back to the first time Stefan had sat in my kitchen and how wound up and excited I'd been. Now I wasn't sure what I was, but it was neither of those. Just fairly relaxed. I felt Stefan was too. However, while we ate, he did jump out of his skin when someone put a leaflet through the front door with a loud clonk of the letterbox. 'Is that Alice?' he said. I actually think he's a bit uncomfortable around her.

'So what do you want to do about our book?' I asked.

'If it's all right with you, I'll sort of rehash some of the earlier sex scenes to finish the story off with.'

I hadn't actually noticed any story. 'OK. And when it's finished?'

'Ah. We'll have to come up with names for ourselves.'

'Right.'

'Then we'll see if anyone wants it. I'm sure they will.'

'Yes,' I said, pretty sure they wouldn't. Having read over a hundred pages of Letitia, I'm not sure I want my name on it, false or otherwise.

'Thanks for your input,' Stefan said.

He was being too nice. Was he still hoping I might come up with the goods? 'I didn't do that much.'

'Listen, why don't we go out one evening this week, when you're in London? See a film or something.'

'Sounds good.'

'Thursday? I'll see what's on. Dinner after or before?'

Much too nice.

MONDAY

Stefan It took me all night. From the moment I arrived back at the flat, I went at it, changing young Letitia to late-thirties Eleanor. In order not to make life too hard for myself, I kept her in environmental studies, but this time as a lecturer. I haven't done this because I want more sexy scenes from Erica, I'm doing it because I want Erica. That was the nicest twenty-four hours I've spent with a woman in years. She's beautiful – especially when she doesn't try – and clever, and such relaxing company. We're even sexually suited. The things she did! Straight out of her fantasies. I adore her.

There was this moment, yesterday, when she took her jacket off in the kitchen and stood there, waiting for me to react to the fact that she was blocked. She looked so lovely, in her little cream cap-sleeved T-shirt and the slightly-too-big black jeans. That silky blonde hair flopping over one big blue eye, the way it does. She seemed a bit nervous, as though expecting me to explode. But all I'd wanted to do was cuddle her. If I hadn't had my hands full of cheese and things, I would have done.

I do so want to go into her office today and present her with the new version of our book; her version, really. But I'll have to leave it, since I can barely keep my eyes open. Also, if Erica and I are going to get serious – if she'll have me, that is – I need to have a word with her daughter first. God, how I'm kicking myself now for the Alice business, as delicious as she was, and probably still is.

Tim At two minutes past midnight, Deborah got a text from Jonathan and came rushing up to the attic to show me. I put my bedside lamp back on and she handed me her phone.

'Why didn't you come?' it said. 'I'm depressed and don't want to go on living. I might hang myself or drown in the sea, I can't decide. Don't feel responsible because I've wanted to kill myself before. Ask my parents. It was nice knowing you. Jonathan Dalrymple.'

I had a horrible flashback to Debbie Clinker's note. 'Do you think he means it?'

'I don't know. I've tried ringing and he's not answering. I've sent him a text too, saying I'm on my way and not to do anything. I don't suppose you'd come with me?'

I was already out of bed and pulling jeans on. 'Of course I will.'

He wasn't dangling from the balcony, which was a huge relief. However, there was no response when we rang his bell, so I began hammering while Deborah called out, 'Jonathan! Are you there? Open the door! Jonathan!'

Silence.

'Shit,' said Deborah. I hammered again, she shouted again, and then the young guy who'd moved into Deborah's old flat came out on the landing and glared at us.

'I'm sorry,' I said. 'It's just that we're a bit worried about Jonathan, your neighbour.'

'I'm not surprised,' he said. 'He's strange, that one.'

'Do you think we could go through to your flat and see if he's left his balcony window open?' asked Deborah. 'He never seemed to close it when I lived here.'

'Yeah, I suppose so.'

I volunteered to check. I clambered over on to Jonathan's balcony and, sure enough, the window slid open. When I stepped inside the unlit room and walked in a straight line, I fully expected to bump into Jonathan's knees.

'Jonathan?' I called out in a pathetic voice. 'Are you asleep? Please be asleep.' I reached the far side of the room, found a switch and lit the place up. When I opened my eyes, I saw it was empty.

'The beach!' said Deborah from the balcony, and off we hurried.

'This is silly,' I said. Our torches were providing mere pinpricks of light in the vast blackness, and both of us were having trouble walking on the soft undulating sand we couldn't see. Deborah had fallen over twice. 'We'll never find him.'

'Jonathan!' we both yelled again.

'No, it's hopeless,' I said.

'Yes,' she agreed miserably, and we headed back towards the streetlamps along the promenade.

Neither of us slept. Well, I may have drifted off for a while on the sofa watching News 24. Deborah wanted it on, just in case. When it grew properly light, around five-fifty, we set off for the beach again but found no sign of Jonathan.

'He could be back at home?' I said optimistically. We tried there and, as far as we could tell from our gentle taps and quiet calls, he wasn't.

Back on the beach again we sat in our inadequate jackets – the sun may have been up but it wasn't doing what it should – and stared out to sea, almost as though we might spot Jonathan's head bobbing or something. Gradually, from around six-thirty, one or two dog walkers appeared.

Deborah said, 'Haven't dogs been banned?'

'Mm. Maybe they think they can get away with it if they come early enough.'

'Should we tell Alice?'

I thought not. I watched a setter shoot along the beach at top speed, and a Labrador retrieve a stick from the waves, again and again. 'Look at how much fun they're having.'

When it got to seven, we hoisted our tired and hungry selves from the damp sand and made our way towards the Paradise Café, praying it was open and warm. Our luck was in: they were just opening up. It wasn't that warm, though. We took a window table, so we could keep an eye on the beach, and had bacon and eggs that weren't quite cooked enough, and tea that could have been brewing since yesterday. 'I love this place,' Deborah said, and I knew what she meant.

When it felt like cigarette time, I went back to the counter and got an iced bun and two more cups of tea.

'Look,' Deborah said, as I put her mug in front of her. She was pointing at a couple of dogs having a tug-of-war over something.

'What?' I said, going back for the rest.

'Oh God,' I heard, and she was out of the café and halfway down the beach before my iced bun hit the table.

'Don't move those!' I told the bloke behind the counter.

'What is it?' I puffed, joining Deborah on the beach. The dogs – one little mongrel, one collie – were growling and tugging scarily, their half-bared teeth yanking what looked like a donkey jacket back and forth.

'Stop!' Deborah shouted at them. She tugged at the jacket and pulled it in the air. The collie let go, while the small dog clung on and left the ground. I gave it a surreptitious kick and it fell off. 'Oh God,' Deborah said. 'I think this is Jonathan's.'

'Really?' There was just too much *déjà vu* going on here. Were we about to find his trousers, one shoe . . . ?

'Oh God. Do you think he's . . . ?' She stared with a terrified expression at the water.

'It might not be his,' I said, rubbing a hand up and down her back.

After feeling in a pocket, then the other, Deborah

pulled out some sort of wrapper and unfurled it. 'Oh God,' she said, turning petrified eyes on me. 'Coronation chicken. Oh God, oh God!'

Deborah We checked the beach. We went back to the flat, got in via the balcony again and found no trace of Jonathan, or of his having been back. I felt sick, though that may have been the breakfast.

'He's got a friend called Clive,' I said, when we were back outside the building. 'Only I don't know where he lives. They might know at the Anchor because he played there.'

'But it's only eight and I think publicans sleep in.'

'We ought to tell the police,' I said.

Tim rolled his eyes. 'Come on, then.'

Sergeant Lillywhite looked as though he'd been propped on the counter all night. Either that, or he'd just arrived and was still full of sleep. He saw us walk in, took a bolstering gulp of something from a mug, tucked it under the counter and said, 'Well, if it isn't Cinders and Buttons.'

It wasn't a good start. We'd agreed I'd do the talking, so after a deep breath, I said, 'We'd like to report a missing person.'

'Right,' said the sergeant, looking straight at Tim. 'And do you have a helpful sketch with you?'

'Er, no.'

'Well, that'll make things easier.' He dragged a pad towards him and took a pen from his shirt pocket. 'Name?'

I said, 'Jonathan Dalrymple,' then gave his address,

age and a physical description, and explained I'd been his neighbour and had become a sort of friend.

'And when did anyone last see him?'

'His neighbour heard him through the wall yesterday. You know, the TV. I saw him on Saturday, early. He was feeling down about his exams and other stuff, and . . .' I could tell Sergeant Lillywhite was about to put his pen away. 'Well, last night I got this text.' I took my phone out and showed him, and the sergeant's face changed from bored and sceptical to slightly concerned.

'I see,' he said.

From behind his back, Tim produced the black jacket. 'We found this on the beach,' he told the sergeant. 'Deborah's certain it's his.'

'And you've had a good search, I take it?'

'Yes,' I said. 'His flat and the beach, anyway. His family's in Spain and, well, he doesn't have friends, apart from one called Clive but we don't know where he lives.'

Sergeant Lillywhite scribbled in silence for a while. 'I don't suppose you have a photograph of the missing boy?'

'Yes I do,' I said. 'That beach photographer guy took one when we were walking along the prom.' I found it in my bag and handed it to him.

'Nice-looking kid,' he said.

'Very.'

'You think?' said Tim tartly.

'If you wouldn't mind us hanging on to this,' said Sergeant Lillywhite, 'we'll go and search his flat and have a good look round Shelcombe for the lad. I expect he'll turn up.' He ripped the top page off his pad and gave me a smile. 'After all, you did.'

I felt too upset and tired to go to work, but I went anyway, thinking Jonathan might just turn up at the arcade. Tim said he'd tell Elspeth he was going to be late, and go and ask about Clive at the Anchor. We decided to give Jonathan the day to make an appearance before trying to contact his sister. All I know is she's at Sussex University.

It was ridiculous to feel so guilty, but I should have found time to visit him over the weekend. However, the rest of Saturday I'd been working, then entertaining Elspeth in the evening, and Sunday I'd been entertaining Elspeth all day. Bloody Elspeth, I thought. But then I felt bad because the two-timing husband she'd adored had drowned at sea and left her bereft.

I sleepily pushed change at people all morning – sometimes getting it wrong – then had a quick lunch break and sleepily pushed change at people all afternoon. Jonathan didn't appear but, just before the end of my shift, Tim did.

'Anything?' I asked, knowing he would have sent a text if there'd been news.

He shook his head, looking even more tired than I felt. 'No one knows where Clive lives. And you?'

'Uh-uh.' I asked him why he had a roll of lino under his arm.

'It's a remnant. Found it in Bishop's. You know, "You name it, we sell it", in Ship Street.'

I knew it well. I'd bought my Debbie padding there. 'I'm not sure you answered my question.'

'Oh. Well, I thought it might go nicely in the beach hut.' From a pocket, he took a Stanley knife. 'Want to come and help?'

I wondered if I'd had enough of helping Tim on the Elspeth front. But he had stayed up all night with me on the Jonathan front. 'I'll be finished in five minutes,' I said. 'See you down there?'

'OK.'

When he'd gone, I tried Jonathan's mobile, as I'd been doing all day. Again, it rang and rang till voicemail kicked in. I forced myself not to cry and had a real yearning for London. Life was so much quieter there.

Erica I was tapping Tim's number into the phone, when a package arrived at the office via courier. It was addressed to me and marked 'Strictly Private'.

Tim could wait. I'd only wanted to sound him out about this client of ours, Neville, that we're having trouble finding a match for. Not many women say they want a man in his late seventies. I wouldn't mind betting he's more than that, but short of asking for a birth certificate, seventy-eight he is. He's an actor – well, was – and he doesn't live a million miles from Shelcombe. I've got Tim's lonely old lady in mind for him.

Anyway, I put the phone down, picked the package up and worked at the several feet of tape wrapped around it. Someone hadn't wanted this coming open. The someone turned out to be Stefan. It was our manuscript again, with a little scribbled note clipped to it: 'You were right. Love, S'.

I went and shut my office door, then got reading. Oh yes, this was more like it. Ha! Good on you, Eleanor. Christ, had I really come up with these things? About two-thirds of the way in, I called Stefan. 'I love it,' I said.

'I love you too.'

'I said "it".'

'And I said you.'

'Oh. Really? Since when?'

'Yesterday. When I was making lunch.'

I laughed. 'That's very specific.'

'I know. It just hit me. I'm crazy about you, Erica.'

'I don't know what to say. Except . . .'

'Yes?'

'It's just that I do value honesty in a person, and I'm not sure you'd score very highly.'

'Oh, Erica. Look, I promise—'

'I mean, is that girl really your niece?'

He groaned into the phone. 'No. No, she's not. But she's history now, honestly.'

'I'm going to have to think about this,' I told him. 'About us. But listen, the book's brilliant. When do you think you'll finish it?'

'Soon. Next couple of days.'

'Truthfully?'

'Oh, right. Couple of weeks. Maybe you could come and help me over the weekend?'

'Maybe.' All I wanted was to get off the phone and think about Stefan's declaration. 'Better go,' I said. 'I'm late for a meeting.'

'Truthfully?'

'Yes,' I lied, but decided it didn't count.

Alice The ridiculous thing is, *I'm* feeling guilty. Mum fancied him, she invited him down that first weekend and she flirted like mad with him, but then I ended up sleeping with him. If doing it on my old candy-stripe carpet counts as sleeping. But then, in London, yeah I did actually sleep with him two nights in a row.

It looks like they're becoming an item, but what the hell's Mum doing? He's such a rat. Telling me he was with an agent when he was with my mother. Once or twice today, I've thought I should just let her know what happened. Thing is, I don't know how serious it is. Mum tends to be mad about a bloke for a while, then you can see her cooling off, and before you know it she's whispering that she's not in, whenever he phones. I suppose I can just hope it fizzles out and in the meantime get through my exams – two more to go – then plan the party for Shelcombe getting a Seaside Award. If I wasn't going off to build latrines, I'd try and get us a Blue Flag.

So, there's loads to think about other than stupid Stefan. And he must be stupid to trust me not to say anything. He's not to know that I'm exceptionally mature for my age and got masses of integrity and sensitivity. The thing I hate most about the Stefan episode is that

I've realised Rupert doesn't really do it for me, sexually. I mean, it's nice. Romantic and intimate, and all that. But . . . anyway, only a few more weeks, then I'll be off to Africa. I love him, though. Obviously.

Tim The first thing I noticed when I let myself into the beach hut was that the small window on the back wall was wide open. Damon said he was going to leave the window till last, since taking the boards off the outside might pose a security risk. Or as he'd put it: 'Kids'll use the place for shagging. I know I would've done.' He was going to make sure it had reinforced glass and a proper window lock before painting it. Maybe even get hold of a new window. Damon always thinks of things like that.

The second thing I noticed was Jonathan, curled up on his side on Damon's pile of work clothes. He didn't look dead, and when I listened hard I could hear long deep breaths. I was reluctant to approach him, wake him up and get punched or something, so instead I walked backwards out of the hut, pushed the door to again and waited with my roll of lino for Deborah to come. She'd know how to deal with him.

It was five minutes before she appeared at the end of the row of huts, but it felt like much longer. I'd spent most of it rehearsing what I'd say to Sergeant Lillywhite. I got up and hurried towards her. 'Jonathan's in the hut.'

She gave me a tortured look. 'Alive?'

'Yeah, yeah. Come on, quick. Before he escapes.'

'Oh God. Oh, thank God.'

'I was wary of waking him up. Thought he might hit me or something.'

'Better that he hits me?'

'Exactly.'

Deborah seemed to know just what to do. She didn't rush in saying, 'Jesus, Jonathan, we've been worried sick!' There were no admonishments when he came to. She didn't do any melodramatic crying or hugging. In fact, she didn't touch him at all, just repeated 'Jonathan,' quietly until his eyes opened. Then she said, 'I was thinking of going to the Paradise Café. Do you want to come?' She waved me out.

'Yes,' I heard Jonathan say. I hid round the side of the hut, then watched them until they disappeared. I assumed Deborah would be all right and got on with laying the lino, alone. A terrible idea, it turned out. I put it down to tiredness. I'd buy another remnant and leave it to Damon. Before locking up, I went over to the little window and tugged at it, trying to get it to shut properly. The window was too big for the hole and wouldn't close, which explained how Jonathan had got in. As skinny as he is, it must have been a tight squeeze, even without his coat. Oh, to be that thin. I looked down at my paunch, got my phone out and dialled Elspeth's number.

'I think I need more hypnotism,' I said.

'Is it the custard creams, dear?'

'Among other things.'

JUNE

THURSDAY

Alice We've decided on Midsummer's Day for the party to celebrate the Seaside Award. It's on a Saturday this year, so loads of people will come and we'll have stalls and things, so we can try and recoup the money we spent on the campaign. It'll be on the beach and there'll be no smoking, no junk food, no cans and, of course, no dogs. Mum suggested getting the Gay City Rollers to come and play and I said, 'Over my dead body.' Anyway, where would they plug their instruments in? We're going to have Rupert's aunt on her harp, which I think is much more in keeping with water and waves.

The council is now employing people to pick up beach litter all day, which leaves me time to prepare for Ghana – jabs and clothes and stuff – and to enjoy my last few weeks with Rupert. Because of Stefan, I'm at Rupert's house a lot now, even though that means putting up with the gloomy Mrs Gerrard. If she'd only get rid of that stiff hairstyle, she could find a lover and pay Mr Gerrard back, and maybe smile every now and then.

I also go to Dad's quite often. He's getting quite good on the piano, thanks to Deborah. After dinner yesterday, they did this really nice duet. It was from some musical by Rogers and someone. Rupert was a bit rude, putting his headphones in halfway through, but I don't think they noticed. Dad always plays with his nose an inch from the sheet music, concentrating like mad, while Deborah watches Dad's fingers all the while.

Afterwards, we played Boggle, which was going well until we all tried to tell Rupert that 'BRO' wasn't a word, but he insisted it was. We showed him it wasn't in the dictionary, and he said the dictionary was too old. The nice jolly atmosphere turned a bit hostile while Rupert dug his heels in. He can be like that these days. I think it's because he doesn't want to study law, but he says it's because I'm going to Africa. In the end, Deborah went and looked at an online dictionary, and 'BRO' was there. Dad and Deborah apologised like mad and I suddenly felt really proud of Rupert. He wasn't the least bit told-you-so. I'm very lucky, really. I could have ended up with a creep of a boyfriend, like Mum has.

Stefan and I avoid each other as much as is possible, now he's staying at Mum's house half the time. A few weeks back, when she'd popped out, Stefan said, really quietly, as though the place were bugged, 'I'm so sorry about what happened between us, Alice. It was a terrible thing for me to do.'

'Yes,' I said, although I don't exactly remember discouraging him.

'And, obviously it would be just awful for your mother if she found out.'

'Don't worry,' I said. 'I won't say a word. In fact, I've forgotten all about the miserable and tawdry episode.' I don't think he liked that.

So now when he's with us, I tend to stay in my attic room with Rupert, or go out, or go to Rupert's. Mum seems happy and in love; not in her usual manic, flash-in-the-pan way. She doesn't flirt or doll herself up. In fact, I haven't seen her breasts in ages. When she stays up in London at Stefan's, Rupert and I have the house to ourselves, which is really nice. Sometimes I think I wouldn't mind marrying him, though I'd probably have to buy him some manuals. I have tried to get him to do some of the things Stefan did, but it's not the same.

Jonathan This afternoon I made a list of the reasons I like living in Elspeth's house, and the reason I don't. One, I've got a room at the very end of the landing upstairs, where it's hard to be disturbed unexpectedly. Two, there's a room in the house called the library, full of books on marine life, which is my new interest. Three, when I've learned some interesting facts about a fish or sea creature, I can go and tell Elspeth all about it and she doesn't sigh or ask me to change the subject. In fact, she usually adds more information. Sometimes I make notes. At the moment we're working through the arthropods, or *Arthropoda*. It's good fun learning all the Latin names. I spend time each evening doing that, then I get Elspeth, or sometimes Tim, to test me.

On my list there's only one reason why I don't like living in Elspeth's house, and that is that Tim forces me to do things I don't want to do. Like shopping for food. Tim is what they call my support worker. I keep telling him I don't need one, but the Social Services and, apparently, my parents think differently. I'm not sure what a support worker is supposed to do, but I bet it's more than cutting the grass and saying, 'Anyone for another cup of tea?' every fifty-seven minutes. I timed Tim the other day and worked out the average. He makes us lunch too, and what Elspeth calls elevenses, and in the afternoon what she calls high tea. Elevenses is a biscuit and high tea is a sandwich. So Tim is useful in some ways, but mostly he sits listening, while Elspeth and I discuss lobsters or clams or some other fascinating thing. He sometimes does crosswords during our discussions, and once or twice he's fallen asleep. No, more than once or twice. Elspeth told me I could talk for England, and I said I hadn't heard of that competition. She said, what she meant was I talk a lot. I don't know why she didn't just say that. Anyway, I think she could talk for England too. If there was such a competition.

When I moved in one week, three days ago, Tim told me I must 'on no account' mention Elspeth's beach hut. They were doing it up for her, he said, but were having to wait for a window to be made. I said I'd try not to, and

Tim said thanks. I'm not very good at keeping secrets. This I know from when my sister used to say she'd kill me if I told Mum and Dad something. I'd forget, that's the trouble. Or else, I wouldn't see the point of lying about a trivial thing that my parents couldn't possibly care about. Anyway, she didn't kill me but she did get grounded a lot and always cried when it happened. I couldn't see what was so bad about having to stay in. Mum and Dad used to say if there was an opposite to grounding, they'd do it to me.

Tonight I'm learning about the *Limulus polyphemus*, which is the horseshoe crab. First I go through Elspeth's books, reading as much as I can find. Then I go on the Internet, which I've got all to myself in my room because, luckily, Elspeth thinks the World Wide Web gives out toxic rays.

Oh, yes, something else Tim does is to drive us to the Oceanarium. I love it there. The first time I went, I kept seeing the fish and creatures I'd been studying. It was fantastic. As we walked through, I told Tim everything I'd learned about each one, because I guessed Elspeth already knew. But when Tim completely disappeared before we were even a quarter of the way round, I had to tell Elspeth instead.

After a while, she said, 'Goodness, you're a walking encyclopaedia. Now, why don't we go and find a peach melba?' I hadn't heard of it and asked if it was a vertebrate or an invertebrate, but Elspeth just laughed and put her arm through mine, which I didn't like much, and said, 'You are a scream, Jonathan.'

*   *   *

Deborah Yesterday I got an email from ex-boyfriend Sean, saying he'd been thinking about me a lot lately, and how lovely it would be to see me because he was really, really missing me. Would I like dinner some time?

After my blood went off the boil, I found myself laughing cynically and saying, 'Wanker,' to the screen. The relationship he left me for eight months ago has obviously soured. What puzzles me about men is why they don't realise how transparent they're being. Sean, I know from his history, can't leave a relationship until he's got a new, or sometimes old, one to fall into. I emailed him saying I'd rather lose a limb, thanks. I haven't heard back.

I told Tim about the email this morning and he wanted to know if Sean was good-looking.

'Er, yeah. In a biggish rugby-player kind of way.'

'Really?' he said, suddenly puffing his chest out. 'Huh.' And off he went to work, or what you could loosely call work. No, I shouldn't knock Tim's job. He's taken a load off my mind and plate, becoming Jonathan's support worker. And it can't be much fun listening to Jonathan talk at Elspeth all day. Tim says she doesn't seem to mind. 'In fact, she's been a lot less melancholic since Jonathan moved in.'

The arrangement was my stroke of genius. Jonathan hadn't wanted to join his parents, tearing up his plane ticket in a fit of temper one day and saying he needed to stay near me. When I called the Dalrymples, they didn't appear that keen to have him in Spain either.

Nobody felt he should be left in the flat, and Elspeth, with her four spare bedrooms and a tendency to get lonely, seemed the answer. Following Elspeth's enthusiastic agreement, Tim talked to Kay, his boss, and she talked to Jonathan. Jonathan went to see his GP, then there were meetings, and eventually Tim found himself with two clients.

The great thing is, Jonathan's taken an obsessive interest in marine biology and forgotten all about me. I passed him in the High Street today and he looked right through me. He once said he had a problem recognising faces when they're out of context. I shouted, 'Hi, Jonathan!' to his retreating back. He turned and stared, and I could almost hear his brain clicking and clunking before he said, 'Ah. Hello.' He came over and started describing the walking catfish – Latin name, average length, habitats – but I was on a fifteen-minute break, so had to be firm with him.

Over dinner this evening, Tim said, 'We're going to try and get an assessment of Jonathan next week. There's clearly some AS there, but perhaps ADD and a bit of OCD too.'

Tim's job is a whole universe away from my 'But *we* don't want to give you *that*!' world. More and more, he talks in capital letters. Usually after he's been to a meeting or on a training day. I tend to just nod knowledgeably.

'Kay thinks he's likely to come up AS only, but I'd bet on AS with ADD.'

'Uh-huh. This salad dressing's yummy. What's in it?'

'Mm? Oh, fennel. I found some in the jungle.'

'Great.' Tim and I have been slowly hacking away at his back garden, gradually unearthing all the things Erica planted way back.

'So, what does he do?' Tim asked, while I sniffed the dressing. 'This muscle-bound Sean.'

'He's not muscly, just biggish. You know, chunky. There's something else, besides fennel.'

'Lime?'

'That's it, lime. Nice.' I put the jug down. 'He's a financial advisor.'

Tim nodded and, I think, tried not to smirk. 'The thing I don't get about financial advisors,' he said, 'is, if they know where to invest money, how come they're financial advisors and not filthy rich?'

'I don't know, you'll have to ask Sean.'

Tim choked and downed some water. 'Is he coming *here*?' he asked.

'No,' I said, then after a pause, 'Would it matter if he did?'

'Of course not. Good grief. Honestly, Deborah, feel free to have absolutely anyone you want staying. Even big fat, two-timing financial advisors, ha ha.'

Like I said, transparent.

Erica Once the sale of Stefan's flat goes through and my office lease runs out, we thought we'd start looking for somewhere abroad. Well, Stefan's idea, actually. With way too much Internet competition, I'm winding down

Opposites, trying to rapidly match up the remaining clients. If they fall for someone they might not ask for a part refund of their annual subscription. There'll be quite a few spare, unfortunately, including poor Neville, I suspect. I keep asking Tim if Elspeth might be interested, but he says he doesn't know how to bring the subject up, so besotted is she still with her late husband.

Stefan likes the idea of Italy and I've sort of stopped resisting, even though I don't speak Italian and don't know what I'd do there. He keeps telling me I'm resourceful, so I'll be fine. I'm quite keen on staying put, to be honest. But now Stefan's got an agent for his book – not our book, though – he sees himself producing novel after novel for the rest of his life, and doesn't feel Shelcombe's a romantic enough spot to be writing in.

I tried to explain that the place is in my soul. I grew up here, fell in love several times here – most recently with Stefan, of course – got married and had a baby here. I like knowing the sea's just round the corner, even if I rarely go near it. I love my house and my garden. If the Italy thing happens, I definitely won't sell up.

This afternoon, I signed on with some local agencies to do temp work, now Opposites has become very part time. Stefan scoffed at the idea but I pointed out that one of us should have a job. He smiled and said, 'You're so practical, Erica. Come here,' and we made love on the sofa, Alice being out for the evening. It was delicious. We really gel, physically, and I love his body; soft yet hard. Stefan only needs to take his shirt off and I'm halfway there. His smell, the feel of his skin, that face. Since I stopped being distrustful, which took a while, I've been letting myself wallow in him, in us.

We're spending practically all our time together, and apart from my initial opposition to the Italy idea, we tend not to disagree, or bicker or sulk. Stefan's surprised by this, since most of his girlfriends have told him he's an awkward and moody bugger. I said, 'That's teenagers for you,' and he laughed.

Tomorrow we're going to London for the weekend. I've got stuff to sort out in the office and Stefan's going to be exchanging contracts and packing. Alice and Rupert will have this house to themselves again. I hardly see Alice these days. I sense she's not keen on Stefan, but not much I can do about that. Anyway, she's off to Africa in a few weeks, to work on some ghastly sounding project in sweltering heat for no money. Just her thing – she'll love it.

Tim The most enjoyable times are when Jonathan hides himself away in his room and Elspeth and I have a good old natter about lowly things, such as the weather, the price of a poncy uncut loaf at the corner shop – 'Over a pound, Timothy!' – and the state of Elspeth's neighbour's front fence.

With Jonathan out of the way this afternoon, Elspeth asked me how the beach party plans were coming along.

'Fine,' I told her. 'I'm trying to talk Alice into hiring a DJ, so we can all dance.'

'Jolly good,' Elspeth said, waving her arms. 'Do you know, a wonderful idea came to me in the middle of the night.'

'Oh, yes?'

'The dinghy. You know, the one in the beach hut.'

I went cold. 'What about it?' The dinghy had long since gone to the council tip. I just hadn't been able to fit it and my car in the garage.

'Well, during the party, we could take people out. Little boat trips.'

'But . . .' I'd gone even colder, '. . . I thought you never wanted to see it again, after, you know, William.'

'Ah, but perhaps it's time to move on. And, besides, I'm sure William would wholeheartedly approve. You see, if we charged for each trip, the money could go to an environmental organisation, such as Greenpeace or Friends of the Earth. People who watch over the seas for us. What do you think, Timothy?'

What I thought was that I must go and find a dinghy exactly like the one William fell out of. But I have no idea what it looked like, never having inflated the bloody thing. My brain was frantically trying to come up with a way out. 'Fantastic idea,' I said. 'Of course, we'll have to get permission from the council. I'll look into it.'

'Would you? In the meantime, I might take her out for a little test run. It'll be jolly painful, Timothy, but I believe it may help lay William's ghost.'

I had to get her off the subject, for the sake of my heart and nerves. 'Have I told you about Alice's summer plans?' I asked. 'She's going to help build latrines in Ghana. I'm worried sick, of course, and wish she'd change her mind. I spent most of last night's dinner trying to talk her out of it.'

'But you mustn't do that! It'll be a jolly good character-building exercise.'

I said, 'I'm not sure my daughter needs more character.'

'These faraway places,' Elspeth went on, 'always sound so much more terrifying than they turn out to be, believe me. One thinks, goodness, Ghana. It'll be so alien. Then when one gets there, it's just like being in Belgium or somewhere.'

'But I've been to Belgium, Elspeth. It's very alien.'

'Ah, ha ha. Yes, that's true.' She got up from her armchair and flattened the back of her skirt. 'Now,' she said, 'where the Dickens did I put the pump for the dinghy?'

I was considering a coughing fit, a wasp sting, a mild heart attack, when Jonathan, bless him, walked through the door and said, 'Look, I printed out an amazing picture of a Portuguese man-of-war.'

'Really?' I said, guiding Elspeth back into her armchair. 'We'd love to see it, wouldn't we, Elspeth?'

'Here,' Jonathan said, handing me the picture. 'Apparently, it's almost as poisonous as the sea wasp, or *Chironex fleckeri*.'

'Wow, sounds fascinating,' I said. 'Sit down and tell us more. Anyone for a cup of tea?'

SATURDAY

Stefan We exchanged contracts late yesterday, aiming to complete in a week's time. This means putting my stuff in storage and moving in with Erica in Shelcombe, which doesn't thrill me. Not the Erica bit, the Shelcombe bit.

Erica I adore, but Planet Shelcombe will do my head in. The tackiness, the smells, those awful families forced out of their rooms for the day, roaming around aimlessly. Fat sunburned bodies in bottom-hugging shorts, kids in tears because they've eaten too much crap and the waltzer's made them queasy. Spring Bank Holiday gave me a taste of what's to come in the summer, and I have to get us out of town before the schools break up. My agent thinks a proposed series would be easier to sell to a publisher, but how could I write another Saul Sanders in such surroundings?

I considered London for us, and Erica was semi-keen, but I know from experience there'd be too many distractions here. Italy appeals more. I speak some Italian, love the warmth of the people and the warmth of the summers. I love the food, the cities, the scenery. It's been hard work, trying to talk Erica out of Shelcombe and into Italy. Almost there, I think. Last night, when we looked on my computer at places for sale in Umbria, Tuscany, Lombardy, her beautiful blue eyes lit up and she said, 'I suppose I could always do a crash course in Italian.' I kissed her and told her I loved her and we fucked on my swivel chair. I can honestly say, it's the best sex I've ever had on that chair.

Erica's at her office today, packing things up. And I'm at home, also packing. Lots of new beginnings. My parents are relieved that I'm finally entering a proper, grown-up, live-together relationship. They met Erica the other week, when they came to London for a musical. Both heartily approved and the following day dropped hints about marriage, which made me think, hey, not such a bad idea. But let's see how we get on in Italy, or just living together in Shelcombe. God, just saying the name makes me quake.

One thing I'm amazed by, as I pack, is how many padded bras I've come to own. As I work my way chronologically through the girlfriends, it occurs to me Erica might be the first not to need one.

Tim Elspeth's sick of the Oceanarium, I can tell. But she keeps saying she wants to see the sea, and the hut's not quite ready yet, so we have to go to Bournemouth.

And if we all go to Bournemouth, Jonathan has to do the Oceanarium, and he insists we go round with him.

There's a very controlling side to Jonathan. He likes people to do what he wants to do. Most of the time Elspeth and I give in, but occasionally we have to force him to come on a big shop with us, or a nice healthy walk, twice round the park. He gets very negative on these outings, criticising anything and everything. Elspeth usually say, 'Yes, dreadful, isn't it?' to him, whilst winking at me. I often think I should give her half my salary.

During a particularly frustrating supermarket shop yesterday, Jonathan managed to always be in a different aisle, so we couldn't ask if he wanted whatever we were considering. Then, at the checkout, he said, 'I don't like that/those,' to almost all the items, while he stood at the end, not helping to pack. After we waited patiently for him to inspect the receipt for two-for-ones, three-for-twos and the correct number of loyalty points, Elspeth said, 'Thank you for your help, Jonathan. Now what would you like to do when we get home?'

'*Cetorhinus maximus*?'

She clasped her hands. 'Ah, the basking shark. Did you know they give birth to their young?'

And then they were off, nattering away, while I steered a trolley of food Jonathan wasn't going to eat, let alone help load into the car or unpack when we got back. Still, at least he wasn't depressed, and neither was Elspeth. On the whole, I reckon I'm doing a pretty good job.

Today being Saturday, I was free, so met Alice for

lunch at Shelcombe's new vegetarian restaurant. We had to queue outside for a while, but it was worth it for the interesting salads alone. After the soup, I decided I'd definitely bring Elspeth here one day. Jonathan I wasn't so sure about. Deborah was right, he does have an odd relationship with food, and anyway, he'd find fault in a very loud voice and I wouldn't be able to come back.

Alice proved hard to please too, poking at her lasagne and saying, 'They should really guarantee organic.'

'Maybe,' I said, then pointed out that she'd probably be eating raw wildebeest in a couple of weeks' time.

She laughed. 'You just can't stop trying to put me off, can you? Anyway, at least it'll be free range.'

'True.'

'You know I really, really want to go and do this, Dad.'

'OK. But you've definitely had all your jabs?'

'*Yes.*'

'And there'll be a contact number, and you'll be able to send emails occasionally?'

'Yes, and yes.'

'What does Mum say? I keep meaning to give her a call.'

Alice shrugged and pulled a face.

'What?'

'Oh, she's cool about it, don't worry. It's just that . . .'

'What?'

'I dunno. I'm a bit worried about *her*, I suppose.'

'Oh? I thought she was in love and happy and about to settle down with Stefan.'

Alice took a forkful of lasagne, chewed, swallowed, had a sip of water and said, 'Quite.'

'You think she's making a mistake?' I've had my doubts too. Deborah's filled me in on Stefan's reputation, then there's Erica's low boredom threshold. Being human, I guess a little bit of me wants it to fail.

'I know she's making a mistake.'

I laughed. 'Oh, come on, Alice. You're not exactly a woman of the world. What are you basing this on, eh?'

She looked hurt and her face grew pink. 'I can't say.'

'Why not?'

'Look, forget it, OK? I'm not worried about Mum at all. She can marry the arsehole for all I care.'

We were cheek by jowl with three other tables and heads were turning. 'Arsehole?' I whispered. 'That's a bit strong, isn't it?'

She was really quite flushed now and looking tearful. She didn't say anything, just shovelled more food in.

'Alice?' I said, putting my fork down and cupping the hand that held her knife. 'Is there something you're not telling me? Us?'

She let go of the knife, swallowed and squeezed my fingers. 'Well . . . yes, I suppose. No, I can't.' She took a deep breath. 'OK. Er, you know when I went on that field trip to London?'

'Yes?'

'Have you finished with those?' asked a young guy with a tray. He leaned across the table for our empty soup bowls, causing Alice to let go of my hand. 'And these cups?'

'Yeah, yeah.'

Alice stood up and pointed at the toilets. I nodded at her, watched the table clearer, then was suddenly alone. What was she about to tell me? Something to do with the London trip. But what could that have to do with Stefan? While my head tried to make a connection, I heard a distant Rupert: *So how come yous was the only person at school what went on a laak environmental studies field trip?* All alone in London . . . days after first meeting Stefan . . . who, according to Deborah, has a penchant for . . .

'That's better!' Alice said, plonking herself down with a huge smile. 'Just a bit PM. Sorry about that.' She scooped up lasagne and looked me in the eye. No sign of tears. 'I think Stefan's been great for Mum. I'm *really* happy for them.'

'Right,' I said. 'Good.'

'Can you actually eat wildebeest?' she asked in a swift change of subject.

'Ah, this I know the answer to,' I said, letting her off the hook, for the time being, anyway. 'Elspeth's eaten it.'

Alice rolled her big brown eyes. 'She would have.'

'Now, now.'

Deborah With only four weeks until peak season begins, I'm manically job hunting. The arcade is becoming busier and busier, and I can't get any work done under the counter. The weekends are absolutely non-stop. How Debbie Clinker stood it all those years, I'll never know. So, the other day, I went to an agency, took a typing test and was told, very politely, that I'm too slow. 'But I type all the time,' I protested. 'I'm a journalist!'

The over-friendly girl called Tanya said, 'Wow, who've you written for?'

I told her I'd worked on *Zip!* and before that on regional newspapers. That I was currently doing a bit of free-lancing.

'Wow,' she said again. '*Zip!*'

It wasn't getting me a job. 'Do you have anything that doesn't involve typing, then?'

'Hotel receptionist?'

I pulled a face. If I wanted tourists, I'd stay at the arcade.

'Chambermaid?'

'Uh-uh. I struggle to make my own bed.'

'Fruit picking?'

'No. Not good in the sun.'

'Wages clerk?'

'Sorry. Number dyslexic.'

Tanya gave up on her computer screen, rested her chin on a hand and said, 'So what was it like, working on a glossy lifestyle magazine?'

I told her it was fun. That it was frantic most of the time, trying to come up with ideas, having to meet dead-lines, but exciting seeing your article in print in all the newsagents. 'Yeah, I loved it.'

'So why are you in Shelcombe?' she asked, laughing. 'Must be a man.'

'No, no,' I said, chuckling along with her. But then I thought about it and said, 'Actually, yes.'

Tim does make me feel safe, cared for, protected. Maybe even loved. I know he secretly lusts after me, and I'm touched that he doesn't act upon it. Not that I don't think about it sometimes, when I'm in the brass bed and he's lying directly above me in the attic. But what if it was disastrous? Then the piano playing and the Boggle and the fun chatty meals would never be the same again. No, it's great the way it is.

When he got back from lunch with Alice today, I proudly showed him my piece on life coaching in today's 'Weekend' section. He picked me up and spun me round, plonked a kiss on my cheek, then sat down and read it.

'Ha!' he kept coming out with, even though he'd read it before. When he finished he said, 'You make life coaching sound like a great job.'

'I know.'

'Satisfying.'

'Yes.'

'Fascinating.'

'Mm.'

'Lucrative.'

'Listen, Tim. You haven't still got all your course material, have you? Assignments, notes?'

'Yes, I have. Up in the filing cabinet. Why? You're not thinking of—'

'Maybe. Is it locked?'

'No.'

'All right if I go and look?' I headed for the stairs then stopped. 'Oh, sorry. Maybe you've got confidential stuff in there?'

'Only the gay porn.'

'That's all right, then.'

I was halfway up the first flight when he called out, 'You don't know anything about dinghies, do you?'

'Can't even swim, remember!'

I heard him swear, then took the rest of the stairs two at a time. Life coaching! Why hadn't I thought of that before?

Erica I know that it happened in a matter of seconds, but when I do a rerun, it's in slow motion, just as it felt at the time. I keep reliving those seconds. First, the funny surprise when I turned the page of the magazine. I was at the hairdresser's round the corner from Stefan's. He'd recommended the place, and as I only wanted a trim, I thought I'd risk it. I was looking at the celeb gossip section of a relatively upmarket monthly. In a sea of photographs, taken at a book launch, there was a girl who looked exactly like Alice, but older and very glamorous in a clingy black dress, red lipstick, high heels. Same length hair, but fuller. She was standing at an angle beside a young guy who was grabbing a handful of her left buttock. Underneath, it said, 'Dominic wasn't saying if this stunner is his new "squeeze"!'

'How amazing,' I said, wishing I could take the magazine to show Alice. It occurred to me that she too could be a stunner if she made an effort. But then, when I was about to turn over, I spotted Stefan. There, in the same photograph, at the same book launch. He was to the rear of the couple, staring directly at Dominic's hand on that buttock. Sort of scowling at it.

Still in slow motion, in that semi-drugged state that comes from being at the hairdresser's, I thought, now there's a weird coincidence: Stefan at a book launch with an Alice lookalike.

I can't quite remember how I got from that point, to seeing that the girl was in fact my daughter. But I did, and a truly horrible sensation seared through my body. I may have wailed, because the receptionist asked me if I was all right. 'Would you like some water?' she said.

I nodded and looked down at the pages on my lap, just to be sure I hadn't been hallucinating. Turning to the front cover I saw it was the July issue, so had only just come out. I scanned the intro at the top of the page. 'Dominic Canon . . . much-hyped first novel . . . May . . .'

May? I delved into my bag; stomach knotted, a horrible sick feeling building up. The girl came back with the water and put it on the table beside me. 'You all right?' she asked again. She stared at the magazine then back at me. 'You've gone dead pale.'

I told her I was fine, pulled my diary out and drank half the water. 'May,' I whispered while I flicked, hands shaking, through the pages. Pages that have become increasingly empty, since I met Stefan and started winding the business down. I found a line with arrows top and bottom, drawn through four days in May. 'Alice on field trip!' it said, almost excitedly.

'Would you like to come through now?' someone was asking.

'OK.' There seemed no point in not having my hair trimmed. In fact, it felt like the perfect place to be when in shock.

As I sat being pummelled and combed and snipped and blow-dried, I did what a woman always does in this situation. I came up with reasonable explanations. Alice had somehow ended up at the book launch with her friends and, incredibly, bumped into Stefan. Or she'd bumped into Stefan in London and he'd said why not come along. Either way, she was too embarrassed to tell Tim and me she'd been skiving off her field studies. Made Stefan promise not to tell. Yes, that was it.

There was some temporary relief, but then I felt that hand on my elbow, shoving me into the taxi. I saw Stefan saying, 'Anywhere you like,' to the driver, Alice coming home all upset and a completely different person. The fictional Alicia, with her avocado breasts. Alice cooking Stefan a non-free-range chicken. The way Stefan and Alice avoid each other. Hardly ever in the same room, and never speaking when they are.

'He-*llo*?' the hairdresser was saying to me, waving a hand in front of my face.

'Sorry?'

'I said, is the back OK?' She was holding a mirror up for me to inspect.

I nodded.

'Are you sure?' she asked, frowning at me in the large mirror. 'It's just that you seem a bit upset.'

'I'm sorry.' I let go of the magazine at last, placing it on the shelf in front of me. 'It's great. Honestly. Thank you.'

I paid, left, stopped at a newsagent's to buy a copy of the magazine, went round the corner into Stefan's road, turned my mobile off, got into the car and, sobbing pathetically, pointed it towards Shelcombe.

When I got home, Alice and Rupert were out, which was a relief. I wanted to talk to Tim, but was afraid Alice would be with him. I'd leave it till tomorrow, I decided. What I had to do now was get very drunk.

Two-thirds of a bottle later, I was almost there. Certainly less upset, which was good, but just as angry, which was also good. I got my diary out of my bag, along with the mobile I'm never going to switch back on. If I hear his voice, I'll throw up. I looked at those May dates again, remembered Alice saying she might stay in London longer, then coming back home and giving me that hug. She was so distressed. What had he done to her?

I leaned over and poured the rest of the bottle in my glass, and when I sat back the diary had fallen open at the end of the year. It was a page full of my scribbled

novella notes: Eleanor gently lashing Steven on the rock.
I reached for a pen and changed 'gently' to 'viciously'.
Then, in the half-inch space at the bottom of the page,
I continued the scene. Eleanor was now wrapping the
long wet strands of shiny seaweed around Steven's neck,
pulling and pulling whilst he wriggled beneath her. A
lifeguard appeared from behind a boulder.

'Hi, I'm Karl,' he said in an American accent. 'Do
you need a hand?' Eleanor took in his six-pack. 'If
you could just hold him down . . . ?' she asked the
hunky blond.

SUNDAY

Tim I was lying in bed this morning, thinking about dinghies. Last night I'd been online for information and come away feeling confused and much more worried. Had William's dinghy been a two-seater, a six-seater? Had it had a motor or just paddles? Information I should have wheedled out of Elspeth, but now I'm avoiding bringing up the subject, hoping she'll forget all about it.

I'd have to just buy a new one and hope it was similar. But where? They were so expensive new, I'd learned online. There was Ken next door, of course. He'd know someone, somewhere. Yes, Ken. The problem was almost solved, I told myself, and my thoughts went back to where they'd been when I first woke up: Deborah slumbering prettily beneath me, albeit on another floor. If we ever slumbered together, which room would we chose? She loves that room, so probably hers. These were silly thoughts, I knew, but I carried on with them until the front doorbell went. I looked at the alarm clock. Eight

258

twelve on a Sunday morning? It could only be an energetic, post-jog Alice.

Deborah and I arrived downstairs at the same time. 'Morning,' we both said.

'Eggs?' she asked, and as I unbolted the front door, I called out not to worry, I'd do them.

'Erica?' I then gasped at the sight in front of me. Hair not sleek and shiny but all over the place. Dark rings under her red swollen eyes. Mouth set in a miserable pout. Before I had time to ask her in, she handed me a magazine and said, 'Page sixteen.'

'OK, so Alice was at a party in London and so was Stefan.' It was more of a question than a statement. I wanted Erica to expand.

Her eyes darted to Deborah, who I could tell was scrambling the eggs to rubber consistency. 'Can we go in the front room?' Erica asked.

'Or the garden?' I suggested.

She almost laughed at the idea, but once outside couldn't believe the change. 'Wow, you've worked hard, Tim.'

'Yes.'

Deborah cleared her throat loudly.

'So's Deborah,' I said. I closed the back door and Erica and I sat side by side on the bench discovered last week, hidden under a weighty jasmine. When I realised Erica was too upset – traumatised, perhaps – to talk, I kicked off. 'I think Alice was trying to tell me something yesterday, about Stefan and her trip to London.'

'Oh?'

'We were interrupted and the moment was gone.'

'I want to kill him,' Erica said.

'Go on.'

When she was through and my jaw was back in place, I took hold of her hand and said, 'I'm so sorry, Erica. But you know, Alice is eighteen. He may be a selfish, thoughtless bastard but unless he raped her or something, he hasn't done anything illegal.'

'I know,' she said, now crying. 'Anyway, he wouldn't do anything like that.' I wrapped an arm around her shoulder and pulled her towards me. 'Why do I always choose the wrong men?' she asked.

I chuckled and said, 'I don't know.'

'Oh God. Sorry.'

'That's OK.' I kissed the top of her head. It was a bit greasy but I didn't mind. 'Shall we both talk to Alice? Later today, maybe?'

'Could we?' She looked up and gave me a snotty kiss on the cheek. 'Thanks, Tim.'

'That's all right,' I said with a heavy heart. Obviously I wanted to hear Alice's side of things and know that Stefan hadn't harmed her physically. I wanted everything to be OK between Alice and her mother, and I wanted Erica to feel better. But I also wanted to get the dinghy business sorted today. 'In fact, let's go now,' I suggested.

Stefan The bedroom door creaked open and my mother said, 'Are you awake, Steven?'

'Stefan, Mum. Remember I changed it twenty years ago?'

'I'm sorry, dear. I'll get used to it one day. Anyway, here you are . . . now where's the table? Can't see a thing in—'

'Don't open the curtains!' I could see perfectly well, so took the mug from her. 'Please.'

'Are you sure? Only it's such a beautiful afternoon. And if you're really doing some soul-searching, won't you need a little light to see what's in there?' She laughed at her joke and I tried to, then she felt her way back across the room, said to come and join them in the garden should I suddenly feel better, and clicked the door shut behind her.

I love my mother. I don't love what she's done to my old bedroom, though. One reason I didn't want the curtains open was the cacophony of colours and patterns I'd have to look at. I'd painted it black, as teenage boys do. And black was how I wanted it now, while I searched my soul for signs of any decent traits. I'd come across a few. Good with animals, good with old people. Hardworking. A decent boss. Honest, when it comes to taxes and the like. A careful and considerate driver. A careful and considerate lover.

I wondered again and again where Erica was, what she was doing, who she was with and how she was feeling – not just about me. I'd never cared so much about a woman before. I wanted Erica to be fine, no matter how much she hated me. But she wouldn't be fine. And she certainly wasn't yesterday, according to the girls at the hairdresser's. I'd caught them just as they were closing and asked if Erica had kept her appointment.

'Dead upset, she was,' said the girl who'd cut her hair. They thought it might have had something to do with a magazine. They showed me. 'She just like stared and stared at this page, yeah? Like all the time I was cutting her hair. She was definitely crying, wasn't she, Tamsin?' Tamsin concurred. Tamsin had the pertest little breasts, but I gave them little thought then, or indeed now, as I lay in the position I'd been in since arriving at my parents' St Albans semi. It had merely been an observation, and not a lust-filled one. A lifetime habit of spotting pert breasts wasn't going to fade overnight.

The photo made me look slightly demented. What had I been so pissed off about? Dominic Canon's hand on Alice's bum? Surely I hadn't felt jealous or possessive about a girl I barely knew? It was impossible to believe now. All I could think was how much progress I'd made in six weeks. All Erica's doing. But now Erica was gone, and I was crying. Crying over a woman. It was a first and, in a horribly painful way, it actually felt good.

Every now and then, I wondered if Erica wanted to murder me again. I'd come across that message of hers whilst packing on Friday. 'If you touch my daughter, I'll kill you!' I'd laughed and torn it up. Rather complacent of me, in retrospect.

I sat up and drank the strong tea, trying to work out how to salvage the situation in an open, honest and adult fashion. I wondered what a truly good person would do. Did I know any? There was Tim. Not entirely neutral, of course, but he might know how Erica was bearing up.

I leaned across and tugged at a curtain. When a beam of light fell upon Monet's *Waterlilies*, hung on rose-patterned wallpaper beneath a daffodil frieze, I thought about getting up and closing them again. But I deserved harsh punishment, so left it and carried on sipping tea, and thinking about phoning Tim.

Deborah The eggs managed to stick themselves to the pan while I'd stood just to one side of the kitchen window, secretly watching Tim canoodle with his ex-wife in the garden. Let go, I urged him. Take that arm away. Don't let her kiss your cheek. Get up! Come in the house and send her home. Cuddle *me*. It was a bit of a surprise to be so outraged. I guess I was just seeing a new physical, romantic dimension to Tim. I liked it. Liked that Tim. I wanted to be Erica. They came in, at last, but then when they immediately left the house together I was gutted.

'Back soon,' Tim called out.

'I'll save you some breakfast!' I replied optimistically.

'Oh, don't worry!'

I sat down with my cold rubbery eggs, catching the end of Sunday worship on Radio 4. It was quite moving, almost uplifting. The vicar called for peace and forgiveness, the organ bellowed, the members of the congregation sang their hearts out. 'Please God, don't let them shag,' I said, adding my own little prayer to the vicar's. 'Or if you do, let it be terrible.'

* * *

Alice 'Oh shit,' I said, when Mum shoved the picture of me, Dominic and Stefan in my face. I could see why they'd packed Rupert off home. 'What magazine is it?'

'Never mind that.'

Dad said, 'Shall I make some coffee?' and didn't wait for an answer.

'Do you want to tell me what happened?' Mum asked.

'Not really.' I couldn't believe the photograph was of me. I looked so sophisticated. 'But what do you want to know?'

'Did you and Stefan have . . . ?' She looked really awful, all pink and puffy. 'Have you and Stefan ever . . . ?'

'Yes,' I said, and she gave this sort of combined jolt and snort.

Dad came over and put his hands on her shoulders. 'Maybe you should start at the beginning,' he said, and so I did. It was never going to be pretty for Mum, so I just went at it. The Gay City Rollers night, the next day on the beach in the dip behind the beach huts, the three nights in London. Not that you could count the last night.

I honestly thought Mum was going to pass out, but Dad kept patting her hand and making her drink coffee. 'Did he hurt you?' he asked.

'What, like hit me? No, of course not. He was quite nice when he wasn't being totally thoughtless, calling me Aggie and locking me out the flat because he was on a date with Mum.'

'What!' Dad said.

Mum looked at him. 'I turned up on his doorstep. He needed to get me out the way, I suppose.'

Dad went, 'Ah, right,' and nodded, as though he'd often found himself in that situation.

Mum said, 'You can imagine what a shock it must have been for him.'

'Yeah,' I agreed. So did Dad. 'Anyway,' I continued, 'I slept on the sofa and left the next day before he woke up. I was a bit nervous because I'd hit him really hard in the face with my Millennium snowstorm thing.'

'That one?' asked Mum, pointing at it on a shelf.

Dad went, 'Ouch,' and we all laughed.

'Where's Stefan now?' I asked, and Mum shrugged. 'Does he know that you know?'

'I don't know and don't care.' She'd started crying and Dad handed her some kitchen roll. 'I'm never going to see him again, so what does it matter?'

'Look, I'm really, really sorry, Mum. It was my fault as much as his – well, almost. Anyway, I reckon he's changed. Changed a lot since you two got together.'

Mum mumbled something about leopards and spots into her tissue, then blew her nose. 'I wish you'd told me, Alice.'

'Sorry.'

Dad said, 'Can I top anyone up?' while he flicked through the magazine. He stopped at a page near the back and went, 'Ha! Just what I'm looking for.'

'What?' I asked.

'A dinghy.' He turned the page round. Some young duke in a wax jacket was in a little boat with two Labradors and a gun in his hand. 'To replace the one that was in my garage.'

I said, 'You mean the one Rupert's got?'

'Pardon?'

'Elspeth's, yeah? Damon asked Rupert to help him get it in his van to take to the tip, only Rupert thought that was a waste so it's in his parents' garage. He's been wanting to try it out, only I said that was a bit spooky because of what happened to Elspeth's husband.'

It's funny, but I don't think I've ever seen Dad so happy. He said, 'Yes!' and punched the air, then stood up and wiggled his hips and punched the air again, then grabbed my face and kissed me on the forehead. 'What a brilliant daughter you are.'

I said, 'Thanks, but I don't think Mum would agree.' I put my hand on top of hers and could feel it shaking. 'You know, Mum, if you feel like getting away, you could always come to Ghana with me.'

'Could I?' she asked. Not the response I'd expected at all.

'Er, yeah, of course. Only you'd have to pretend to be thirty because that's the upper age limit for the project.'

'No problem,' Dad told Mum with a wink. He was heading for the front door. 'Will you two be OK? I might just go and call on Rupert.'

'You won't tell him about Stefan?' I called out.

'Duh!' he said. I think it was an impression of me.

MONDAY

Tim 'Now, Rupert,' Mr Gerrard had said last night while Damon and I were loading the dinghy into the van, 'less of that long face. You know you won't have time for boats when you're studying law.'

Since it hadn't been Rupert's dinghy in the first place, I couldn't feel bad about nicking it back. Also, I know from Alice that Rupert's monthly allowance would run to a brand-new dinghy. I slipped him a tenner compensation, and by seven-thirty, William's last vessel was back in its rightful place, beside all the rest of the paraphernalia – deck chairs, Primus stove, ice bucket, etc. – on top of the pale green marble-effect lino, fitted beautifully by Damon. All we needed was to test the dinghy for punctures.

So, late this morning, after I'd made an excuse to Elspeth, that was what we did. Damon brought along a pump, and much interest was taken by Brian, next door but one. 'Oh dear, dear. In a bit of a sorry state, isn't she?'

I wondered why cars and boats are always 'she' and carried on pumping with my foot.

'Nasty scuff here,' Brian pointed out. Damon took over while I went and looked. 'She wouldn't get through an MOT if she was a tyre,' he added helpfully.

Eventually, the dinghy was fully inflated and, thanks to the heat and the pumping, I was gasping for a pint. Damon said he wouldn't say no either, and we asked Brian, who obviously liked to make himself useful, if he wouldn't mind keeping an eye on the boat while we nipped to the pub. I was slightly uneasy, as Brian struck me as the kind of guy who'd rub away at that scuff, just to prove a point. He said, 'I don't suppose she'll go far on her own, but right you are.'

The Lobster Pot was air-conditioned and the lagers were morish, so Damon and I ended up spending a while there. He moved on to lemonade as he was driving, but I stuck to lagers. We talked a good deal about Shelcombe United, which seemed the only common ground. When we left the bar at around three, we both expected the dinghy to have shrivelled to its previous state. What we didn't expect was for it to have disappeared.

Jonathan Tim didn't come today because he had a family crisis, so after lunch, Elspeth and I played chess. But not for long because I was so much better than her, what with playing the computer on the highest level all the time.

I was about to go back to my room, when she said, 'Let's go to the shops. We seem to have run out of so many things over the weekend.' When I said, couldn't we wait for Tim and go tomorrow, she said, 'It'll be fun, Jonathan. We'll take a walk along the prom too, and perhaps the beach. Come along, put some old shoes on. Ones you don't mind getting wet.'

I've only got two pairs of shoes, and it took me a while to decide which ones I didn't mind getting wet. They're both black trainers, and identical, which didn't help. In the end, I went for the ones on the left, because I prefer things on the right to things on the left. Just as I prefer even numbers to odd ones, and playing the black pieces in chess.

On the way, Elspeth and I talked about chess moves. I went through the most recent game I'd played against the computer, hoping she might learn a bit more, so we'd be better matched in future. When we reached the prom- enade she said, 'You are a puzzle, Jonathan. You've a photographic memory when it comes to chess, but you never remember to put the toilet seat down!' She laughed, so I don't think she was angry about the toilet seat. Then she said, 'Ah, yes, smell that sea air. Isn't it wonderful?'

All I could smell was fried onions, coming from a burger stand. I told her, and she said, 'Mm, makes one hungry, doesn't it? Come along, let's have a paddle.'

When I told her I'd never ever been in the sea, she said telling fibs wasn't nice. I said, 'No, honestly. Mum and Dad always tried to get me in, but I couldn't see the point and didn't want to, and so they'd let me sit and draw diagrams or write equations in the sand with a stick. I liked doing that.'

Elspeth said something I couldn't quite hear about the standard of parenting these days, then she was taking her shoes and socks off and rolling the bottoms of her corduroy trousers up. 'Shoes off,' she said. 'Last one in the water's a jellyfish!'

I actually wouldn't mind being a jellyfish. I think being an invertebrate might be fun. When Elspeth was paddling in the water and I was blocking out her voice, I found a stick and sat down on the sand and drew a vampire squid. The funny thing about *Vampyroteuthis infemalis* is that its fins are up near its eyes, and so they look like huge ears. When I'd finished, I wanted to show Elspeth, but she wasn't in the water any longer. Instead, she was running towards the beach huts. There was something I wasn't supposed to tell her about her beach hut, but I couldn't think what, so I carried on making my drawing better and waited for her to come back.

Deborah Tim told me all about the Erica, Stefan, Alice business over an early rushed dinner last night. It was the first Sunday he hadn't cooked a roast. I thought he was remarkably blasé about my former boss's degenerate and slippery behaviour, but I could tell his mind was on the rediscovered dinghy. It would probably hit him later, I decided. After bolting his food down, he knocked back the last of his water, wiped his mouth with his serviette and rushed off to Rupert's house.

He was back by nine, and when I suggested a game of Boggle, he said, apologetically, that he was emotionally and physically drained and went straight to bed. Why physically? Were things back on with Erica?

Anyway, this morning he was perky again and determined to get the dinghy inflated. Or so he said. I heard him making an excuse to Elspeth on the phone and would have followed him when he left the house, if I hadn't had to go to work. 'A family crisis,' he'd told her, and I couldn't help wondering, crudely, if it was the boat or his ex-wife he'd be pumping.

But my mind was put at rest when, during my lunch break, I wandered down to the beach and saw Tim and the dinghy in the distance. All this effort for Elspeth. I hoped she was going to appreciate it.

Back at work I was full of nice warm thoughts of Tim. Such a lovely man and more attractive by the day. I had this horrible feeling that if something didn't happen between us soon, it never would, and then he'd take up with someone else – ex-wife or whoever – and I'd spend the rest of my life beating myself up. Perhaps I'd sneakily seduce him during some shared activity. I couldn't do it with food. Boggle?

Tim 'How *could* you?' I said to the useless Brian. 'An old lady and a hopeless kid?'

'Don't think I didn't try and stop them,' Brian said in his defence. 'But she's not a woman to argue with, that one. Told me it was her property. I could tell the kid didn't want to go, but then she said summat in Latin, I think it were, and he couldn't get in the boat quick enough.'

I swore again and all three of us scoured the bay with hands held over our eyes. Apart from an inept para-surfer, we saw nothing. No distant blobs, nothing. They'd been gone almost an hour, apparently. I felt sick. I yelled, 'ELSPETH!' several times. Then, 'JONATHAN!' as his hearing was probably better. 'Jesus,' I said, falling on the sand and burying my head in my hands. 'Jesus, Elspeth.'

Damon said, 'Maybe we should notify the coastguard or someone?'

'How?' I asked, looking up again.

Damon wasn't sure and neither was Brian. After standing and examining the bay from left to right, then right to left, I realised there was only one thing for it.

'Ah,' said Sergeant Lillywhite when I walked in. Damon had gone off to some job and Brian was picking his wife up. 'Now let me guess.'

I nodded and he dragged a pad towards him. 'Name?'

'Jonathan Dalrymple.'

'Again?'

''Fraid so. Also, Elspeth Fitzgibbon.'

'And you suspect a suicide pact?' he said, not quite managing a straight face.

'This time it's serious. Honestly.' I summed up what had happened and he took notes.

'Hmm,' he said, rubbing that chin. 'We wouldn't normally alert the coastguard this soon. You say she was a marine biologist. Pretty used to boats then?'

'She's eighty-fucking-one,' I said. 'He's nineteen, special needs, can't swim and has suicidal tendencies.'

'All right, all right. Keep your hair on. Does the boy have a phone on him?'

'I tried that on the way here. Not much of a signal mid-Atlantic, I guess.'

'Now then,' the sergeant said, propping himself on his elbows and giving me a patronising look, 'why don't you go and check again, give me a tinkle if they're not back, and I'll alert the coastguard.' He eased himself up again and wrote down a number for me.

'Thanks for nothing,' I said snatching it from him. Childish, I know.

Deborah I could see immediately that something was wrong.

'Elspeth and Jonathan have gone missing,' panted Tim through the glass. 'In the dinghy.'

'Shit,' I said, pulling my wig off. I let myself out the booth and told the boss I had to go. As there were no other members of staff around, he had to take over. That's my job gone, I thought, following Tim outside. The first thing we did was to stand and scan the sea. 'Have you got your lenses in?' I asked.

'Yes.'

'Have you reported them as missing?'

'I tried. They could be halfway to Africa for all Lillywhite cares.'

'What about lifesavers and lifeboats and stuff?'

'There's the coastguard, but I don't know how to contact them directly.'

'Isn't there a pamphlet in the beach hut? Phone numbers and things.'

'Ah. Brilliant. Probably out of date, but let's go.'

Tim broke into a trot and I followed. Nice bum, I thought, when I should have been worried sick about Elspeth and Jonathan. Nice long legs, and quite a graceful running style. When we arrived on the beach at the bottom of the steps we saw, in the distance by the huts, an over-turned dinghy just at the water's edge, and somebody face down in the sand, inches from the waves. Tim howled, 'Elspeth!' and got to her just before I did. He landed on his knees beside her tiny cardiganed body, rolled her over, pinched her nose and went straight into a kiss of life.

All I could say was, 'Oh God, oh God, oh God,' arms wrapped around my stomach. But then a little leg came up and booted Tim firmly on his nice behind.

His head rose and I heard Elspeth gasp, 'For heaven's sake, Timothy.' She pushed him aside and sat up. 'What's come over you? Can't a gal lie on the beach without being molested these days?' She brushed herself down and smoothed her hair. 'Goodness.'

'You're alive!' he said, hands clasped.

'Why on earth wouldn't I be? Now help me up, there's a good chap. And no more smooching!'

'Look,' came Jonathan's voice. We turned and found him sitting on the step of the hut, a large red bucket between his legs. 'It's a conger eel.'

I went over and peered in the bucket and couldn't help screaming. It was revolting. Jonathan seemed hurt, so I apologised and said, 'It's great.'

'I think it must be a baby,' he told me, proudly stroking the awful thing underwater. 'The current rod-caught World Record is a hundred and thirty-three pounds, four ounces. I could convert it to metric if you like?'

'No, don't worry.'

Tim said, 'Why's the dinghy upside down in the water?'

'Ah,' said Elspeth, 'more conger eels. Underneath. Absolute beauties, aren't they, Jonathan?'

'Do you want to see?' he asked me.

My knees went weak and I said I had to get back to work.

'I simply adore what you've done to the hut,' I heard Elspeth say as I wandered off. 'An awfully nice chap called Brian said he'd have gone for a navy again, not mint green. He was terribly helpful getting us launched, wasn't he, Jonathan?'

Tim 'Have you ever played strip Boggle?' Deborah asked me. We'd had dinner and were now carrying on drinking.

'How does that go?' I said, not thinking. My mind was still on the embarrassing snog with Elspeth.

'Well, if you lose a game . . .' she said, filling my glass with white wine again. How many I'd had I wasn't sure, but what the heck, it had been a stressful couple of day~

'. . . you have to take an article of clothing off.'

'Right. Sounds fun. Have you ever played ˈ

'No. But what do you think?'

'What do I think about what?'

Now she was filling her glass again. To the brim. 'We could maybe have a game?'

Some odd and unexpected things have happened recently, but this was the oddest and most unexpected. 'Come on,' she said, standing. 'Let's leave all this.' She waved an arm above the table. 'We could play in my room, then we won't be overlooked.'

'We could?' I said, possibly frowning, possibly waiting for Deborah to realise what she was saying.

'Where's the Boggle?' she asked.

'On the fridge,' I said, still waiting for normal service to resume.

Down came the box. 'Coming?' she asked over her shoulder.

I would have been ridiculous not to go.

I sat at the foot of the brass bed, she was at the top. We each had a pillow behind us. After five games, Deborah was fully dressed and I'd lost both socks, plus shirt, trousers and my watch. Just before the trousers, I asked if contact lenses counted and she said, 'No,' quite firmly.

So there we were, curtains closed, playing by candle-light – Deborah in jeans, T-shirt and, presumably bra and knickers, and me in just underpants – when I was saved by the phone bell. I told her I should go, in case it was a distraught daughter or something.

'Hello,' I said, down in the hallway.

'Is that Tim?' I was asked.

'Stefan?'

'Yeah. Hi.'

'Ha!'

'Oh, you know then?'

'Yes, I know.'

'Look, I'm really phoning to find out how Erica is.'

'Ha!' I reiterated. 'How do you think she is, you slime-ball? One thing I can tell you is, she never wants to see your creepy child-molesting face again.'

'Alice isn't a child.'

'She's *my* child.' Christ, I was suddenly fuming. 'Now piss off for ever, will you!' I slammed the phone down and headed back to our strange game. But then I stopped at the foot of the stairs and looked at the phone. I went and picked it up and dialled 14713.

Stefan 'Hello?'

'It's Tim.'

'Oh, hi,' I said, bracing myself.

'Sorry about that.'

I breathed out. 'That's all right. I'm sure I'd be an outraged father too.'

'Anyway, are you OK?'

'Not really. But more importantly, how's Erica? I've been worried witless about her. And not just for my sake.'

'She's not that good, but she and Alice have talked it through and seem to be all right with each other.'

'Thank God for that, at least.'

'But she's taken it badly, Erica. Not much I can do to help. What on earth made you . . . ? Oh, never mind. I suppose when Alice decides she wants something, she goes all out for it.'

'Mm, she did invite herself to London. But I should have said no.'

'Like her mother in that respect. God, the way she chased me. Scared off my then girlfriend. Determined wasn't the word.'

'Um, Tim?' I said before he stopped empathising.

'Yes?'

'Well, the reason I was phoning was . . . well, I thought you might have some idea of how I can go about, you know, a reconciliation.'

'You'll be lucky,' he snorted.

'Oh.'

'But, I dunno, I suppose you could try a letter. Much more dignified, and somehow more personal than an email. Easier than a phone call. Not that Erica's answering her phones.'

'A letter, you think?'

'Uh-huh. Might be worth a try.'

'Right.' I knew Tim had been the person to call. 'Well, thanks. Thanks a lot. I hope I didn't get you in the middle of anything?'

'Er, actually, yes. You did.'

'Sorry.'

'Better go,' he said and we hung up.

I went through to the sitting room and asked my

parents if they had a writing pad and envelopes. Silly question. 'Blue, pink, plain white or ivory?' asked Mum, opening a drawer. 'Lined or unlined? Oh and look, I've got these ones with flowers and sayings on.'

'You choose,' I said. She was a woman after all.

Tim Back in Deborah's room, I found her under her duvet, just one candle flickering, the Boggle boxed up. 'Oh,' I said, a bit relieved, a bit disappointed. 'Game over?'

At this she smiled and slowly pulled the quilt back. 'I thought I was bound to lose the next four games,' she said, utterly naked.

'Oh, yeah?' I gulped.

She stretched across the bed and gently tugged my last item of clothing down my thighs. 'And I expect you'd have lost the fifth.'

I reached for my wine glass and took one final, quite enormous glug. 'Almost certainly,' I said, stepping out of my smalls.

Alice Mum and I spent most of the afternoon and evening at Gran's house. At five on the dot we had ham salad. The ham came from a tin and the salad items weren't mixed up. Lettuce next to radishes, next to cucumber, next to sliced tomato. In a tumbler, in the middle of the table, were sticks of celery, and if anyone wanted cheese, we helped ourselves to Dairylea triangles. There was salad cream and a pile of white bread, already buttered. We each had a cup of tea next to our plates. I love tea at Gran's. I think Mum does too, because it reminds her of being young and carefree, without a series of broken relationships behind her.

Gran and I did most of the talking. Gran asked me all about my exams, and what I was going to do in Africa, and could I speak the language, and how was Rupert, and did he ever get that speech impediment sorted out. Mum didn't say much, just stared at the condiment set a lot. But at least she ate.

'Are you all right, love?' Gran asked her every now and then. 'I've never seen you like this before, Eric.' Mum hates being called Eric, not surprisingly. 'I've got us some chocolate teacakes for afters.' Mum bucked up a bit. 'Always were her favourites,' Gran whispered to me.

We ate the teacakes in Gran's tweedy three-piece suite, which has wide seats and fat arms and wings, and which leaves just about no room for anything else in her lounge. There's a huge TV, though, and Gran always likes to catch the local news. It was hard to be interested in Shelcombe's proposed inner ring road, so I thought about Mum, and about Stefan. She was obviously missing him like mad. It was hard to imagine how Stefan was feeling, but if he was miserable too, then someone should do something. Me, I guessed. I might hate him, but who else ever does anything round here?

FRIDAY

Erica This extraordinary letter came from Stefan yesterday. Extraordinary because the sheet of writing paper had a border of cornflowers around it and, printed top left in a very curly red font, was 'Making friends is quick work, but friendship is a slow-ripening fruit.' On drugs, was my immediate reaction. However, what he actually wrote seemed more Stefan-like: how sorry he was, what a truly terrible person he was, how he didn't deserve someone as wonderful as me . . .

I didn't get to the end because I hadn't had a coffee, and because seeing his familiar handwriting was making me come over funny. Once I'd made a drink, I went straight to the computer and looked up my stars. 'You are having to deal with the consequences of a hastily entered-into partnership. When will you ever learn, Aries?' Bloody cheek. This was the astrologer who told me to go for it, six weeks ago.

I clicked, fairly reluctantly, on Stefan's sign – remembering a friend once saying, 'You know you're over a man when you stop checking his horoscope.' 'Gemini: A youngster will help make one particular dream come true this week.' That sounded like Stefan. Which niece this time?

Now fired with caffeine, I went and read the end of his flowery letter. He wanted to meet and talk. He'd be happy to come to Shelcombe. Or perhaps somewhere in London, if I preferred. He was staying at his parents' but was picking up emails and London phone messages. Towards the bottom of the page he actually begged me to meet him. I went back to the computer and wrote him an email of two carefully chosen words.

I've felt so much better since doing that, but then in another way I haven't. So final. But that's how it has to be. He took advantage of my daughter, then wooed me. I have to keep reminding myself of that fact, because every now and then it feels almost unimportant, particularly as Alice and I are getting on much better now. 'Yeah, but that was *old* Stefan,' she says when what happened comes up.

It's funny, Tim's sticking up for him too. He came round to see how I was on Tuesday and spent the evening saying things like, 'He's a changed man, these days.' Or, 'He's basically a really nice bloke.' Or, 'He's not the type to go into hiding. I'm sure you'll hear from him soon.' How Tim has suddenly become an expert on Stefan, I don't know.

No. It's over. Has to be.

Today, I'll ring the employment agencies. See if

anything's come up. I'll type and file for the rest of my life and tell any man who shows an interest where to shove it. Stefan and his antics and his slow-ripening fruit (avocados again?) have put me off for ever.

Tomorrow, I'll go to this wretched beach party of Alice's and pretend I'm fine. She wants me to read palms, of all things. 'Just make it up,' she said when I protested. 'All for a good cause.'

Sunday I'll spend working on the garden.

Monday will be the first day of the rest of my life, as they say. Without Stefan. Without that place in Italy. Without 'Oh my God, you're the best, Erica' sex. Without his soft-but-firm chest against mine, or his tongue working its magic, ever again. Without those once-sweet but now sick-making declarations of love.

Good. I feel better now I've got a plan.

Tim Having managed, since Tuesday, to take it in turns to be out each evening, Deborah and I were now being overly polite during an unavoidable dinner.

'Mustard?'

'Yes, please. No, after you.'

'Good steak.'

'Yes, isn't it?'

And so on.

There were unusually long silences. So many, that I asked if she'd like *The Archers* on. 'Please,' she said quickly.

It was hard to know what was causing our discomfort. Sex, of course. But why? I fancy Deborah like mad, and had enjoyed myself enormously on Monday night. Although I did wonder, both during and afterwards, if we were only doing it because she was tiddly. Maybe she hadn't enjoyed it that much. I thought she had, but who knows with women?

I decided to try and put myself in her place. She'd been the initiator, I'd gone along with it. I'd then retreated to my own bed at one o'clock because I knew I had to get up early and didn't want to disturb her. I'd then left the house just as she was getting up, in order to check on Erica before going to Elspeth's. It could be, I thought, that Deborah's detecting a lack of passion and enthusiasm on my part. Fairly understandably. The trouble was, the more days went by, the longer we sat quietly listening to *The Archers* and then *Front Row*, the harder it became to do something passionate and enthusiastic. I got up and filled the dishwasher.

'No, I'll do that,' she said. 'You cooked.'

'That's OK. Perhaps you'd like to make the coffee?'

'Yes, of course.'

It was awful, and I didn't know how to start making it better. I had this sinking feeling and pictured her quietly moving out. Polite handshakes goodbye, promises to keep in touch.

'I'll go,' I said, when the doorbell rang.

It was a relief not to be in the same room for a while. I opened the front door and saw a vaguely familiar face there. A woman of around forty. Tall, dark and anxious-looking. 'Are you Tim?' she asked.

'Yes.'

'Elspeth's support worker?'

'Has something happened to her?' I asked. She'd taken that bloody boat out again.

'No, don't worry.' She was very well spoken, and expensively dressed in some kind of arty linen suit, pale green. She wore leather, gold-studded flip-flops and bits of gold jewellery. I'd seen her before somewhere. 'I just wondered if I might be able to have a word? I know it's Friday evening, and I really ought to have phoned first. Sorry. I decided in the end just to turn up. On your doorstep. My name's Willa.'

She held out a hand, which I took. 'Tim,' I said, but of course she knew that. 'Come in.'

'Thanks.'

'Would you like a coffee?'

'No, thank you. I won't keep you long.'

I racked and racked my brain on the way to the kitchen, then ushered Willa in first and said, 'This is Deborah. Deborah, this is Willa.'

Deborah put whatever she was holding down and came over with hand outstretched. 'William's daughter?' she asked, smiling for the first time today.

Of course, the woman in the photograph.

Now Willa was aghast. 'How did you know? Surely Elspeth didn't tell you?'

Deborah went to a drawer and pulled out the photo. 'No she didn't. It's just that you and your father look so alike. And now I know you're called Willa . . .'

Willa took the photo and said, 'But—'

'Please, have a seat,' I said. 'Can I get you anything other than coffee? Wine? Soft drink?'

'I'm fine, thanks.' She stared at the photo while she lowered herself on to a kitchen chair. 'Where did you find this?'

Deborah said, 'At Elspeth's.'

'I can't believe she's kept a photograph of Daddy and me.'

'No?' I said.

'You see, Elspeth wouldn't acknowledge my existence. I imagine she's never mentioned me?'

'Er, no.'

'No. She knew about me from the start. Daddy owned up to the affair, the pregnancy. But she absolutely refused to let Daddy see me.'

'Really?' said Deborah, as we too slid on to chairs, either side of our guest. We were all ears.

'Daddy . . . William . . . had a brief affair with my mother. It was during one of the rare periods when he and Elspeth weren't working together. She was back in England, Daddy and my mother were in Nova Scotia. Anyway, I was the product.'

'Right,' Deborah and I said together.

'Mummy wasn't married, by the way.'

'Ah,' we both went.

'Where did you grow up?' asked Deborah.

'Bangor. Mummy taught at the university. Retired a couple of years ago.'

I did the calculations. Willa's mother was about twenty years Elspeth's junior. And William's, presumably.

'Daddy did get to see me occasionally, over the years. Secretly, that is. It was difficult for him, though, as he and Elspeth tended to do everything together.'

I said, 'Yes, I got that impression.'

'They occasionally had blazing rows about it. About me. I think Daddy longed for her permission to see me but it was never forthcoming, so we had to meet up in secret. Sometimes he'd go off on a pretend golfing weekend. He had an older sister Elspeth couldn't abide, so he'd say he was visiting her.'

'Listen, are you sure we can't get you anything?' Deborah asked.

This time Willa nodded. 'Perhaps a glass of wine.'

We gave her wine and she continued. I could tell Deborah was as gripped as I was. 'Elspeth found a set of photographs, taken on my twenty-fifth birthday. Daddy said there was the most ghastly scene, and to make things worse, she'd discovered them on their wedding anniversary.'

'Oh dear,' said Deborah. 'Poor Elspeth.'

Willa shot her a disapproving look and continued. 'Anyway, he played down the number of times he'd seen me over the years, and she tried to make him vow never to contact me again. It was the worst situation he'd ever been put in.'

'I can imagine,' I said.

'He made her a sort of promise, fingers crossed behind

his back, as it were, and then tried to salvage their anniversary. He bought champagne, fois gras, all the trimmings, and, as it was a beautiful day, they went down to their beach hut. Do you know the one?'

'Er, yes.'

'But it was hopeless. The day was ruined, perhaps their marriage was ruined. They argued in the beach hut, and again outside the beach hut, and then Daddy said he was going to take the dinghy out. Apparently, the last thing Elspeth ever said to Daddy was, 'Oh, drop dead.''

Deborah and I looked at each other, the cold realisation that something wasn't quite right here, hitting us both. We turned to Willa, wide-eyed, waiting for an explanation.

'Well, Daddy did drop dead,' she said. 'Three weeks ago.'

Jonathan I'm going to study biology and chemistry for two years, then become a marine biologist. My parents have agreed to support me. My dad said, 'Could you put Elspeth on the phone? We really need to discuss your rent.'

But Elspeth said she didn't want rent. 'He's terribly useful around the house,' she told my father, winking at me. I'm not sure I'm very useful, but Elspeth tells me I'm getting better. The other day she said, 'It's just a case of trying to think of what the other person – i.e. me – might like, or might like done.' I have tried, but how am I supposed to know what Elspeth's thinking or needing, when I can't even remember to tie my shoelaces? 'You're an absent-minded genius,' she told me. 'I've come across many in the science world. Brilliant but adorably hopeless!'

So this evening, after we'd had the salmon and potatoes and salad that Elspeth made, and after she'd washed up and done her little chores, as she calls them, and we were sitting watching a documentary together on the not-very-interesting topic of child drug addicts in South America, I looked at Elspeth and tried to imagine what she might like or need. It was a bit of practice. But it was hard. In the end, I said, 'Is there anything you'd like?' and she jumped about ten centimetres in her chair, then landed again.

'Goodness!' she said. She leaned across and squeezed my knee, which I didn't like, but didn't mind as much as I usually do. She was smiling at me and her eyes were a bit red and she was blinking a lot. 'Just your company, Jonathan,' she said. But I wished she hadn't said that because I wanted to go and look up conger eels on the computer again and make more notes. What I did was to count in my head to 88, because that's my favourite number – it's so neat – and then I went to my room.

Deborah 'What an amazing story,' I said, when Willa had gone, leaving us shell-shocked in two armchairs.

'Incredible.'

'What do you think we should do?'

Tim said, 'About the letter?'

'Mm.' William had written Elspeth a letter during his short terminal illness, explaining everything and apologising. He always wondered if she'd felt responsible for his death, after her last words to him. Willa, her mother and William had all waited to see if Elspeth would try to contact Willa to say her father was missing, presumed drowned, but it didn't happen. 'I think that's when Daddy realised he'd made the right decision. He was retired by then. He changed his name and grew a beard and lived very quietly with Mummy and me, and then just Mummy, until he died.' Willa, reluctant to post the letter directly to Elspeth, had felt obliged to at least pass it on to someone close. With no family left, Tim was next in line. She'd got his name and contact details through the social services.

'I don't know if we should give it to Elspeth,' Tim said. 'Imagine the shock. The anger.'

'Not to mention the humiliation. She has rather built William up to be a minor god.'

'Do we tear it up?'

I sighed. 'That doesn't seem right either.'

'No.'

'Let's sleep on it,' I suggested.

Tim smiled, wriggled in his chair and twiddled his fingers. 'Your bed or mine?'

I waited a couple of beats, just to put him on edge. I don't think Tim's ever going to be Mr Passion, but he'll do. 'Yours,' I said. 'Then maybe you won't desert me in the middle of the night?'

'Oh. Sorry. Thought I was being considerate.' He got out of his chair and came and took my hand. 'Strip Boggle?' he asked.

'But you're rubbish.'

'I know.'

SATURDAY

Alice I think Rupert's aunt's harp must have been over-strung or something, because when she went off for a break, the strong sea breeze took over and music, of sorts, continued. We all stood around watching it for a while, laughing but a bit spooked.

Not that I had much time to stand around, what with making sure everyone was having a good time and, more importantly, spending money. All the stalls selling stuff – plants, hand-made pots and jumpers, cakes and jam – were giving ten per cent of their profits to the campaign, so we'd, hopefully, be in the black by the end of the day. Then there were the games, mostly for kids, and one or two other stalls, like Rupert's, which we'd get a hundred per cent of. Honestly, the time I've spent this week getting volunteers and helping wrap presents for bran tubs and things.

On top of that I had to track down Stefan, who was at his parents' in St Albans, and talk him into turning up today, as a nice surprise for Mum. He said, 'She hates my guts, but I'll try anything.' I think he's probably all right, Stefan. Or maybe not. I don't know. Anyway, about three o'clock, he sent me a text to say he'd arrived and where should he go? The Lobster Pot, I texted back, and to let me know when he was there.

What's great about these kinds of celebrations is that you get all sorts involved. Even Rupert's dad had torn himself away from his sordid life to run the Treasure Island stall. Elspeth and Jonathan were showing a dinghy full of fish and other creatures to kids and their parents for 50p per person. Jonathan seemed to be talking non-stop. Dad and Deborah were running the organic drinks stall, and Mum was Mystic Madge, telling people's fortunes in a little tent covered in stick-on stars. How I was going to get her out of there to meet Stefan, I didn't know. She had a constant queue outside the tent.

I had no idea where Rupert had got to. He'd been collecting all his friends' unwanted CDs all week, plus the CDs their brothers, sisters and parents didn't want. At twelve o'clock he set up his stall and by two all the CDs had sold except for the Gary Glitters. If he was at the Anchor drinking the profits, I'd kill him.

When Stefan let me know he was at the Lobster Pot, I risked letting things carry on without me and went to talk to him. It was annoying, when I walked in, to see how attractive he looked. But, trying very hard not to fancy my mum's boyfriend, ex or otherwise, I sat down beside him and said, 'OK, here's the plan . . .'

* * *

Tim 'Got any Coke?' people kept asking.

'I wish we had,' I wanted to say, but instead told them it was all organic and quite delicious, especially the cranberry and pear. Some just headed off to the front and came back with cans. Still, we were doing well, filling biodegradable cup after cup at 50p a pop. I wasn't that keen myself, despite the great selling job I was doing. I had a couple of cans of lager and was taking sneaky swigs.

While we served, Deborah and I held a whispered discussion out the sides of our mouths about Elspeth. Should we or shouldn't we show her the letter? Would now, while she was distracted and happy, be a good time? And where was it?

'In my pocket,' Deborah said, patting a breast.

'You won't take that jacket off?'

'In this wind?'

This morning, we thought tossing a coin might be the answer. We tossed one. Heads, we'd give her the letter; tails, we'd burn it. It came up tails. 'Best of three?' asked Deborah and we tossed twice more. It came up tails.

I said, 'I think it's trying to tell us something.'

Deborah nodded. 'But if we don't give her the letter, she might always feel responsible for William's death. I mean, imagine telling someone to drop dead, and then they did.'

'Yeah, but at the moment she believes William didn't deliberately leave her. That must be reassuring.'

We'd been going on like this all day. Completely torn. And the longer it went on, the harder the decision became. In the end, I decided to go and have a chat with Elspeth. Jonathan said he'd be fine on his own and so I took her into the beach hut I still had the key to, and sat us both in deck chairs.

'So you like the improvements?' I asked, waving an arm around.

'It's quite, quite beautiful,' she said. 'And thank you so much, Timothy. But, you know, it doesn't really feel like my hut any longer.'

'Oh.' Oh dear. She was pissed off.

'That's not a criticism, Timothy. And stop looking so nervous. I'm not going to bite your head off.'

'Sorry.'

'I know we've still got the deck chairs and the other bits and bobs, but somehow none of it conjures up William and that last ghastly day together.'

'No?' I cleared my throat and thought, here goes. 'Do you want to tell me what happened?'

'No, Timothy, I don't. Well, perhaps just a little.' She clasped her hands in her lap and stared straight ahead. 'We had a terrific tiff.'

'Here?'

'Yes, here.'

'About . . . ?'

'Oh,' Elspeth said, rotating her thumbs, 'something quite minor.'

'Right.'

'I said something dreadful, he stormed orf with the dinghy, and I never saw him again.'

'That must have felt—'

'You know, Timothy, it's so very strange that his body wasn't washed up somewhere. Don't laugh, but I do sometimes wonder if he faked his own death.'

'Oh, Elspeth! Surely not?'

'He . . . well, he had someone he wanted to spend time with.'

'Oh dear.'

'No, not another woman. Well, not really.'

'Ah. So, er, how would you have felt if you'd discovered he had faked his own death?'

Elspeth turned her stare on me. 'Oh, I'd have killed myself, without a doubt. What's kept me going all these years is a vision of William rowing his way back to tell me he loved me and was sorry, then suddenly getting these horrific chest pains. "Elspeth, my darling . . ." I hear him calling across the waves. "Elspeth . . ."'

'Burn it,' I told Deborah, handing her the matches I'd just bought.

'Are you sure?'

'*Quick.*'

'OK, OK.'

Erica Weary of telling people they'd soon be coming into good fortune, hearing welcome news about a family member or crossing water, I was about to take a break, when Stefan of all people walked in, shocking me to my core. He looked gorgeous; I looked ridiculous. Alice had forced me into a kaftan someone had run up. It had a pattern on it that wasn't quite paisley, but almost. I wore a matching bandanna and lots of black around my eyes. I wasn't surprised when he laughed.

At the filthy look on my face, he then said, 'I've paid a pound to the girl outside, so I'm afraid you'll have to do me a reading.'

'Sit down,' I said, controlling my fear quite admirably. 'And give me your palm. Not that I want to touch it.'

'Oh, Erica.'

I grabbed at his right hand and turned it upwards. 'Ah,' I said, examining it. 'Interesting. It's the first one I've had like this today.'

'What do you mean?'

I think he was trying to get our knees to touch under the tiny table. I inched my chair back and said, 'You see, all the other palms have shown honesty, loyalty and a strong sense of right and wrong.'

'And mine doesn't?' he asked, going along with it. 'Not even a trace?'

'Um . . .' I peered again, then took hold of his left hand and examined that too. 'No.'

'Oh dear. How about love? Can you see any of that?'

'Quite a lot, yes. But only of the self.'

'So is there any hope?' he asked. His eyes were on my face, I knew, but I was damned if I was going to look at him and weaken.

'Hope of what?'

After a hefty sigh, he said, 'Of getting you back, Erica. Of getting you to forgive me and love me again.'

Someone had stuck a knife through my ribs. It hurt. A lot. But I was determined to be resolute. 'No,' I said firmly, this time looking him in the eye. 'None at all.'

'Oh, for Christ's sake, Mum,' said Alice, barging through the tent flap. 'Get over it, will you? Poor Stefan's come all this way to beg you to take him back. He obviously loves you like mad. Tell her, Stefan.'

'I love you, Erica.'

'He's desperately sorry about what happened, aren't you, Stefan?'

'Desperately. I told you in my letter.'

'And I'm sorry too,' said Alice. 'Which I must have mentioned a zillion times.'

I let go of Stefan's hands. 'What's the time?' I asked, leaning back and pulling the bandanna off.

'I dunno,' Alice said. 'About four.'

Stefan looked at his watch. 'Five to.'

'I didn't realise it was so late. Listen, I've got to go and meet someone.' I stood up and pulled the kaftan off over my head. 'Excuse me.'

He was in a three-piece suit and cravat, which I found endearing, waiting in the bar of the Lobster Pot as arranged. 'Lovely to see you again,' he said. 'Can I get you a drink?'

'Thanks. A gin and tonic, please.'

'Double?'

'Good idea.'

He went to the bar in his dapper outfit with his dapper walk and I wondered how any woman over sixty could resist him. He may have shrunk an inch or so, as people do, but he was still a good five-ten. Slim, but not scrawny, with a good healthy glow from all the golf he plays. A handsome face with a strong nose. Short white strips of hair each side of his otherwise bald head, a perfectly trimmed white moustache. Quite a catch.

While he was gone, I sent Tim a text – 'He's here!' – then tried not to think about Stefan while I waited for that gin. Impossible, of course. Bloody, bloody Stefan. And Alice. His turning up must have been her doing. Which was kind of thoughtful, but it was all way too soon. He looked adorable and it would have been so easy to fall into his arms. But Stefan, I decided, is going to have to wait. If he's still around when, or if, I feel all right about the situation, then fine.

'Great,' I said when the drink was placed on the table in front of me. 'Thank you, Neville. Now, tell me what's been happening on the dating front since we last spoke.'

'Not a lot,' he said. 'One lady who wanted to go to bed on the first date. Can you imagine? That wasn't through your agency, don't worry.'

'I should hope not!' I said, and he laughed infectiously. He was a bit of a tonic, Neville. I wondered if I'd made a mistake and should bag him myself, but it was too late. Tim and Elspeth were heading our way, Tim with a surprised expression.

'Erica!' he said. 'Fancy bumping into you!'

'Tim! How nice. Won't you join us?' I wondered if we were being a bit over the top, but carried on being bubbly. 'This is my friend, Neville. Neville, this is Tim.'

Neville stood up and shook Tim's hand. 'Pleased to meet you.'

I said, 'And this is Tim's friend, Elspeth.'

Elspeth proffered a tiny hand, which Neville took, raised to his moustache and kissed. 'Charmed,' he told her. 'And may I say what lovely eyes you have.'

'Yes, you may,' said Elspeth, patting her wispy bits of hair back in place and laughing. 'But forgive me if I take it with a pinch of salt. They used to be aquamarine, you know.'

'And, indeed, still are.' Neville looked at Elspeth as though she were the most beautiful woman in the world. He eventually let go of her hand and said, 'Do sit here,' pulling a chair out, 'beside me.'

'Thank you,' she said, running her eyes up and down him. 'Gosh, one feels positively underdressed. I've been showing folk various sea creatures on the beach. I do apologise if I whiff!'

Neville took a deep breath. 'I smell only delicious flowers on a dewy summer's morn.'

'Oh, ha ha,' said Elspeth. 'More like stinky crabs on a seaweedy beach. Now, is anyone going to fetch me a glass of stout, or do I have to go myself? Timothy?'

'Actually,' said Tim, 'I'm going to have to dash. Sorry. Um, Erica, would you mind . . . ?'

I looked at my watch. 'Golly, twenty past four. I think Alice is expecting me. Neville, would you mind . . . ?'

'Did I hear you say stout?' he asked Elspeth. 'Surely a woman of your beauty and breeding drinks nothing but champagne?'

She whooped again. 'Of course that's what I meant to ask for. Do make sure it's a good one, though. None of that ghastly Asti business.'

Neville bowed and said, 'As the lady pleases,' and we left them to it.

'Pass me the sick bag,' Tim said outside.

I shook my head at him. 'You know, Tim, you could learn a thing or two from Neville.'

He looked at me. 'Really?'

'Really.'

Jonathan I was disappointed that we hadn't got any starfish in our collection. I like starfish. Most of what we had was caught by a fisherman that Elspeth talked to a few days ago, and it was all a bit of what he called 'pot luck'. Just things that got stuck in his nets. What I did was to take photographs along to show people the huge variety of creatures living just off the beach, or sometimes on it. I think they were very interested, and I was really enjoying myself, especially after Elspeth went off with Tim for the second time and I didn't have to bother taking 50p off everyone. Some people only had ten-pound notes.

When Elspeth came back with an old man who looked like he'd just been to a wedding, she was wearing a hat that said 'Kiss Me Quick, Shag Me Slow', and was behaving a bit stupidly. She kept giggling and then she took her shoes and socks off and got in the dinghy with the eels and crabs and things. The old man laughed a lot too. He clapped and said, 'I do like a spirited woman.'

I shouted, 'Mind the sea slugs!' to Elspeth and she got out and said sorry, and then she and the old man walked in a very wobbly way to the beach hut. They started singing 'Oh, I do Like to Be Beside the Seaside' together and I wondered if they were on drugs. I checked all the sea slugs were OK. They were.

Alice I stayed in the tent with Stefan while he cried. Not embarrassing big-sobs-type crying, thank God. 'Do you think she meant it?' he asked.

'Hard to know with Mum. When she goes off a bloke, that's usually it.'

He sniffed again and I handed him Mum's bandanna. 'Thanks,' he said, dabbing at his nose with it. 'We had such plans. Italy and all that. Now I'll have to find somewhere to live. Alone. Without her.' Either he really was heartbroken, or he was putting on a brilliant show. 'No woman's ever made me feel so miserable.'

I remembered sitting crying on his doorstep when I was locked out, and suddenly felt less sorry for him. 'Oh, come on,' I said. 'It's not the end of the world.'

His face told me otherwise, but how genuine was all this? I decided to put him to the test, leaning forward and squeezing his knee through his nice black brushed-cotton trousers. 'Listen, why don't we go to my house? Just you and me, mm? The place'll be empty . . . We could, you know?' I bobbed my eyebrows and did a sexy pout.

'Oh, Alice, my love,' he said, his hand landing on mine, 'have you gone completely off your rocker?' He lifted me by the wrist. 'And what kind of a daughter are you?'

'It was just a test,' I said sharply. 'Honestly, Stefan, as if I would really *do* that. Huh!'

He shook his head. 'Unbelievable.'

'I was *testing* you.'

He carried on shaking. 'I won't tell your mother, don't worry.'

'Oh, for fuck's sake,' I said, getting up and storming out. I can't think why I bother sometimes.

SUNDAY

Stefan I managed a little breakfast at the hotel, then wandered aimlessly round town, along the front, along the beach, round town again. I found, to my surprise, a great little vegetarian café. It was busy, as was the rest of Shelcombe, but not one of its customers was yelling at a child. Their coffee was good, so I ordered a second and even considered eating.

For want of anything else to look at, I scanned the notice board. They were doing Brecht at the Exchange and a fireworks concert was coming up in July: Mozart, Handel, Jagger and Richards. Interesting combination. You could learn Pilates, go to baby massage classes, order boxes of organic food from someone called Bethany. In August was the first ever Shelcombe Music Festival: bhangra, soul, West African, funk, reggae. The Shelcombe Women's Christian Feminist Group was planning to reclaim the night on the beach next Friday. There was a choral society and a history society and, coming soon, a series of talks on Kant's *Perpetual Peace*. To say I was astounded would be an understatement. Just yards away people were buying inflatable bosoms.

So, maybe it wasn't such a bad town, after all. Ironic, really. Now that I know I can't stay, the place is growing on me.

I ordered some lunch, then found myself with a table-mate – a young hippyish guy – and we got chatting and I sort of opened up to him. He was very sympathetic and said, behind a hand, that he might have just what I needed, if I knew what he meant. I declined. Nice bloke, though. Plays drums in some local band.

I think I felt worse for having been in the café. When I got in the car to head back to London, I wanted final memories of Shelcombe to be fat thighs and fried onions, not Kant and coriander and friendly drug peddlers.

After packing up the last of my stuff in the flat, ready for it to go into storage, I headed with a leaden heart for St Albans. My parents said I could stay on till I'd found somewhere. I know they're deeply disappointed in me, although not totally surprised that the Erica thing hasn't worked out. When I arrived, Mum fed the three of us neck-of-lamb stew – her speciality, and always good.

We were settling down afterwards for the usual prolonged bout of telly watching, when the phone rang. Mum wanted to know who on earth that could be, as she always does, then came back and handed me the cordless.

'Hello?' I said.

'It's Alice.'

'Oh. Hi.'

'You OK now?' she asked, rather sweetly.

'Not really.'

'Hmm. Listen. Now don't laugh, only Mum's thinking of coming to build latrines in Ghana with me . . . I said *don't* laugh.'

'I'm sorry.'

'Only if we both went we'd need someone to look after the house for us while we're away. It's for six weeks. Interested?'

'You're not telling me your mother would let me—'

'I'll talk her round. I've already slipped it into conversation.'

'And she said?'

'Not repeatable. But don't worry. I told her we could probably get you to pay holiday-rate rent of six or seven hundred a week, and she looked a bit more interested, especially as she hasn't got a job.'

'Right.' Seven hundred a week? I could rent two places in Umbria for that. I knew I'd pay it, though.

'Then, you know, when she's been away and had a good long think, and I've worked on her a bit, and if you've taken good care of the house and garden and stuff . . . well, maybe she'll have a change of heart.'

'Why are you doing this, Alice?'

'Oh, that's easy. Guilt.'

'Ah.'

'Yeah, that reminds me. There'll be absolutely *no* inviting women back here for the night, OK?'

Shelcombe women? 'No worry on that score,' I told her. 'There's only one woman in my life.'

'I was thinking . . . they've still got loads of witch doctors in Ghana, so what I might do is take a photo along and get one of them to put a spell on you. Like, I dunno, for every time you're unfaithful to Mum, you lose like a tenth of your hair.' She laughed evilly. 'How about that?'

'Fine by me.'

'Anyway, she's just back from doing a shop. Better go.'

I put the phone down in a mild state of shock. I'm not sure I've ever known an eighteen-year-old like Alice. And I've known a few. A born organiser with her heart in the right place, but truly scary. I examined myself in the gold curly-framed hall mirror. I've been lucky on the hair front, so far. I ran a hand through it roughly, then examined my palm. Two brown hairs sat there. Was that normal?

Deborah I was told on Friday morning that I'd be out of a job soon. In the afternoon, some men came and fitted two cash machines inside the arcade. This week, some other guys are coming and installing change machines. Slotsa Fun will keep the booth going for a while, until customers get used to things. Hey ho, I thought, redundant again.

However, for the past week, I've been wading through Tim's life coach course, plus his notes and assignments. All of which, combined with the research I'd already done for the article, led me to believe, round about Wednesday, that I could set myself up as a life coach, no problem. By the end of the week, I had cards printed and scattered around town in shop windows and one or two other places. Tim could never bring himself to advertise like that. 'I just sort of relied on the Yellow Pages ad,' he said, which might explain why he had only four clients in eighteen months, including Debbie.

No, Tim is definitely cut out for a more caring, less competitive role in life. For caring he is, primarily. Smooth and suave and overly romantic, he definitely isn't. Last week he stopped mid-lovemaking and said, 'You did switch the iron off?'

I'm mad about him, though. He's funny and attractive and, perhaps most importantly, he makes me feel safe. For example, I know the house won't burn down while we're having sex.

Erica Of course I can't go to Ghana. Alice can be persuasive, but not that persuasive. Me building latrines while Stefan lives in my house? I was almost going along with it for a while. Then, this evening, I discovered my passport was about to expire and Alice remembered it would take me six weeks or something to get all my vaccinations, and I came to my senses and Alice's enthusiasm began to wane and we didn't mention it again.

No, I'm going to stay put. I've got temp work, starting tomorrow. Some firm in the business park. It'll be fine. I'll be fine. No more trudging up to London or trying to conjure up clients. And no more men. Not for a while. I suppose there's just the very slimmest chance that one day, a long, long way off, I'll make up with Stefan. No there isn't. What am I saying . . .

Before bed, I went online and checked my stars for the week ahead. 'Monday's new moon brings the opportunity to heal rifts in one close relationship.' Not what I wanted to hear. 'Take the initiative, Aries, and things will sizzle between you once more.'

Hmm. I took myself off to bed, where I flicked through a gardening magazine but couldn't find anything of interest. I looked over at the clock and saw it was 00.23, which meant it was now Monday. New moon day. 'Sizzling' sounded good. Should I give him a call? Would I feel demeaned and embarrassed?

Sod it, I thought. Who wants to just temp in the bloody business park and potter in the garden for ever and ever? I reached for the phone and dialled. He answered almost immediately.

'Hi, Kurt,' I said.

'Hey, Erica. Great to hear your voice. Howya doin?'

'Fine. You?'

'Good, yeah.'

'Still seeing that, er . . . ?'

'Uh, no.'

'No?'

'She was a little, well, young.'

'Ah. Anyone else on the scene?'

'Not that I can see. How about you?'

'Uh-uh. Listen, I was thinking of coming to New York.'

'Great, hon. When?'

'This week.'

'Fantastic! You wanna stay with me?'

'Could I?'

'Sure.'

'That's brilliant. Thanks, Kurt. I'll let you know when I've booked a flight.'

'Do that.'

'Meanwhile . . .'

'Yeah?'

'I was wondering what you're wearing?'

'Ah! OK, well I'm in a pair of—'

'Take them off?' I asked nicely.

'Oh, come on, Erica. You can do better than that . . .'

MONDAY

Tim I woke up five minutes before the alarm was due to go off and thought about the day ahead. I was to go to work, of course. Today, with the weather forecast being good, I'd take Elspeth and Jonathan out to the country, no matter how much Jonathan protested. The outing might depend upon Elspeth feeling better, though. I suppose hangovers are like broken bones and pneumonia – harder to get over, the older you get. She looked pretty rough when I popped in yesterday.

She and Neville had hit it off in a big way, and had hit the champagne in a big way too. After putting Neville in a taxi and carrying Elspeth upstairs late Saturday, I said to her, 'Stick to stout from now on, will you?' but she was asleep already.

It would be great if those two got it together, so long as they laid off the booze. Apparently, Neville wants to teach Elspeth golf, which would be good for her, health-wise. I sometimes think she spends far too much time in a dark and stuffy bedroom, being shown things on Jonathan's ever-glowing screen. He makes her watch him play chess against the computer for hours on end. Never when I'm there, though. She says she doesn't mind because it keeps her from gloomy thoughts.

This evening, Deborah and I are going to have a romantic candlelit al fresco dinner to celebrate having returned the garden to its former state, and better. It's been relentless hard work – you take a day off and a hundred weeds appear – but it's increased the value of the house by ten thousand, and helped me lose my tummy. Although the tummy thing could have been Elspeth's hypnosis or being in love, or both. I smiled to myself at my good fortune, leaned across to push the alarm button off and got up to make tea.

Ten minutes later, with the curtains open on a gloriously sunny day, Deborah and I sat sipping from our mugs and taking in the sea view. We nattered about the events of the weekend and went over the letter business again, deciding we'd absolutely done the right thing but feeling bad about knowing what Elspeth didn't. We agreed that Neville might be just what she needed. 'He's very handsome,' Deborah said, and I came over a bit jealous. 'In a beaky kind of way.'

There was a comfortable silence, during which I continued to feel lucky to be alive. I had a great house, a fabulous garden, an adorable woman and a regular income from a job I really loved. OK, quite enjoyed. Yes, life was good, and getting better. I felt pretty sure

Deborah was happy too, as she stared at the horizon and sighed contentedly. When our peace was interrupted by the bedside phone, I put my mug down and stretched across for it.

'Hello?' I said.

'Oh, hello,' came a familiar voice. 'I, er, saw a card in the vegetarian café. For Jasmine, the life coach?'

I said, 'Hang on,' in a deep, very gruff, hopefully disguised voice and passed the phone to Deborah, one hand smothering the mouthpiece. 'Someone for life coaching,' I whispered. 'I *think* it's Stefan.'

She pulled the same face I was pulling, shook her head and whispered, 'Hang up.'

'OK,' I mouthed, pressing the off button, then reached down behind the bedside table to the telephone socket. 'Just in case he tries again,' I said, yanking it out. We waited for the other phone to ring downstairs but it didn't. I relaxed, leaned back against my pillow again and turned to Deborah. '*Jasmine?*' I said.

'Mm. Jasmine White.'

'That's terrible.'

'No, it's not.'

'It's what we did the inside of the beach hut in.'

'Don't lie.'

'It's true.'

'Well, maybe I'll change it. Anyway, White's better than Cash.'

'No it's not.'

'Yes, it is.'

'No, it's not.'

'Listen, this is silly. We don't argue.'

'Yes, we do,' I said, and we both laughed. I looked over at the time – not too bad – and felt under the duvet for Deborah's thigh. 'Toast or a shag?' I asked, then realised how unromantic I sounded. Neville would never have come out with that. I turned and gazed at her, lovingly. 'You know, you have beautiful eyes, Deborah.' I tried to think of a brown equivalent of aquamarine. 'The colour of . . . the Thames,' I told her. 'No, not the Thames. Didn't mean that.' I tried to think what kind of brown Deborah's eyes were as I stared into them. They brought to mind Butch, our old dog, but I couldn't tell Deborah she had the eyes of a Jack Russell. Or could I?

'I think I'll go for the toast,' she said.